W9-AUZ-223

WITHDRAWN

Through A Glass Darkly

G·K
Hall
&Co.

Also by Gilbert Morris
in Large Print:

The Honorable Imposter
The Rough Rider
The Iron Lady
The Remnant

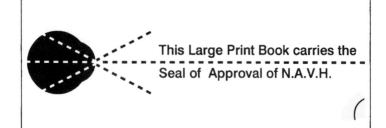

Through A Glass Darkly

Gilbert Morris

G.K. Hall & Co. • Thorndike, Maine

Published in 2000 by arrangement with Bethany House Publishers.

G.K. Hall Large Print Inspirational Series.

The text of this Large Print edition is unabridged.
Other aspects of the book may vary from the original edition.

Set in 16 pt. Plantin by Warren S. Doersam.

Printed in the United States on permanent paper.

Library of Congress Cataloging-in-Publication Data

Morris, Gilbert.
   Through a glass darkly / by Gilbert Morris.
     p. cm.
   ISBN 0-7838-9009-5 (lg. print : hc : alk. paper)
   1. Amnesia — Fiction. 2. Large type books. I. Title.
PS3563.O8742 T494   2000
   813'.54—dc21   00-023516

Dedication

To Steve Laube,
who made this one possible.

Contents

Fire. Heat.

White hot.

Raging flames.

Choking smoke.

Panic! Flee!

Nowhere to run.

Walls of fire.

Surrounded.

Terror. Pain.

Dear God, help!

Blackness.

The Awakening

ONE

EVERYTHING was white and clean. The eleven men in the long white room were all staring at the wall, not saying anything. Except for the one directly across the room, who was staring at me. He wasn't very loud, but he kept saying over and over again in a low voice, "Emiliano Zapata . . . Emiliano Zapata."

A sudden noise made me jump. Over to my right I saw one of the men in white squatting on the floor and flapping his arms like a chicken. My forearm tensed as I tightened my grip on something metal in my left hand. An orange liquid spurted all over my chest, ran down my hands, and then spattered the brown tile of the floor by my feet.

A shadow fell on my hands, and I looked up. A very big man with a black face was grinning down at me in an odd way, and he kept glancing anxiously over his shoulder to the door at the end of the room.

"Hey, Champ, you done went and spilt yo' sody pop," he said.

9

His voice sounded familiar, and he even looked a little familiar. But it bothered me that he kept looking over his shoulder, waiting for something . . . someone. . . .

"Whut you do a thing like that for?" he asked, smiling again, nervously looking over his shoulder.

"I don't know."

When I spoke his mouth opened, and he grunted as if he'd been hit in the stomach. His eyes got big, and he began to pace, seemingly unconcerned with anyone in the room but me. The more he looked at the door at the end of the room, the more nervous I became.

I held the metal can that the orange liquid had come from in front of my face and began reading whatever was on it: *Packed by Western Bottling Los Angeles, CA 90069. Under the Joint Authority of Sunkist Soft Drinks, Inc.* I read that over and over, but it didn't mean anything. It did, however, take my mind off the white room and the men in it, including the big man who kept looking at the door.

For a long time I'd been hiding in some kind of dark, safe place. The bright room was making me nervous, and I had closed my eyes and almost retreated back into the dark when I felt a heavy hand on my shoulder. I opened my eyes and saw the big man.

"Come on, now, Champ. You don't be goin' nowhere."

I could feel that my eyes were wide as I stared

up at him, and he sort of smiled again.

"You 'member ol' Perry, don'cha? Ol' Perry, he ain't never let you down, has he?"

Before I could answer, the door to the room flew ajar, and the man entering through it was very heavy and very short. He slowly walked toward me, his fat jiggling with each step. The big man with the hand on my shoulder, Perry, he called himself, leaned down to me.

"You 'member Doc Kimpel, don'cha, Champ?" Then looking up at the fat man, he said, "He can sure enough talk, Doc. Ain't no doubt 'bout it."

The short man's face was round and white, with lots of chins falling on his blue checked shirt. He had light blue eyes that were watching me carefully, and as he approached, he smiled just a little.

"Perry, why don't you leave Adam here and come back after a while?" I must've looked afraid, because his eyes cut back to me, and he added, "It's okay. Perry will be right outside."

The man, whom I presumed to be a doctor, since the big man had called him "Doc Kimpel," sat down across from me at the table. His fat quivered and shook as he settled himself.

For a long time I looked at him, and he just looked back, not saying anything. He tore off a piece of lined yellow paper from a pad he'd carried in with him and began folding it over and over, looking up at me from time to time. I watched his fingers, fat like sausages, form it into

11

an airplane. He looked at me, then drew his hand back and threw it. It sailed through the air until it hit the wall and fell to the floor.

He leaned slowly back in his chair and locked his fat hands behind his neck. He seemed to be watching my every move, and I guess I was watching his too.

"You're feeling better today?"

I didn't know how to respond to his question. I wasn't sure how I was feeling. I wasn't sure where I was. I searched my mind for something to compare today with, but there was nothing.

"You don't remember me?"

"No," I said. Just that simple word seemed to spark something in him, and he shifted his large body forward so he leaned on the table.

"This is a hospital," he said. "You were very badly hurt." He eyed me carefully. "But you're going to be much better now."

He got up slowly from his chair and walked to look out of the window. For a minute he blocked out all the light coming in through the window, and he stayed still so long I thought he'd forgotten me. Finally he turned around, walked back, sat down on the edge of the table, and looked down at me.

"You were badly burned. You don't remember any of that?"

I just looked at him, trying to recall being burned, but I couldn't remember anything like that.

"Don't worry about it, Adam. It'll come to

you." He paused, as if thinking about something important, then said, "Adam isn't your real name. We didn't know what your real name was when you were brought in, so we just called you Adam. Can you remember your name?"

I began to tremble. It seemed wrong for me not to remember. I got up and began to walk a little, but he didn't seem bothered by it. I walked over and picked up the paper airplane he'd thrown, then walked to the window. Following a sudden urge, I threw the airplane. It sailed across the room, then dove into the tile.

The doctor talked awhile about how hard it was to make good airplanes, but he didn't say anything about me. I listened to him. I didn't have much of anything in my mind to think about other than that.

I don't know how much time passed, but I finally asked, "Why can't I remember anything?"

The doctor still seemed impressed at my being able to speak. "Like I said, you were very badly burned, Adam. No one thought you'd even live. You had to have several operations, skin grafts. The pain was . . . apparently . . . unbearable." He looked away for a moment, then looked at me again. "So . . . you just sort of went away."

That statement confused me, and he must have noticed because he added, "You didn't actually *leave* here. Your body was here, but part of you left."

"You mean — I'm *crazy?*"

I looked down at my hands. They were square and brown and thick. I could feel the doctor looking at me.

"The pain caused you to go down inside yourself —" he picked his words carefully — "into a place where you wouldn't have to deal with it. You couldn't run from the pain physically, so you ran away in your mind. Understand?"

I thought about what he was saying for a while. I knew that place. It was a dark place with no sound and no noise. I sat down across from the doctor again, and he gave me a pleasant smile.

"You're coming back to the real world again. That's why I called you Adam. I knew you'd come back someday, and you'd be a new man."

"Adam from the Bible . . ." The phrase shot out of me without thought.

The doctor's eyes grew sharp, and he asked, "You know the story of Adam?"

I thought for a minute, and the story sort of flowed into my mind. I knew it well, every detail. I looked up at the doctor and said, "He didn't have any yesterdays." A fly buzzed around my head, and I reached out and caught it. I held him in my hand, feeling him crawl around inside.

"I never saw anyone who could do that!" the doctor exclaimed. "Catch a fly on the wing!"

It bothered me the way he stared at me. I didn't want to be different. After a little while I opened my hand and let it fly away. The doctor was quiet for a while too. Finally he said with an edge of authority in his voice, "Adam, try not to

14

worry about what's going to happen. The more relaxed you are, the quicker you'll get your memory back."

I thought of the dark world where I'd been and didn't want to go back there. But I wasn't sure I wanted to be here either. A simple question nagged at me, and finally I said it aloud. "Who am I?"

The doctor hesitated, then spoke slowly. "I'll tell you what we know about you, though it isn't much. Two years ago you were found in a forest fire not far from here."

I looked around, wondering where "here" was. The doctor quickly added, "Louisiana State Hospital. Jackson, Louisiana." He paused and searched in his pocket, retrieving a bat-tered-looking pipe with a curving stem and a big bowl. He took a kitchen match out of another pocket, raked it across the top of the table, then stuck it into the bowl of the pipe. When he had it going, he blew a small cloud of purple smoke and watched it thoughtfully. "We work on very special cases here. You made medical history, Adam. You're in all the textbooks now — espe-cially those written about plastic surgery."

He suddenly rose, came around the table, and grabbed me by the arm. I stood obediently, and he walked me over to the other side of the room to a large window with a heavy reflection. The window seemed out of place, as it didn't appear you could look out it or even through it. "Take a look at yourself," he instructed.

15

I peered into the glass and saw a tapered face with a broad forehead, high cheekbones, and a chin with a deep cleft. The nose was high bridged, and the mouth was wide. Small scars puckered the skin up a little around the eyes and along the hairline . . .

. . . looking like someone else.

The doctor caught my expression and said quickly, "You have to remember, the plastic surgeons didn't have a lot to work with. Your face had been burned, though not as badly as your hands, and your cheekbones were damaged. They didn't have a picture to work from or anyone to tell them what you'd looked like before. They did a good job too," he said observantly. "Except for some tiny little scars, nobody would ever guess what a mess you were when you first came here."

I turned from the reflection, not wanting to see myself anymore. The doctor led me closer to the door that he'd entered. He looked up at me and said, "We were all waiting for somebody to come looking for you." The statement seemed to bother him. He puffed rapidly on the pipe, took it out of his mouth, and stared at it. "Nobody came," he said slowly.

He couldn't look me in the eye, and he jammed the pipe between his lips again, then shook his head. "We tried everything — Missing Persons, FBI, even a psychic — but nobody could find out a thing." He then grinned at me and said, "But now you'll be able to tell us some-

16

thing." He may have caught my unknowing expression because he added quickly, "You'll begin remembering things pretty soon."

As he continued toward the door, he reminded me suddenly of a friendly hippo. "You go with Perry. Later today you and I can get together and find out more about you. All right?" When Perry came in the doctor said, "You take care of Adam. Bring him back about three this afternoon."

"Want me to go put 'im back in Ward C?" Perry asked.

"No. Get him in one of the singles."

"Hey, maybe he can stay wit' me. I gotta extra bunk in my room."

"That's fine. Get him back here by three." The doctor gave me a sudden and intense look, then smiled. "You'll be fine, Adam."

Perry pulled at my arm, so we went out of the long white room and down the hall. "We get you settled in my place, and then we have some fun," he grinned.

We went to get my clothes, and I was glad I didn't have to stay there any longer. There were four other men in my old room, one of them very old with brown spots on his hands, the others sort of middle-aged. They all just stared at us. Perry helped me get my clothes and shaving things; then we left. We walked down another long hall, then went outside across an open place with some grass and flowers. I noticed some of Doc Kimpel's paper airplanes on the grass and was afraid that the groundkeeper would come and scold me. But nobody looked at us, and we went into another building. I followed Perry to a room on the second floor with two single beds, each with a nightstand and a chest of drawers.

"Bathroom down the hall, Champ," Perry said. "Put your stuff on that bed. This is your room now." There wasn't much to put away — a few white uniforms, some well-worn underwear, socks, two pairs of rubber-soled shoes, some shorts and T-shirts, and some shaving things.

"Put on them workout clothes, Champ," Perry instructed. So I put on the shorts and the white T-shirt and one pair of the worn tennis shoes. Perry had changed into shorts. "Come on, now. We ain't had us no good workout for a couple of days now."

I followed him out of the room, and we went to another old building. This one was made of weathered red bricks covered with moss. Vines stretched from the ground to the roof. A power line ran from the roof across to another building, and a red squirrel with stuffed cheeks ran across it. Perry unlocked the door and we went inside. He threw a switch, then looked at me, his eyebrows lifted. "You 'member dis place, Champ?"

I looked around at the high ceiling with skylights letting the sun filter through to the hardwood floor, then at the square platform with ropes around it. Around the wall I could see some machinery, but I didn't know what most of it was. But I saw one thing that I recognized. I walked over to a large wine-colored bag hanging by a steel cable from an arm attached to the wall. I tapped at it with my fist. "I . . . I remember this."

His laugh echoed in the big room. He reached into a box beside the wall and pulled out some limp padded gloves. Shoving one pair at me, he said, "I reckon you *ought* to 'member this here bag! You done spent what seems like weeks off and on hammerin' at it!"

He helped me put on the gloves, saying, "I 'member whut you look like when you first come here — like a plucked chicken! All new skin, pink and kind of splotchy like a crazy quilt. And weak as a kitten! Why, you couldn't hardly hold your hands up when I fust got you, Champ!" He finished tying the laces of the gloves, then stepped back. "Now see if you can hit that bag like I done taught you."

I faced the bag with my hands raised. Something seemed very familiar about it. Without thinking, I dropped my left hand and shot my right forward. It struck the bag, making it fly backward, and a dim memory flickered through my mind. It wasn't much — but it was the *first* thing that'd come to me from a blank past, so it sent a sort of thrill through me. Perry caught the bag, held it, and I began to hit the bag with a series of blows — left . . . left . . . left . . . *hard* right — and the blows were all in a perfect rhythm that had obviously come from long practice. Perry grunted as I kept the bag jumping, and finally I knew that the series was over. And a word came to me:

Combinations! I repeated the word out loud.

"Right!" Perry nodded, a pleased look on his face. "That's *good,* Champ!" He slapped me on the shoulder, his eyes bright with excitement. "When you come here, all skin and bones and wouldn't say nothin', all the shrinks gave up on you. All 'cept Doc Kimpel, I mean. He tells me to get you in shape, 'cause one day you gonna come out of it. And I been training you real good! Why, you could make a fighter yet! You a little old — maybe thirty or so. But you got the moves, just like I had."

"You were a fighter?"

"A *con*tender!" he grinned. He had a round face, and his teeth were white against his black skin. "If I could've got past Simmons, I could've been the champ!" He suddenly stopped smiling and got sad. "But I jus' wasn't good enough. Ain't many who is, Champ." Then he brightened and looked pleased. "I think maybe *you* could be real good. You're downright easy to train! I tell you to do sit-ups, you do sit-ups like *forever!* Once I told you to do push-ups, and then I got busy and forgot all 'bout you. When I come back in thirty minutes, you *still* goin' up and down, jus' like a machine!" He rolled his big shoulders and laughed. "Ain't no trick to get a dude like you in shape — jus' have to be sure not to overtrain and get you all muscle-bound."

Something was reaching at me out of the past

20

just then. It came scratching at my mind — a faint ghost tapping on a windowpane — trying to get inside. I stared hard at the square with the ropes around it. "I remember *that*. We . . . we *spar* in it."

"Hey, man, it's really comin' back, ain't it, now?" Perry grinned in delight. Picking up a pair of shapeless gloves, he pulled them on and slapped his fists. "How 'bout we go a few rounds?"

We got into the square with the ropes. Perry put his hands up and shuffled toward me, suddenly throwing a punch at my head. I picked it off with my left hand without even thinking about it. It was easy. I knew I'd done it over and over a thousand times.

"Hey, that's sharp!" Perry laughed. "You ain't forgot that, have you?" He began circling me, throwing punches from different angles, but I caught them all on my gloves and my shoulders.

"Now — you throw a few at me," Perry said. "See if you can dish it out." He watched me, and there was sort of a flashing light in my mind. I had looked at this black face, traded punches with him many times. It felt good to have *something* seem familiar.

We moved around for a while, and finally Perry dropped his hands. He stood there looking at me with a funny expression on his face. Finally he said, "When you come heah, you weighed 'bout a hundred and fifty pounds. Couldn't hardly lif' your hands. I made you into a real fighting machine. You're exactly six feet one, and you weighs two hundred and eight pounds. And you done learned all I know about *how* to fight. You can spar, all right. . . ." Then he suddenly glared at me, and I wondered what I had done wrong. "But lots of folks calls themselves fighters who can't do nothin' but dance around for a few rounds. Whut I wants to know is, can you fight?"

I stared at him, not knowing what he was getting at. "I don't know, Perry."

His forehead ridged up, and his brown eyes fixed on me. Finally he nodded. "Well, you're gonna know in about two minutes! Now, listen to me. You been learnin' *how* to fight for quite a while. Now I wanna see, can you *do* it?" He squinted his eyes, put his hands up, and there was a hardness in his eyes I hadn't seen before. "Git your hands up, 'cause I'm gonna do my best to put you down — you hear me? If you don't stop me, Champ, I'm gonna bust you up, and we ain't playin' this time!"

He suddenly dipped his chin behind his thick shoulder, and his left arm shot out, catching me high on the head so hard I staggered back against the ropes. I saw the right hand coming and got a hand up, but it broke through, catching me on the mouth. I tasted blood as I floundered back, falling to the floor. When I got to one knee, Perry was glaring at me with his hands still lifted.

"Git up! We ain't playin', I tell you!"

I shoved myself off the floor just in time to

catch a barrage of blows, but this time I was able to ride with them by going backward. He caught me with a combination — a hard left to the temple, then a left to the cheek, then that big right hand caught me in the stomach, knocking the wind out of me.

But something happened to me as he was driving me backward. I forgot the dim memory of sparring, and from someplace deeper down inside me something took shape. It came from so far down I couldn't even call it a memory, but whatever it was, it took over my body for a short time.

I took two more hard lefts to the face; then I planted my right foot and swung for Perry's face with a whiplike blow that traveled all the way up through my leg. It practically whistled through the air and exploded right in Perry's face, driving him back with his hands flailing. He went flat on his back, and I stood over him waiting for him to get up. My face must have looked pretty mean, because Perry took one look at me, then slowly shook his head.

He climbed to his feet, staring at me with an odd expression in his coffee-colored eyes. "I guess you was a fightuh of *some* kind 'fore you got here," he said softly. I looked at his bleeding lip, and he said, "Ain't nothin', Champ. I was cut up lots worse in other fights."

I pulled off one of my gloves, then the other. We climbed down, and Perry tossed the gloves into the box. When he turned to face me he

23

looked thoughtful. "I guess you know a little more 'bout yourself now, Champ. You got some killer in you. I taught you to box, but I didn't put *that* in you. Some dudes got it, some ain't. That's why I never made it in the ring. I could box and I could take a punch. Could do it all, 'cept what I just seen you do."

"Do?"

"You come aftah me when I had you beat, and if I'd've got up, you'd have put me down again, no matter *whut* it took. And that's whut lots of folks ain't got in 'em, Champ. But you got it." He was staring at me with a funny look in his eyes, so I couldn't tell if he was happy or mad. Finally he shrugged, saying, "Well, let's us work out. . . ."

An hour later we left the building, and as we walked along, I said, "Doc Kimpel told me after I was found nobody ever came looking for me. I felt bad then. Nobody ever came. Was I that bad of a man?" I shrugged and after a little bit said, "I guess I'm just a . . . a nobody man."

Finally I whispered, almost to myself, "Perry — *somebody* should've come. . . ."

Going to Meet the Man

TWO

I KNOCKED on the door, and Doc Kimpel said, "Come on in." When I stepped into his office, it was cluttered with books and papers. I guess he saw other patients, but I'd never seen anyone else in the office, except a cleaning lady once. She must not have done much cleaning, but I don't think it was her fault. Maybe he kept seeing me because he was interested in my case. We'd spent lots of hours together the past four weeks, sometimes just talking, or taking tests — *lots* of tests! The thing was, they weren't tests you had to *pass,* so there was no pressure during those times. And Doc never seemed to expect anything out of me. The other doctors were always pressing me, but Kimpel never did.

As soon as I stepped into the office, I saw a big man standing by the window. It bothered me, but Doc said quickly, "Adam, this is Lieutenant Cossey from Missing Persons, New Orleans Police Department. I'm hoping he'll be able to help us."

Cossey put out his hand and I took it. He was

tall with beefy shoulders and a bull neck. He was chewing the soggy remains of a cigar, and when he took my hand, he caught me off guard by giving it such a squeeze that it ground the bones of my hand. I tightened my grip, but he squeezed harder, his smallish eyes getting narrow in his red face. He kept squeezing harder, and I just kept tightening my grip to keep from getting crunched. I thought maybe I could have outmuscled him, but I didn't. His face got a little redder, and he let go with a grunt. "Glad to know you . . . Smith." He had a high-pitched voice that didn't go with the muscles, and the way he said "Smith" was funny. He chewed on the cigar, puffed at it, then said, "Hear you been talking some."

"Yes." He had coarse black hair that came down low on his forehead, and his whiskers made tiny black dots. He didn't like me. I could tell that by the way he bit his words off and by the hard light in his eyes.

"It all just came back to you, huh?"

"Well . . . I know where I am, but I still can't remember anything about my life before I came here."

"Can't remember your name — or where you came from? Nothing like that?" He took in my face with a scowl. "That's funny. I'd think if you weren't nutty anymore, you'd remember things like that."

"I've already explained that to you, Lieutenant," Doc said sharply. I could see he didn't

26

like the way the policeman acted. "This isn't at all unusual. Many people with amnesia have a very slow recovery. Adam's making good progress." His voice had an edge as he added, "If you'd give him a little help, it might make things easier."

Cossey stared at him, then at me. He shifted the cigar in his teeth, then shrugged. "Okay. What you wanna know, Smith?"

"Well . . . anything you can tell me. Were you in charge of my case when I was first brought here?"

"You ain't *got* no case," he grunted. "I'm from Missing Persons — and you ain't missing."

"Nobody reported me missing? Isn't that unusual?"

"We don't *know* that nobody reported it," he said. "All we know is that nobody filed a report that *fit* you."

"But —"

"Look, you were found in Louisiana, but you may have skipped out on your family in, say, Detroit five years before that. Maybe there was a missing person report filed then, but you think I got time to go back and check all the reports?"

"I never thought of that," I said, looking him directly in the eye.

"Yeah? Well, did you ever think there might be a good reason *why* nobody ever came looking for you?" Cossey, with an exhaust of gray cigar smoke trailing out of his mouth, glanced casually out the window and hunched his big shoulders.

27

"Lots of guys don't leave much of a trail because they don't *wanna* be found."

"Wait a minute!" Doc Kimpel sat up, his face turning red. "You're implying that Adam had a criminal past? You don't have any evidence for believing that!"

"I got no reason to think any different," Cossey shrugged. He ground the cigar out in an ashtray on Kimpel's desk, then straightened up. "Look, Smith, I got no reason to think you're a fugitive. I'm just saying lots of guys lay low because they don't wanna be public. I'm just giving you a few possible reasons why nobody came to claim you." He looked straight at me, adding, "*If* you're telling the truth about this amnesia stuff — and I've seen that bit before! — I'll tell you one thing. You'd better start remembering things pretty fast, because I don't think you're gonna get much help from the law."

"Somebody *must* be looking for him!" Kimpel insisted. "People don't just disappear without somebody reporting them."

"Some people just aren't missed."

"Don't ever start believing that, Adam." Doc bit the words off angrily, shaking his head from side to side, making the fat ripple on his face and neck.

I was feeling pretty bad, but I tried not to let it show on my face. I seemed to be getting pretty good at that. "Maybe Lieutenant Cossey is right, Doc. Maybe if I found out who I was, I'd be worse off."

"*Somebody* is better than nobody!" he said with determination. Then he swung to Cossey. "I want some help on this, Lieutenant. I want you to find out who this man is."

Cossey gave him a half smile, then spread his meaty hands out. "How?" he asked.

"You *do* find people, don't you?" Doc snapped sarcastically.

"Not too many," Cossey answered sourly. "Besides, this thing is at least two years old. Before my time with the department — and there wasn't much to work on *then*. It sure won't be any easier now." He looked at me, and I saw that he was shifting his ideas around. Finally he sighed and shrugged his shoulders. "Look, I guess maybe I ought to tell you I came here pretty well convinced that this whole thing was a cover-up for something, but that don't change things too much. I still don't have any idea of how to go about finding out who you are."

"But that's what you *do!*" Doc said angrily.

"Yeah? Well, let's just go through what it is I *do* when someone needs finding." He held up his hand and took hold of his index finger. "Number one — we get a picture of the missing person." He turned toward me and demanded, "You got a picture of what you used to look like?"

Doc looked uncomfortable. "Well, not exactly . . ."

"Way I understand it, Smith here was burnt to a crisp. You told me how they had to build his face back with all kinds of plastic surgery. And they didn't have any way of knowing what he looked like before the fire — so they just made him a nice face, right?"

Doc Kimpel shifted around uncomfortably. "His face wasn't burned as bad as his hands and arms. They figured out he was facedown, so the fire didn't ravage his face completely. Besides, there are a great many new techniques in laser repair and laser cosmetic surgery."

"They didn't do surgery on his face?"

"Well, yes," Kimpel admitted. "He had a lot of broken bones on one side of his face along with the burns, so they had to work on that. They also discovered that he probably breathed in the fire and smoke, because his voice box was roughed up a bit too."

"So he looks *and* sounds different from before the fire?"

"Well — they had no other choice," Doc argued feebly.

"Okay, no picture," Cossey nodded grimly, then grabbed another finger. "Number two — fingerprints. We got government files, industry, schools, prisons — lots of places we can check fingerprints." He suddenly reached out and grabbed my left hand, moving faster than I would have thought he could. Turning it over he demanded, "What am I supposed to do about *this?*"

I looked down at the tips of my fingers, which were smooth. No prints at all.

Doc explained quickly. "They had to do grafts

with skin taken from his side. You wouldn't expect fingerprints after that!"

Cossey dropped my hand and fished around for another cigar. He found it, then took his time taking the cellophane off, dropping it with ceremony into the trash. Digging a kitchen match from his shirt pocket, he raked it across Doc's desk, then touched the blue flame to the end of the fat cigar. When it was glowing like a tiny furnace, he shook the match out and tossed it onto the floor. After a few quick puffs, he pulled it out of his mouth and studied it, then lifted his head, saying roughly, "I don't expect much of anything. What I'm trying to tell you is that you'd better not expect much either." He stared at me and then took a third finger. "Number three — past history. We get notified a person is missing, we check where he worked, his habits, his sex life, his religion — a thousand things. And with you, Smith . . ." He puffed slowly at the cigar, then shook his head. "With you we got nothing."

"I guess you're saying if I don't remember, it's no go?"

"Like I said, there's not a lot I can do."

"Maybe we could hire private detectives," Doc muttered.

Cossey gave him a nasty grin. "If you got a bundle and want to get rid of it, that's one way. They got nothing to work with either."

"That's all you can say?" Doc Kimpel demanded.

Cossey picked up his shapeless hat and moved

31

toward the door, trailing blue cigar smoke. "You got my number, Doc. Get me something to work with, and I'll get at it. But you gotta give me more than this." He suddenly came back to stand before me, stuck out his hand, and when I took it, he grinned broadly. "That's a pretty good grip you got there, Smith. You could have made me holler when we shook — but you didn't. Ain't too many can do that to me. Good luck. You'll need it."

He turned and went to the door but paused to look at me one more time, adding, "There's worse things than not knowing who you are. Lots of guys blow their brains out because they *do* know who they are." He walked out, and we heard his heavy tread as he walked away.

Doc Kimpel looked toward the door and then slapped his hand on his desk, sending books and papers flying. "Useless flatfoot!" he muttered. "A drain on the taxpayers!"

I sat down and looked at him. "I guess he's okay, Doc."

He stared at me, then cooled down some, settling his bulk back in his chair. "I suppose so." He kept watching me, but I was used to that. "This bother you much?" he asked abruptly.

I thought about it, then shook my head. "No. I guess we both knew it'd be this way. If there'd been an easy way, it would have turned up before now."

"I suppose so." He heaved himself up with a grunt, moved to stare out the window with a blank expression, then turned to me. "You want to do some more tests?"

"What's the use? Do you think they help?"

"I don't know," he sighed. He stared at me and finally began folding a piece of paper like he always did. "I've just about given up my profession on account of you, Adam. I can't quit thinking about you. Must have read twenty books on amnesia, and nothing helps! We've tried association tests, we've tried truth drugs. . . . We've even tried hypnotism. We've tried everything I can think of and still got nowhere." He dug his smelly old pipe out and got it going, and I could see that he was thinking hard. Finally he looked up and said, "Adam, I don't think you really understand how far you've come since you came here."

"I understand I've got no more memory than a stump."

Waving his pipe in the air, Kimpel said, "Listen to me for a minute. I may use some words you're not familiar with, but I want you to get an idea of how bad off you were the first time I saw you." He stood up and punched the air with his pipe as he recited his case.

"You were catatonic at first — totally unresponsive to *anything*. Then you finally became *semicatatonic* — that is, you showed traces of awareness of your surroundings, had a limited response to audio stimuli and tracking eye movements. Phase Three" — he jabbed at me with the pipe almost angrily — "you became *functional, but nonparticipatory* — that is, you could feed yourself and walk, go to the bathroom. From that you finally became *functional*. You could participate in more activities, but you never spoke. Now you've got *selective amnesia*. You're functional and self aware, but large blocks of information and memory have been blanked out."

"Maybe we've learned something," I shrugged. "I know what I *know*. I know boxing and baseball. I've read Robert Frost a lot." I thought for a long moment, then added, "I know the Bible pretty well. All that must mean something —"

"Sure, sure!" he interrupted. "But do you know how long it would take to get all that put together? We don't have anything that's *you* — the real person we're looking for. And I think I know why."

When I looked at him, waiting for him to go on, I saw that for the first time since I'd known him he was nervous. He threw the airplane he'd been folding at the wall. It performed a perfect loop and glided to a smooth landing on the floor. Kimpel stared at it for a long time, then lifted his eyes to me.

"Adam, I think you're still hiding. You hid in that 'dark place' you told me about to keep away from pain, but you've still got some sort of hiding place. Maybe you're trying to hide something."

"Hide what?"

"I don't know, but most people have some things they'd like to hide. That's why I'm in business. Remember what Cossey said: 'Lots of guys blow their brains out because they *do* know who they are.' " He then said quickly, "Maybe I'm wrong, Adam, but it could be you've put your identity in a box. As long as you don't know who and what you were, you don't have to face up to yourself."

I sat silently. There were no words to express what I felt, but even if there had been, I wasn't even sure what I felt.

"It's just a theory," he continued nervously. "I'm probably way out of line." Then he grinned with a tired expression. "I've got to shoot you some line of garbage to keep your spirits up, but such things do happen. Some people go to a lot of trouble to *forget* who they are."

"Well, maybe I'll never have to worry about who I am." A thought that I hadn't spoken aloud came to me, and I cleared my throat. "Doc, do dreams mean anything?"

Instantly Doc's eyes lit up, and he leaned forward eagerly. "Dreams? I think they can be very helpful sometimes. I don't put as much reliance on them as some in my field; still, they can be useful. You haven't told me of these before."

I didn't like thinking, much less talking, but he was waiting, so I shrugged and said, "It's not really a dream, Doc — not a real one. I mean in some dreams a fellow does things, like in a movie. They have a beginning, a middle, and an end."

"But your dreams aren't like that?"

"Not really." I wished I hadn't brought it up now, but it was too late, so I tried to explain what it was like. "It's like I'm in some kind of fire, Doc — a bad one."

Doc's rotund face was swept by disappointment. "You *were* in a fire, Adam — a terrible forest fire. And it's no wonder you have bad dreams about that experience. Most people would."

"No, it isn't a forest fire. I know that much. I mean, in a forest fire there'd be lots of woodsmoke and crackling of burning tree limbs. But in this dream there's none of that."

"What exactly is it like, Adam?"

"It's . . . it's hard to say." I closed my eyes and tried to bring the dream back — exactly the opposite of what I usually tried to do. Always when a memory of it came to me, I tried to push it aside as quickly as I could. Now I waited as Doc sat there as quiet as a stone. Finally I said, "It only lasts a few seconds . . . or that's what it seems like. I'm in this wide open space and there are . . . machines."

"Machines? What kind?"

"I don't know. They're just there. I think there are other people there too, but I don't see any of them. I can hear them yelling, but I can't understand —" I cut my words off as my heart began to pound inside my chest. I opened my eyes and looked down at my hands trembling. I clenched them together so Doc wouldn't see I was scared.

"All of a sudden the air is filled with fire. It comes rolling over me like a big ocean wave, only instead of cold, green ocean water, it's yellow and red and searing hot." I could see it in my mind's eye, and then I heard my own screaming. I took in a deep breath, focused on Doc Kimpel, and said as simply as I could, "I begin to scream; then I wake up."

Doc came over and stood in front of me and said, "I'll have to think about this, Adam. I want you to tell me every time you have this dream, and I want to know if anything new shows up in a dream. All right?"

"Sure, Doc."

I turned and he waddled with me to the door. "I'll see you tomorrow, Adam." He reached out and gave my shoulder an awkward pat, adding, "We won't give up."

"Sure." I left him at the door watching me go down the hall. I knew he'd go back to his desk and fold paper airplanes, worrying over what to do about me. It gave me a pretty good feeling when I thought of Doc Kimpel.

Perry was waiting for me in the gym, and I threw myself into the workout, trying to drown the thoughts that kept swarming in my mind. I pounded at the bag until my arms were made of lead, then worked on my stomach and legs until I was gasping. Then Perry and I went at it with big gloves and headgear until both of us were staggering.

Finally Perry gasped, "Whut . . . you . . . hear . . . in Doc's office . . . make you . . . so mad?"

I leaned against the ropes and waited until I got breath to answer. Earlier, Perry had caught me with a solid right that had sent little purple and red spots dancing in front of my eyes, and I shook my head to clear it.

"There was a policeman there from Missing Persons. He said there wasn't much hope of finding out who I am."

"Most cops can't find their own nose with both hands!"

"I guess this is a pretty good one, Perry. And if he's right, it means I probably won't ever know who I am."

He gave me a sideways look but didn't answer. We showered, dressed, then wandered over the grounds, not talking much. The sky was blue, hard enough to scratch a match on, and dirty white clouds marched across it. The grass was green enough to hurt your eyes, and the azalea bushes were bursting with cherry red blooms. Across the street two of the staff were playing tennis, making a *poinging* noise as the ball went back and forth. One of them dove for a shot, missed, and fell down. He got up, laughing at his own clumsiness.

"Sort of peaceful, ain't it, Champ?" Perry said.

He stopped and we watched the game for a

while. Finally I saw he was looking at me in a peculiar way. "Why are you looking at me like that, Perry?" I asked.

A smile split his broad lips, and his brown eyes glinted. " 'Cause I know you ain't gonna stand around here and look at no scenery, Champ. You gonna split, ain't that right?"

I sort of chuckled, as if the thought hadn't crossed my mind. But it had, many times, late at night when all the lights were out and I found myself staring into the darkness trying to answer questions that I wasn't sure even existed. "Where would I go, Perry?"

"I figure you might mosey around lookin' for whoever it is you us'ta be. Don't reckon you plan on stayin' in *this* place for the next forty years."

I looked back at the gray building, and the impulse that had been growing in me for a month got stronger. "No, I don't think I'm going to do that."

"You mebby want some company?" Perry asked. I looked at him, surprised, and he shrugged his bulky shoulders. "Thought I might tag along with you. Kind of like to see whut you turn out to be."

"Quit your job here?"

He threw back his head and laughed. "Why, Champ, this here is my own private hotel! When I gets tired or broke, I come here and work a little. I get rested up, saves me a few bucks, and I go out again." He stopped grinning then, adding, "I jus' can't make up my mind, Champ, whether folks is worse off in here" — he waved a big-knuckled hand toward the buildings, then toward the gate — "or out there. But I guess if you go, I'm about ready to make a try on the outside again."

I thought about that while the green tennis ball shot back and forth, sometimes so fast it looked like a blurred line. I wondered if I could play tennis, but it didn't seem familiar. Finally I said, "Kimpel will have a fit when we leave!"

For several more days I chewed on it, not saying anything to Doc. Every day we had an hour like always, but I could see the games we were playing meant no more to him than to me. He kept saying things like "someday" and "when you remember," but I could tell he didn't really have much hope. The dream came back five times, and I told him about it each time, but there was nothing new. I could see it irritated him, and once he said, "If we knew what that dream meant, we'd be able to open up a lot."

"Maybe it's hell."

Doc stared at me with a shocked expression. "What do you mean by that?"

"Well, there's fire in hell, right? Maybe I was an evil man before I lost my memory. Maybe it's God's way of telling me that's what's waiting for me."

Doc shifted in his chair uncomfortably. He dug out his pipe and lit it. He took a few puffs, then glared at me. "So you believe in a literal hell?"

"I guess I do . . . or did, at least. I know the Bible says it's real."

"And you believe the Bible?"

"Haven't thought about it. I do seem to know it pretty well."

"You *must,* or you wouldn't have come up with that particular interpretation of your dream."

I saw that he was troubled about this, and that bothered me. "Do you believe in the Bible, Doc?"

"Haven't made up mind yet. Anyway, this isn't about me." He seemed very defensive and shifted his bulk around as he changed the subject. "I think you've got a strong religious background, Adam. I'd like to know what sort of beliefs you had."

I wondered if I still had them. "Well, I'm like a slate that's been wiped clean, Doc. All the things on the slate are gone. So even if I was religious before the fire, that's all gone. I'll have to start all over, won't I?"

Doc fussed with his pipe, then shook his head mournfully. "That's a theological problem, Adam. It would take a wiser man than I am to answer it."

I saw that he was really shook up, so I said, "Well, don't sweat it, Doc. You know, I remember a verse from the Bible that says, 'All things work together for good to them that love

41

God.' That's in the book of Romans, chapter eight, verse twenty-eight." He looked startled, and I felt a little startled myself. I didn't even have to think about it. It was just there, like an index ready to be searched. I sort of smiled at Doc and said, "That's the King Jimmy."

"King Jimmy?"

"King James Version. Well, I gotta go, Doc."

Perry and I talked a lot, of course. He'd been at the hospital this time for quite a while and was growing restless. We kept up with the workouts, but I noticed he was giving a lot of thought to something.

About a week after Cossey's visit, we were stretched out on our bunks listening to Perry's stereo. He had an old turntable, with a whole stack of records going way back, and he was amazed that I knew the names of most of them. They were a mixed bag — jazz, popular, light classical. That night, he put the disk on, and after the first few bars, I said, "Glenn Miller. 'In the Mood.' "

He whistled. "Right on! You're too young to be around when that was on the box. Wonder how you know all this stuff from the '40s and all the old-time jazzmen like Jelly Roll Morton and Earl Hines?"

I didn't answer and he didn't press it. Finally when the record ended and Sinatra started singing, "Down Mexico Way," he asked abruptly, "Hey, Champ, you still thinkin' about splittin'?"

"Can't stay forever, Perry. I know it sounds nutty to think I could find out something about my past when even the law can't, but I've got more motivation, as Doc would say."

We lay there until the record ended, and then Perry said, "You goin' out into a mean world, Champ. That scare you?"

"Well, not as bad as the thought of staying here."

Perry laughed deep in his chest. "You're right about that! Listen, Champ, I been thinkin' about how we might make out. You got any coins — money, I means?"

"Money? No."

"You thought about how you gonna live outside?"

"Get some kind of job, I guess."

"They don't come easy these days. Even guys with a trade ain't workin' steady. And you ain't qualified for most of them government programs."

I knew he was headed somewhere, so I asked, "What's your idea, Perry? You been trying to work up to telling me for a week now."

He lay there silently, and then he said, "Well, I been thinkin' a lot, but I don't know if you gonna go with it."

"What is it, Perry?" This was the one human being in the world I trusted, apart from Doc. "If you've got any plan at all, it's better than anything I've got."

"Well, I lay it out for you, Champ. All you got

43

to do is say no." He sat up and leaned toward me, a thread of excitement in his husky voice. "I think you could make some nice change in the ring."

I rolled over and stared at him. The only light in the room was a tiny lamp on the table, but I could see the glow in his heavy-lidded eyes. "Be a prizefighter?" It sounded so silly I laughed. "You've got to be kidding! I've never fought in my life . . . as far as I remember. I'd get killed!"

"Not if we do it right," Perry said, and there was none of the customary humor in his voice. "Champ, I know fightin'. It's what I done for a long time. I seen lots of guys get chopped up, and plenty of them got their brains scrambled. But you ain't got no idea of how *good* you is, and how bad some fighters is! You got the size and strength, but mos' of all, you got the reflexes. And dat's whut it takes — reflexes. Most fighters don't stay in shape, but I been training you for nearly two years. You ain't had a drink or a cigarette or a woman. You is in the best shape of anybody I ever seen."

"But, Perry, they're professionals!"

"So will you be when you gets the first purse from a promoter. Now, look, I'm tellin' you flat, you can beat most guys. Not the big ones, the contenders. But the prelim boys — why, you can have them, I tell you!"

We talked for a long time, and finally I said, "Well, we can give it a try, Perry. If it doesn't work, we won't be any worse off, will we?"

44

It sounded wild to me, but the more Perry talked, the more I thought it might just work. I took a day or two to mull it over; then I went to see Doc Kimpel and told him I wanted to leave. He had a fit, just like I knew he would, telling me I needed treatment and would regress if I left the hospital. But we both knew the therapy wasn't doing me any good.

"But it takes money to live outside," he said. "You don't have any."

"I'll make out." Perry's idea, I knew, would sound crazy to Kimpel, so I kept quiet.

Finally he said, "Have you got some ideas about finding out who you are, Adam?"

"I'm going to do some looking around."

"What can you do that the police haven't already tried?"

"Start talking to the people who were around when I was picked up. The guy who found me, maybe."

"Why, it's been two years! That guy's long gone. Anyway, what could he tell you? He was just a volunteer fire fighter."

"Probably nothing, but I won't know until I talk to him. Maybe I'll go to see Cossey. Or I'll read old newspapers. I must have left a vacancy *somewhere*. Right now I'm like a bird that's wandered from its nest. A man needs a place, Doc."

"But you're not a private investigator, Adam. At least not now anyway."

I grinned at him. "But I'm *motivated,* Doc. That makes a lot of difference."

45

He grunted unhappily. "You'd better forget all that and stay here. Learn a trade, start making friends. Find a girl and get married."

"How do you know I'm not already married?"

"Doesn't count," he said quickly.

"I think maybe it does. When a man takes a wife, the two become one flesh."

He gave me a funny look. "From the Bible?"

"Yep." Then I asked him directly what had been on my mind for some time. "You don't think I'm ever going to get my memory back, do you, Doc?"

He looked out the window at a blue jay perched on a wire, then turned his eyes toward me. He studied me for a long time, then said quietly, "I do think you will, Adam, but there's no guarantee. You can't count on it."

"Then I've got nothing to lose."

His face was sad, and I knew he'd gone beyond professional interest in me. That made me feel pretty good. I had two friends, and from what I could pick up, that was better than most people had.

We had several talks after that, but two weeks later when Perry and I were ready to leave, I went to Doc's office to say good-bye. He handed me some papers, saying, "I've made you an identity . . . of sorts." He went over the items as he handed them to me. "Louisiana driver's license; this is an ID from the hospital; this is a Social Security card; . . ." He went through all of them, and I was surprised at the completeness of it.

"How'd you get all these?"

He waved his hand in the air vaguely. "Oh, I have ways." Then he said, "Adam, this is going to be a very strange time. As I've already said, I do still believe your memory will be restored at some point. However, until then, you will be in the dark and confused, unaware of the specific details of your former life. Yet paradoxically you will find that most of your knowledge of the rest of the world will be intact. As you move through each day, you'll 'remember' the oddest stuff, and that sense of déjà vu will occasionally be a surprise. You'll be literally discovering yourself bit by bit, and every new scrap of information will be another piece in the puzzle. Eventually you'll have enough pieces to start seeing the whole picture. I wish I could give you more to go on. . . ."

He sighed and continued, "Look, here's some money. And here's my number. Use it! I want to hear from you every week, you hear? Call collect and come back if you need to. If you need a recommendation, use those names I've given you." A grin pulled the corners of his lips up. "As far as these papers are concerned, you've been an employee of this hospital for the last couple of years, and that'll help you get a job. Did they fix you up with clothes and things?"

I nodded at the new brown suitcase by the desk. "Sure." I wanted to say something about how I felt, but finally all I could do was grin as best I could and say, "Well, thanks a million,

Doc. I'll be in touch."

He put his hand out, and as I took it, he said, "I hear Perry's going with you." I nodded and he made a sour face. "The blind leading the blind! Don't let him get you in trouble, you hear?"

"Don't worry, Doc. Well . . ." I picked up my bag and walked to the door, then stopped to look back at him. He still looked like a beached whale in a wrinkled white suit, but I realized at that instant how much I'd leaned on him. I knew there weren't going to be many Kimpels in the world. "So long, Doc." That was all I could say, and it wasn't enough.

Perry was waiting for me, carrying two expensive-looking American Tourister suitcases. As we went out the gates and headed toward the bus stop, he took one look back. He grinned and shrugged his shoulders. "If it gets too bad outside, we can come back." Then he lost his smile and muttered in a gloomy voice, "Champ, sometimes it's safer and a whole lot easier bein' crazy than goin' out there in that dog-eat-dog world."

Fighter

THREE

WE arrived at the Greyhound station in New Orleans a little after seven that night. Perry led the way to the Deluxe, an old downtown hotel, and got us a room. He'd been there before, I knew, because the desk clerk called him by name. When we got up to the room, Perry threw his suitcases on one of the two beds and opened them up. "These my fancy threads, Champ," he grinned and began pulling out colorful shirts, silk handkerchiefs, socks, jackets, and slacks, and putting them in drawers and on hangers. Some of them were so bright they almost hurt my eyes. He opened a small box and removed a gold ring with a large sparkling stone and slipped it on his little finger.

"Is that a real ruby?" I asked.

" 'Course it's real!" he nodded, holding it up to admire the glitter. "This here is my insurance. Can always hock it for couple of big ones if my luck run thin." Then he said, "Let's hit the sack. I wanna be down at King's pretty early tomorrow."

I didn't sleep much that night. The bed was

good, but Perry's idea, which had sounded at least *possible* at the hospital, seemed ridiculous to me now that it was time to put it in action.

We got up, ate two Western omelets apiece at the Waffle House, then took a cab straight to a rough-looking section of New Orleans not too far from the hotel.

"Here we is," Perry said, waving his hand at a fading sign that read *KING'S ATHLETIC EMPORIUM*. It was squeezed between a video game parlor and a shabby adult movie theater. A stairway led up to the second story of the old red-brick building.

I stared at the murky entryway with a bad feeling. "Look, Perry, this won't work. I'm not a fighter, and all those guys are professionals. They've been at it for years! And you said yourself I'm too old."

He stopped and leaned against the wall, then said easily, "We done been over this ten times already. I'm telling you it'll be okay. You're gettin' nervous, but *I* know whut this fightin' business is. I done it all, Champ. I fought over fifty bouts, I wuz a sparring partner, and later on I done a little managing. And I know how *good* you are, and how bad some fighters are. Most of the guys you gonna meet is doped up or boozed out or wore out. You'll see."

"Well, I don't —"

"Com'on, lemme show you whut it's like," he snapped. He marched up the stairs and I followed him.

50

The stairs led up into a huge high-ceilinged room with three full-sized rings in use and all sorts of weight machines around the walls. The air reeked of cigar smoke, sweat, and rotting wood. A boom box growled out an angry-sounding rap, and the weight machines made a constant banging racket.

"There's the man," Perry said in my ear. We walked over to a tall, lean black man with a shaved head, dressed in a fancy shirt with more colors than a peacock. He turned to see who was moving close to him, and his lips curved into a thin smile when he saw Perry.

"Well, Jester, here you are. You been doin' some time, am I right?"

"Naw," Perry said, sliding his hand down his silk sleeve. "Been out huntin' the Great White Hope, Brother King. And here he is."

King's half-lidded eyes looked me up and down, and his grin faded. "Perry, you lost your mind? In the first place he's too old, and in the second place — which I should have put in the first place — when you start messin' with white bread?"

"I'm gonna exploit this white bread, Brother King." Perry winked confidentially. "Use him up, overmatch him, take all his purses, then throw him away and go get myself another one."

"Fade away," King said with a laugh. "I know you're pretty good picking up talent, Perry, but not this time."

Perry looked around the room, and his eye settled on a thick-bodied fighter who was demolishing a heavy bag with punches that seemed to explode. "That Grady over there?"

"Sure. What about it?"

"Let him go a couple rounds with Smith. Then you can make up your own mind about this boy."

"Him against *Grady?*" The thought seemed to amuse the tall black man. Lifting his voice, he called out, "Grady, come on over here. You two, get out of the ring," he ordered the two fighters in the center ring.

The black fighter who came to stand before King was so muscular he almost waddled, and his neck was so thick it appeared he didn't have one. The rest of him was built to scale.

"Grady, you want a free sparring partner?" King asked.

Grady's eyes got narrow as he looked at me and said, "This one?" He looked at King and asked, "You kidding or something, King?"

King laughed. "Get him dressed out, Perry. We'll give the boys a treat."

Perry took me to the dressing room, and while I was changing, I waited for him to tell me something, like how to fight the big man. But he just said, "Don't let Grady hit you, Champ. He'll scramble your brains for sure."

When we got back, everybody in the gym had stopped work, and the boom box was shut down. Grady was in the ring, looking at me, and the whole crowd seemed to be grinning. Perry gave me a shove, muttering, "It's just another sparrin' match, Champ."

I stood looking down at the faces and saw that all of them were waiting for me to get murdered. Then King called out, "Perry, you want Grady to go easy?"

Perry yawned, exposing two gold teeth. "Tell him to take his best shot."

He leaned over against the apron of the ring and gave me a wink. My stomach was fluttering, and my knees felt funny; then I heard a bell and Grady came out toward me. He was big and kind of quick — but not as fast as Perry. I let him back me up, catching his left on my gloves, and tapping him with my own left. When I caught him so easily, a little sound of surprise ran around the audience, and Grady got mad. He came in harder and faster, but I just backed away catching his blows easily enough. Any one of them would have killed me, but he was too slow. I glanced down at Perry, and he was grinning at King.

"Grady slowed down quite a bit in his old age, ain't he, Brother?"

I think Grady heard him, because he came blowing in with both hands. My back hit the ropes, and I picked a spot right on the center of his heavy chin, ducked a vicious right that would have decked a rhino, then set my feet and gave him a solid right. It caught him coming in — so it must have been like getting rammed in the face with a railroad tie. He went down on his back, and after the solid *thump,* his head made against the floor, there was a sudden silence in the gym. He wasn't out, and he got to his feet almost at once. His eyes were glazed, though, and he couldn't find me for a minute.

"Okay, Grady, that's it," King called out quickly. He turned to stare hard at me, an odd look in his eyes; then he said to Perry, "Come on, we'll rap a little."

I was left high and dry in the ring, not knowing what to do. Grady stared at me for a minute, then crawled down from the ring and stalked away toward the dressing room. I felt silly up there, so I got down and went over to the big bag and punched it. Nobody said anything to me, but they were watching pretty closely.

Perry came out of the office in about ten minutes and said, "You got a fight, Champ. Four-rounder next Saturday right here in New Orleans. Now, you work out for a spell. I pick you up in 'bout two or three hours."

He left and I spent most of the morning training. The work felt good, and several times King stopped by and watched as I went at it steadily. He didn't say a word to me, but I noticed him talking to several guys who dropped by, nodding in my direction. Finally I showered, got dressed, and waited for Perry to come, which he did at about noon.

Perry winked at me, saying, "Come on, I'll introduce you to the best Cajun cookin' in New Orleans." He said the name like the locals:

Nual-lens. We walked for a long way until we got to what Perry called "the Quarter — where all the tourists come for kicks." We walked down Bourbon Street, and Perry pointed out places to stay away from. "Used to be good here — old Dixieland bands like Papa Celestin's and Sharky Bonnamo's. Ain't nothin' now but these imitation country bands — kids who never seen a farm! They wear designer jeans, vinyl vests, and frilly white shirts like they wuz all movie stars!"

I felt funny looking at some of the pictures in the windows. Perry noticed my discomfort. "Stay outa these places, Champ. Used to they wuz only burlesque stuff — that waz a long time ago."

The restaurant Perry took me to looked like it was ready to fall apart. It was made of old gray boards and had screen windows. We went inside, and Perry was greeted by a heavy woman with impossibly red hair.

"Perry Jester! Where you been?"

"Just enjoyin' life, Anna." Perry jollied the waitress for a while, then ordered for both of us. We had fried catfish and big bowls of shrimp gumbo. "Taste familiar to you, Champ?" he asked.

I thought about it for a moment, then answered, "I've definitely had it before." Picking up the oversized bottle of Tabasco sauce, I layered the top of the gumbo. "I think this will make it better."

"You done learned to eat *right*." As we pitched

55

into the food, he talked about our prospects. "We got it made, I tell you!" he said with a laugh. "When you put Grady down, you got some respect."

"Isn't he a good fighter?"

"Oh, he's tough and he's strong — a good club fighter. Lots like that around, and they're all right for fillin' a slot on the card. Ain't never goin' nowhere, Grady ain't, but he do put up a scrap. Thing is, he ain't been put down more'n two or three times. He's just tough. People see so many movies, they think you can knock a man down easy." He plucked up a whole jumbo shrimp, dipped it in red sauce, then popped it in his mouth and chewed it before adding, "You see two dudes in the movies swimmin' in water, and one of them knocks the other one out. Ain't no man alive can do that! Got to have your feet planted. But you can hit, Champ, and that's what promoters are always lookin' for. Someone who can put the other dude *down*."

I shook my head and said, "There's got to be more to it than that, Perry."

"Yeah, they is. You ain't never gonna be champion 'cause you ain't hungry. But you can make some easy money fightin' in prelims. You could make good money bein' a sparring partner. But main thing is, you want to keep your brains from being scrambled. I could over-match you, and you'd get minced. But if we take it easy, we can go a pretty long time pickin' up some easy money. But it's your say."

I thought about it, then nodded. "Well, I'll try it once; then we'll see."

That was on Monday. By Thursday I had settled into the Deluxe and the routine at King's. Perry came and went, but once he saw that I was all right, he dropped in only to sleep. He was gambling, and the games took place at night, so mostly he slept when I worked out. He had plenty of money and gave me more than I wanted for myself.

"You earn it soon," he grinned. "Us managers have to take care of our stable, now, don't we?"

I got pretty lonely just sitting around the room every night, and finally I called Doc Kimpel. It was pretty late, but I caught him at his office, and he gave a little shout when I told him who it was.

"Adam! Where have you been! Why haven't you called?"

He sounded like a mother hen with one chick, and I grinned as I thought of him stretched back in his chair like a benevolent but irritated Moby Dick. "Only been four days," I said.

"Well, *tell* me about it," he snorted. "What has that screwball got you into? Drugs or organized crime?"

"Neither one, Doc. I can't answer for Perry, but I'm keeping my nose clean. You'd be proud of me."

"You have a job?"

"Well . . . sort of. I'll tell you how it works out

after next week." We talked for a while, and he seemed almost as glad to talk to me as I was to him.

Finally he said, "Adam, there's a man I want you to go see. He's in Baton Rouge, and I think he might be able to give you some help."

"A detective?"

"No, he's a teacher — a professor of English at LSU."

I grinned at that. "What's he going to do — teach me to diagram a complex sentence?"

There was a moment's pause and then Kimpel chuckled. "How do you happen to know what a complex sentence is? Most people don't." Then he hurried on, saying, "What Henry Sweeting does is specialize in linguistics. He's the best man in the country — maybe the world — at spotting accents."

"Oh. You mean he can tell what part of the country I may be from?"

"Maybe. It's not an exact science, but I think you ought to see him. We went to undergraduate school together, and I gave him a call. Get in touch with him and see what he can do. He said he'd have his office open this weekend. Might be able to fit you in."

I scribbled down Sweeting's number and said, "Great . . . and thanks, Doc. I'll call you soon as I see him." I hung up feeling good. Someone was on my side.

The next morning I called LSU, and a woman gave me an appointment to see Dr. Sweeting at three the following afternoon. I quit working out about noon, and King stopped me on the way out. He had a skinny girl with red lips draped on one arm, and he took off his shades when he stopped me at the door.

"You leaving early today, Smith," he said. He didn't talk like most of the gym rats. His speech was quick and clear, and his eyes were sharp as needles. "You are about the hardest working white fighter I've ever laid eyes on." He gave me an odd look and said softly, "You know, I don't usually take on a heavyweight myself, but in your case I might make an exception."

"Perry's taking care of me."

He laughed at that and gave his girl a squeeze. "Perry will be back in the nuthouse or in jail before you know it, Smith. He's all right but he's crazy. Now, *I* can do you lots of good. The crowd will pay to see a white heavyweight who can hit."

"I'll stick with Perry, King. Thanks anyway." He put his shades on after staring hard at me as if I were some kind of exotic specimen.

"Loyalty — that's a fine thing," he murmured. Then he let a smile touch his thin lips. "Pretty expensive, though. You change your mind, let me know. I'll see that Perry gets a cut."

I told Perry that night about Doc's call, and he gave me money for bus fare. He seemed preoccupied, and I figured he'd been losing money at poker.

The next day I took the Greyhound to Baton

Rouge. The trip only took about an hour and a half. For a long stretch the highway was built over water — Lake Pontchartrain, I found out. Once I saw an alligator sunning on a log, grinning at something. The big cypress trees had lumpy bases, and people were fishing around the base of the piers. When I got off at the bus station in Baton Rouge, I walked outside and found a cab. "Can you take me to LSU?" I asked.

The cabby's name was Boudreau Doucett, and he gave me a running description of what was wrong with LSU from the minute I got in his cab. But he also pointed out the sights. He was a small man with a dark complexion and a funny accent.

"Hey, ain't I seen you three or two times? No? Well, you gonna watch youself at LSU! I don't like that place, me!"

Just before we got to the parking lot where he let me out, Boudreau waved his finger at me. "You wanna be *careful,* you! Boys down here make the gators look sweet! It's got one of the highest crime rates in Baton Rouge."

Somehow he made it seem like it was my fault, so I got out and said, "I'll be careful."

He said, "You better be, you! Eight bucks fifty." I gave him ten and told him to keep the rest, and he became even more protective. "Thanks. Now, I wouldn't move around this crazy place after dark, me. Rapers, muggings, no tellin' what — and look at that!" He waved his hand at a cop who had stopped a student with a massive overload of books and was writing him a ticket.

"Jaywalking!" Doucett said with a horrible curse. "Place is crawling with fuzz all day givin' tickets for jaywalking, and after dark Jack the Ripper wouldn't be safe! Well, you watch it, you hear me, man?"

I assured Boudreau that I heard him and finally managed to move away toward the large cluster of buildings that seemed to be my best bet.

It took thirty minutes to find the English Department and then the office on the third floor with *Dr. Sweeting* on the frosted glass. I went in, and the face of a skinny young woman with large glasses slowly emerged from behind a paperback novel, a picture of an overmuscled guy with long blond hair on its cover. She asked in a nasal tone what she could do for me.

"I have an appointment to see Dr. Sweeting."

She looked down at a pad on her desk and said, "You Adam Smith? Go through that door."

She lifted her book, and I noticed that she moved her lips when she read. When I went through the door, the man sitting at the walnut desk got up and came to me. He was fairly tall, almost six feet, and very thin. His suit looked as though it had been picked up at a garage sale, its frumpiness exaggerated by a crooked little bow tie. He was younger than I had expected, maybe thirty-seven or so, and his hair was black, uncut, and ruffled from the way he kept pulling at it.

He'd grab it with both hands as if trying to lift himself into the air. But he had a good smile, and his eyes were friendly as he greeted me. One thing I'd learned quickly was to read eyes. You can fake a grin with your lips, but not with your eyes.

"Adam Smith? I'm Henry Sweeting." He gave me a nervous handshake and then motioned to a chair. "Sit down, sit down!"

"Sorry to take your time —" I began, but he interrupted me by falling into his own chair and trying to pull his hair out.

"Kimpel called me last week, said you'd probably come by. Haven't seen him in a couple of years."

He kept up a running stream of talk, all the while getting me settled; then finally he paused long enough for me to get a word in. "Doc tells me that you know about my problem."

He nodded. "He thinks a lot of you."

"Well, I guess I owe him a lot. He tells me you might be able to help me a little."

"A *little* is about right, I'm afraid," Sweeting frowned. "Some of the press did a story on my work a few years ago, and after they got through with it, I was a modern day Henry Higgins."

"Able to place any man in London within three blocks just by his accent."

Sweeting stared at me, nodding slowly, and said, "That's about it. You know about *Pygmalion*?"

"Yeah, I guess I do! It's George Bernard Shaw's play about a linguist who takes a young woman off the streets of London and teaches her to speak so well that she could pass for an aristocratic lady."

Sweeting pulled at his hair and said, "Most people just know the movie *My Fair Lady*. Anyway, my work is like that of Professor Higgins. I work with two things — dialects and names."

"And you can tell where somebody comes from?" I asked.

"It's not that simple," he protested. "Look, let me give you a little lecture about my work. It won't hurt you any more than some of the boring messes they have on TV these days."

I said, "I'd like to hear it," and he got up and handed me a large book; then while I glanced through it, he began his lecture, just as if I were a class.

"That book you're holding is a linguistic atlas. It's primarily a book of maps showing the speech habits of different sections of the United States. This sort of thing has been going on since the latter part of the nineteenth century. George Wenker in Germany, Gillieron in Denmark, and other scholars in most civilized societies have been adding to it. Han Jurath published the first significant study of this nature in America called *Linguistic Atlas of New England*."

He walked around the desk and stood in front of me, tugged on his hair, then sat down in the chair beside me and pointed at the page I had flipped to.

"As its name implies, a linguistic atlas is a collection of maps identifying the prevalence of particular speech forms by geographic region. For example, different regions will tend to use different words for certain objects." He paused and asked, "What would you call the appliance we use to keep our food cold?"

"A refrigerator or an icebox."

Sweeting pointed down at the page and said, "Look at that. See? Right there." I looked at the list of words on the page as he said, "You probably come from west of the Mississippi River. If you'd come from anywhere except the South, you'd have called it something else — maybe a *fridge*."

"Yeah, well, I come from the South, then?"

"Not necessarily," Sweeting said quickly. "You may have had a mother born in the South who used that term, or you could have done basic training in Fort Sill, Oklahoma."

"But . . . how does that all help?" It sounded pretty farfetched to me, but I was ready to try anything.

"It works like this, Adam. If you want to get a reading on where you're from, we can do a series of tests. Some of them involve the choice of terms, such as you've just seen. Then there's pronunciation." He looked at me with a smile, then took a pen from his pocket and wrote *greasy* on the margin of the page. "How do you say that?" I said the word and he gave a big grin. "That's the southern pronunciation again. You said 'greez-ee,' and that's west of the Mississippi again. If you had come from another area, you'd have said 'grees-ee.' "

"The South again?"

He waved his hand carelessly in the air and stated with an air of authority, "I decided *that* before you said ten words. The problem is to find out which *section* of the South. Just recently I have been very successful in dividing up the South Midland, which extends south along the Ozarks into a form of what I call Mountain English. And I've broken this up into areas like southern Illinois, Missouri, Arkansas, eastern Oklahoma, and eastern Texas. After that I may —" He broke off suddenly and said truthfully, "Well, you don't want to hear about all that."

"It's very interesting," I said sincerely.

"I'll bet! But here's one more thing we can test you for, Adam — job and nationality. If you know certain terms, you'll be a jazz musician. If you know other terms, you'll probably be a race car driver. And, of course, if you know what *chutzpah* means, we'll know you're Jewish."

"What does it mean?" I asked.

He gave a wry grin. "I guess it means you're not Jewish, which I was already pretty sure of." He got up and asked, "You want to give it a try?"

"What can I lose, Doctor? How long will it take?"

"Oh, we can take care of it tomorrow. I'll have

a graduate student give the battery of tests; then I'll try to interpret the results. Be back here about nine in the morning."

"Thanks a lot, Dr. Sweeting."

"I can't promise anything, you know," he warned me. "It will probably be very general."

"I appreciate it no matter how it turns out," I said. I went out, and the receptionist was now reading a thick textbook. When she looked up and saw it was only me, she dropped it and whipped the steamy romance out of her drawer.

I saved money by getting a cheap room at the Majestic Motel, which was anything but. After I'd paid the twenty-five dollars, I walked around Baton Rouge until I got hungry. As little as I knew, I realized that the city was sick, maybe dying — at least the section I was in. The stink of death wreathed the aging apartment houses that seemed to lean against one another for support; the bleak smell was a compound of fear, poverty, anger, bad cooking, bodies packed too close together — all overlaid with the smog that fell like a hazy soup out of the sky.

Some of the sections were white, others were black; they all were haunted by the same vagrants. Old women with purple hair clutched brown grocery sacks and kept their purses hooked under their arms to keep them safe from the punks that circled the streets like barracuda. Drunks with trembling hands and empty faces often erupted from back alleys or deserted buildings to ask me for a buck. A pack of tough young kids followed me, trying to decide if rolling me would be worth the struggle. I guess I looked a little hard to handle, so they veered off looking for crippled prey — someone they could beat down with bicycle chains for a slick pair of Nikes and a few dollar bills.

I stopped at McDonald's and ate a Quarter-Pounder and some fries, and it was dark by the time I got back to the motel. I tried to watch television, but it was boring. I found a hard-cover Bible, placed by the Gideons, which seemed vaguely familiar, in the drawer of the nightstand and instinctively turned to the Gospel of Mark and read it straight through. I'd read it before — that much was clear. I knew what was coming before I read it. When I got to the end when Jesus was put on the cross, it made me feel strange — sad and alone, yet strangely comforted, as if He would understand my situation. What had *He* felt like, dying like that? I wondered. Finally, I put the light out and lay awake thinking until I dropped off to sleep.

Sometime that night the dream came, in full color and stereophonic sound. It was exactly as before, except that this time, just as the wave of flame swept over me and I started screaming, I heard voices. This was new. Unfortunately, the voices were so garbled and distorted that I couldn't make out any of the words. But even as I woke up gasping for breath and trembling, I realized that I had not been alone in whatever hellish inferno composed that dream.

I never did get back to sleep, but tossed and turned until dawn, then got up and went to breakfast and ate blueberry waffles. Afterward I went back to LSU to take the tests. A young graduate student who looked more like a football player than an English major administered them. He was a talky Texan named Billy Roy Simmons, and we got along fine. I took the written part in the morning, and then Billy Roy and I went to the school cafeteria. I got his life story — which was pretty lurid the way he told it — but when I didn't have much to say he seemed disappointed. I knew Sweeting hadn't said anything to him about my situation.

All afternoon he had me pronouncing words in front of a tape recorder. It wasn't bad, but I was ready to leave when we finished at four. Billy Roy said I ought to come to the big game that night, and I told him maybe I would. When I said good-bye to Sweeting, he told me he'd get back to me when he had something.

When I got back to the hotel in New Orleans, Perry was there. He gave me a bleary look and asked, "How'd it go?"

"Oh, I took a lot of tests. Probably won't help much."

Perry looked as though he had a headache and was unhappy. "You supposed to be at the gym. Us'ta be I could count on you. You gettin' pretty uppity."

"One day won't matter. Where you been?"

"I been gettin' an education," he snapped,

68

then he made himself grin and lay down on his bed. "I always thought I was the best poker player in New Orleans, but they's a new man come in since I been gone. I gets him the next time, though."

He wasn't wearing his fancy ring, and I made a guess. "Must have been a pretty expensive lesson?"

He laughed then, and his old humor came back. "You ain't wrong 'bout that, Champ. But we wins us some money in a few more days."

I thought about it and said, "I got an offer from King on Friday. To manage me — even said he'd cut you in for a piece of me."

Perry's white teeth flashed against his dark skin, and he gave a tough laugh. "Wouldn't be King if he didn't try to do me in." Then he turned to look at the ceiling and asked idly, "Whut you gonna do 'bout it?"

"What do you think I'm gonna do about it?" I was irritated that he even had to ask.

An odd look crossed Perry's face, and he stared at me silently for a long time. "Champ — you ever notice that I'm black?"

"What?"

He sat up on the bed and swung his legs over the side. His face was serious as he said slowly, "You gonna get me hurt, Champ." He shook his head as I started to argue. "Oh, I know you won't do it on *purpose*, but you done made me change one of my rules: Don't trust Whitey. I done made that rule a long time ago, and now you done messed me about, and I can't help trustin' you. And that's all right, 'cause you jus' like a baby. I mean you ain't *got* no past, and you can't remember how and why to hate black folk. But the thing is, if I gets to believin' in you, I probably do it with another white bread, and that's gonna get me ruined!"

I thought about it, then shrugged. "Well, maybe I'll let you down, and you can go back to the way you used to be."

"Maybe, but I doubt it." He watched as I undressed and started for the shower. "You worried about fightin'?" he asked.

I stopped and looked back at him. "I'm trusting you to keep me safe. Then I'll probably trust another black guy, and he'll wipe me out." I slammed the door, but I could hear Perry laughing like crazy.

No word came from Sweeting the whole week, and on Saturday morning, the day of the fight, we slept late and didn't go to the gym. "We just float around and take it easy today," Perry said. "You is sharp as a razor, Champ. If you don't have no mind trouble — like freezin' up — why, we got us a piece of cake!"

We just walked around for a long time that morning; then in the afternoon we went to a movie. Later I couldn't remember the name of it, but it had lots of cars blowing up and people sleeping together. Perry asked me when we came out how I liked it.

"I didn't." There was no doubt in my mind.

"Why not?"

"Too much sex and violence. I guess it's just not my thing, Perry."

Perry gave me an odd look. "You get that stuff at a Dallas Cowboys football game." When I didn't comment, he shook his head. "You got funny ideas, Champ. Whoever raised you put some old-timey ideas in your head."

We ate a hearty lunch at Ryan's: a couple of thick steaks and a good run at the salad bar. "That's all you git till after the fight," Perry warned, but I didn't really eat much at night anyway.

At five he said, "Let's go."

We went over to a bulky old red-brick building with quite a few people milling around in front. The dressing room was a long, low-ceilinged sort of room with lights hanging from cords and ranks of battered green lockers along one wall. Perry led me to one of them, opened it with a key, then laid out my gear — black trunks, black robe, black shoes. They were all new and I had to grin. "Looks like I'm going to a funeral, Perry. Hope it's his and not mine."

He stared at me, then broke out in a broad grin and hit me on the shoulder. "That's *good!* You ain't got bad nerves. Some guys break out in a rash just puttin' their gear on."

He kept talking to me all the time — mostly about fights he'd had — and from time to time, other fighters and their trainers and managers

71

would come in and begin to get ready. They were a pretty quiet bunch except for a huge white fighter, apparently half drunk, who at the top of his lungs kept telling raw stories about his "success" with women.

At seven the loudspeaker came on, and a tall middleweight followed his handlers out. After a while he came back breathing hard, his eyebrow bleeding. Another fighter went out — this time the big one who did the talking. Perry began kneading my shoulder muscles.

"We next," he said quietly.

Maybe if I had a better memory I'd have been nervous. As it was, I didn't have a lot of bad past experiences to push against me, so I thought with a sudden flash of humor, I guess there's worse things than not remembering anything.

Finally the door opened, and I looked down to watch the loud fighter come back, but he didn't walk in. His face was a bloody mask, and he was carried on a stretcher by four men. They rolled him off onto one of the tables, his head flopping loosely as they worked on him.

Finally it was time, and I followed Perry to the door. He stopped just before we went out and said, "I ain't told you nothin' about this guy you fightin' 'cause I didn't want you to be making no fancy plans. Whut you do is stay with him for the first round. He can't touch you, and you got my word on it. Then when you see whut it's like, we'll decide whut you gonna do."

I followed him into the darkness — a thick,

black sea of smoke smelling of stale beer. I got into the ring, and for just a moment when I looked out at the crowd, I almost panicked. I could see the faces pretty good, and they were after blood — mine, if the other guy could give it to them. There were women there too, with glistening eyes and painted lips, screaming like banshees, every bit as bloodthirsty as the men.

Perry said, "Ain't they a purty sight!"

I grinned at him. He pulled my robe off and the referee came over to check my gloves. Perry pushed me toward the center of the ring, and I stood arm's length from the man I had to fight: Leon Pulaski. He had heavy shoulders, and his eyes were almost pulled shut by the little scars at the corners. His ears were in pretty bad shape too, looking like hunks of dough glued to the side of his head. He had slate-colored eyes, dull and without expression, and when we wheeled and went back to our corners at the ref's word, I had the feeling that he hadn't really seen me.

The bell rang and we met in the center. The crowd started yelling at once, and Pulaski began bobbing and weaving, throwing a pretty good left out of a crouch. I'd never seen anyone do that, so I waited for him to straighten up, but he didn't. Finally I tried a left that bounced off the top of his head and hurt my hand. We circled the ring, and the crowd got louder as I let him bull me around. This went on for about a minute, and the crowd began shouting and cursing.

Then Pulaski straightened up and caught me

73

with a hard right to the temple that drove me against the ropes. It wasn't bad, but he followed it up by wrapping me in his thick arms, and we went reeling around the ring like two drunks. The trouble was he was beating me to death in the process. He could hit me in the kidney with a left, give me a rabbit punch with his right that sent purple spots flashing through my head, and stomp down hard on my instep, which hurt the worst of all.

I was trying to get loose, and I guess the ref was trying to break us up, but he hung on like glue for over a minute and made a wreck out of me with his barroom tactics.

Finally the ref peeled him off, and I just stayed away from him until the round ended. When I sat down, Perry was laughing like crazy.

"What's so funny!" I spat out my mouthpiece and glared at him.

"You is funny," he giggled as he washed me down with a sponge. "You two look like you is in *luv!*" He fell against me in helpless laughter, and I shoved him away. Then he came back and said, "Now you know whut to do?"

I glared at him. "Yeah, I know what to do — I'm going to stomp on him!"

Perry laughed and slapped me on the back as the bell rang. "That's whut we come for, Champ."

I was really mad at Perry for not telling me what to expect, and I was pretty mad at myself for getting wallowed all over the ring in front of that sorry crowd. And so I erupted when Pulaski again crouched down in that bobbing stance. I drew a left jab, then sent a wicked left hook crashing through his guard. It caught him right where his head joined his neck. The light in his slate-colored eyes went out as if I'd thrown a switch. He dropped his hands, and I had no trouble at all laying the big right, right on the button. When he went down, everyone in the house could see he was made of rubber. His head struck the canvas with a *thump*. Then he just lay there, not moving a muscle. The referee didn't even bother to count. He just motioned me to the center of the ring and raised my hand. The crowd broke loose in screaming and jumping up and down, but I didn't care. I knew they'd have made the same noise if I'd been lying on the floor.

On the way back to the dressing room, people kept reaching out to pat my shoulder, to touch me, and they were all screaming at the top of their lungs. I was just glad to get away. When we got to the table and Perry was taking the tape off my hands, King came drifting up and handed Perry a few bills.

"Little bonus in there, Perry. He done good." Then he looked at me and asked, "You be ready in two weeks? A six-rounder in Mobile?"

Perry looked at me and I nodded. "Sure, we be ready," Perry said. I went to the shower, and afterward we went out and walked along the street back to the hotel. It was pretty quiet and I was thinking hard.

Finally Perry said, "Well, now you know, Champ. You kin do it if you want to. But you don't have to."

We didn't say much else until we were both in our beds. "Perry?" I said.

"Yeah?"

"It's a bad way to live — hurting some poor guy."

"You got that right," Perry agreed.

I kept on thinking about it. "I can't live on you forever. We'll do the one in two weeks; then we'll see." He didn't answer and I asked him, "Perry, did you like to fight?"

"Hated every round of it, Champ," he answered at once. "Happiest day of my life wuz when I quit." He lay silently in the darkness and said, "I take care of you, Champ. You won't get punchy, and God willin', you won't get all cut up. It's a way to make money . . . there's worse ways." A thought came to him, showing in his eyes like a ghost, and he shook it away, adding, "I tried some worse ways my own self. Way I see it, you got a long way to go lookin' to see who you used to be. Fighting don't take much time, so you got some freedom. And you kin do it in mos' places. So if you think you kin stand it, I take care of you."

"Well," I muttered sleepily, "guess you got your hands full. I need a keeper, don't I? Good night, Perry."

"Good night, Champ."

D. K. Wolfe

FOUR

TWO days after the fight, I got a call from Professor Sweeting's office asking me to come in at my convenience. I took the bus to Baton Rouge as soon as I could catch one, and the professor was glad to see me. He looked exactly as he had the last time I'd seen him, same crumpled suit, making him look like an unmade bed, same bow tie, and same wild hairstyle he achieved by trying to lift himself off the floor with his hands.

"Well, you didn't waste any time," he said, getting up and pushing me into a chair. "I'm afraid you're going to be disappointed in the results of the tests."

"Well —"

"Oh, we've pinpointed a few things," he added quickly, then turned to pull a sheaf of papers off his cluttered desk. "I'll skip the technical section and get right down to the significant data." He slipped a pair of horn-rimmed glasses on his thin nose and peered over them with a stern expression. "Now, Adam, I must warn you that linguistics is not as precise a science as, shall we say, biology. Give me a few years and it will be, but for the present, all we can do is expose a few *trends*."

He wandered around the room for the next ten minutes talking about things I didn't fully understand, reading statistics and excerpts from papers he scattered all over the room, and finally I interrupted him. "That's very interesting, Dr. Sweeting, but can you give me any *specific* help? I mean, am I from America, for starters?"

Caught off guard in the middle of a series of obscure references to the syntax of the Aztecs, he glared at me, then had to grin.

"Sorry about that." Then he said abruptly, "Oklahoma."

"That's where I'm from?"

"You're either *from* there, or you've spent a lot of time there. Almost certainly." He sat down and looked at me with a strange glow in his mild blue eyes. "You know, Adam, this is the first time my profession has ever had any *practical* use — always before it's been just a theory. But I've spent an enormous amount of time on your tests, and I feel sure you come from the Southwest. And although it could be Texas or northern Arkansas, I'd stake my reputation that you've spent a great deal of time in Oklahoma, most likely in the eastern part of the state."

"Hey, that's *great!*" I grinned at him. "It's the first real help I've gotten."

"Well, Oklahoma is a big place," he said quickly. "And I can't really pinpoint your local roots any closer."

I could tell he was finished, so I got up and stuck out my hand. "You've done a lot and I appreciate it, Dr. Sweeting. Well, I'll be on my way."

He followed me to the door. "I'd appreciate it if you'd let me know how it comes out," he said.

"I'll do that."

I left him then and went back to New Orleans. As soon as I got off the bus, I went to the gym to meet Perry. He was watching a couple of middleweights push each other around in a brotherly sort of way in one of the rings. When he turned toward me, I could see that he hadn't slept much. His eyes were sunk back in his head, and his voice was a little blurred.

"Where you been?" he muttered.

"You get any sleep last night?" I asked. "You look awful."

"Naw, I never," he grunted. "I ain't quite got the hang of that stud who think he invented poker, but pretty soon I get him figured. Then I clean his plow."

I'd never known Perry to be depressed, but I could see he was in pretty bad shape. We spent the rest of the day at the gym, then went to eat. While we were finishing the dessert, I told him about Sweeting and what he'd said about Oklahoma.

Perry listened, and when I'd said it all, he drank his coffee and looked right at me. "I guess you tellin' me you gonna go to Oklahoma."

"Well . . . I might go take a look."

He shook his head and said suddenly, "You ain't gonna do no good. But I guess you gotta try it." He reached into his pocket and pulled out a thin roll of bills, counted them, then gave me a few. "You hafta ride a bus both ways. Be back two days before the bout."

"I can get by without this," I said.

"No, you take it. Time you get back I'll have plenty more. Just keep in shape, you hear me?"

"Yeah." I looked at him and asked, "You want to go with me, Perry?"

He grinned at me and shook his head. "Not this trip. You get this outa your system, Champ. I'll stay here and pick up some green."

He didn't say anything else, but the next day he walked me down to the bus station. "Ain't got nothin' else to do," he insisted. "Besides, a country boy like you might git on the wrong bus."

"I need to make one stop before the bus leaves," I told him. "Won't take long."

He just smiled, but when I told the taxi driver, "Police Department," his eyes opened wide. I waited for him to argue, but he just gave me a tight grin and settled back in the cab.

We got out at the large new building made of white marble and bronze that looked like a savings and loan, and I found Missing Persons without too much trouble. When Perry saw where we were, he grinned suddenly but said nothing as we went inside. It was on the second floor, and when I asked for Lieutenant Cossey, a white-haired sergeant pointed at a door with a sign: *MISSING PERSONS*.

When we went in, Cossey was sitting at a cluttered desk, his hands locked behind his head, staring at the ceiling. He slowly looked down, and when he saw me, he got up and said, "Well, if it ain't Mr. Smith." We shook hands, and he gave me a good hard shake, but then he stared over my shoulder and his eyes widened.

"Jester!" he snorted. "What you doing here?"

"I with him, Massa," Perry grinned and touched his forehead with a kind of short bow.

Cossey stared at him, then at me. He went back to his desk, sat down, and rammed a smoldering cigar between his teeth. Then he grinned at me and said, "Where'd you pick Perry up?"

I couldn't think of anything to say, but Perry piped up. "I'm jus' a pore ol' colored person tryin' to git along with my white folks," he said, his eyes mocking Cossey.

"I bet! You're a credit to race relations, Jester." Cossey grinned sardonically. "I reckon you were the first to integrate leg-breaking on an interracial basis in New Orleans."

"A man is poor indeed if he don't do something for his folks," Perry said humbly.

I wasn't sure about any of this, but I said, "Perry's been a good friend to me, Lieutenant."

Cossey stared at me, then at Perry. Finally he puffed at the cigar and said, "Jester, I hear you been trying to take Ralph Deparma at poker. Let

81

me give you some free advice. Avoid evil companions."

"Oh, he ain't so bad, Lieutenant."

"Yeah, I know, he's done some good things. And Hitler was fond of dogs, too." Then he looked at me and said, "What can I do for you?"

I told him about the results of the test, and he listened without a word. When I had finished, he sat there, his brow ridged with thick lines.

Finally he said, "I've got something gnawing at me, but I can't get a handle on it." He puffed at the cigar, sending out huge clouds of vile smoke.

"You get them cigars secondhand?" Perry asked, fanning the smoke.

"If I smoked good ones, you'd think I was on the take," Cossey answered. Then he said, "I know there's something I should tell you, but it's hiding out. I'll think of it after you're gone."

"You want to give me the file — the one on me, I mean? And does it have the name of the guy who found me?"

He heaved himself out of his chair and walked to a bank of battered gray filing cabinets. After running down the alphabet, he jerked a drawer open, pulled out a thin manila envelope, and handed it to me.

"That's it. You can't take that one, but I can have copies made if you want."

"I'd appreciate it." There were only about six sheets of paper inside; then I pulled out something wrapped in a small envelope. "What's this?"

"That?" He looked at it and shrugged. "Pieces of melted metal — on a belt buckle maybe."

I opened the envelope and looked at the rough, irregular blobs of metal. One was obviously a wristwatch, but the other was harder to identify. It was gold and was more or less round with some rough edges on two sides that might have been clips for a belt. "They found this on me?"

"Yeah. Everything else was burned." He shrugged and said, "We ran it through the lab, but aside from tellin' us it was gold, they couldn't say nothing that meant anything. You can take it with you if it'll do any good."

"Won't that get you into trouble?"

Cossey grinned broadly. "Who's gonna know?" He sobered and gave me a direct look. "Look, Smith, even when a missing person is reported, nothing happens. Local police forces have higher priorities. Who needs a lot of interviews, a lot of forms to fill out? People get killed and buried all the time all over the country. Who cares? They're just bones in shallow graves that pretty soon become deep graves, and nobody cares. And a guy that wants to disappear, why, it ain't hard to get lost."

I knew he was telling me to forget about finding out who I was, and he wasn't a bad guy. "Sure, I know. Well, thanks a lot, Lieutenant."

"For nothing," he grunted. "When you get to Oklahoma, write me and give me an address or a phone number. There's something eatin' at me, but . . ." He paused, then finally shrugged and glanced at Perry. "You keep fooling around with scum like Deparma, Perry, you're gonna wind up with a tag on your big toe."

"I surely do appreciate your concern, Mr. Policeman." Perry grinned and nodded his head. "And I will surely take it up with my pastor at the next meetin'." Perry's eyes were still mocking Cossey. He looked around the office and added innocently, "You has a fine department here, sho does!"

Cossey spat into a battered cuspidor beside his desk and said sourly, "Oh, sure! Apart from splits based on political, racial, religious, and ethic tensions, we're one happy family." Then he glanced at me and said, "Look, you think of anything I can do, let me know, okay?"

"Sure." I turned to go, then stopped and said, "Thanks a lot, Cossey. I'll let you know when I get settled, but I'll be back in two weeks." I grinned at him, and let him have it without warning. "Perry is my manager, you know, and he's got me a bout lined up in a couple of weeks."

Cossey stared at me as if I'd grown two heads; then he gave a tremendous laugh and shouted, "Jester, get outa here before I lock you up for intent to corrupt!"

When we were walking toward the bus station,

Perry said, "You know, for a honky, that ain't a bad cop."

My bus didn't leave for nearly an hour, so Perry and I walked over to the terminal. I asked him how he got to know Cossey and he just grinned and said, "We wuz two ships that passed in the night, Champ." I knew he wasn't going to talk about it, so we talked about the fight that was coming up, and he told me to find a gym of some kind and work out every day.

The terminal looked like a mausoleum, and the guy I bought the ticket from had a serious case of dandruff, making an oddly attractive pattern on his dark blue shirt. We still had a few minutes before our bus left.

Perry said, "You tell Doc Kimpel you goin' on a trip?"

"Say, I didn't even think of it!" A bank of telephones were lined up on one wall, and I walked over and called collect. After a little wait I got him, and after "Hello's" and "How you doing's," I told him about what Sweeting had said and that I was going to Oklahoma.

He was quiet for a long count, then, "Where in Oklahoma are you going, Adam?"

"Oklahoma City, I guess."

"Look, why not go to Tulsa?"

"What's in Tulsa?"

"D. K. Wolfe's in Tulsa. One of the sharpest lawyers in the country — and owes me a favor. I'll give D.K. a call and you can go do some talking. I think you might get some help if there's

85

any help possible."

"Well . . ." I thought it over for about ten seconds and said, "Tulsa will do me fine. D. K. Wolfe, you say?"

"You got a pencil? Here's the address and phone number."

I jotted it down on a piece of the phone book, then ripped it off and put it in my billfold. "Thanks, Doc. I'll write as soon as I get there. And I'll be back in two weeks anyway."

"I want you to come and see me when you do," he insisted, and we agreed on a time and hung up.

Perry was munching peanuts and swigging a Sprite when I finished, and we shot the breeze until the bus got in. "Take care, Champ," he said, and I saw that he waited until the bus left. Like a mother hen with only one chick, old Perry!

I spent the next eighteen hours bored, cramped, sleepy, and longing for the next rest room. The diesel fumes oozed through the seams of the bus and took away my appetite, and when I did eat at one of the bus stops, the sandwiches tasted vaguely like an inner tube. A drunk got on in Little Rock and threw up right behind me, so that took care of any hope for the rest of the trip.

The Ozarks were pretty, but when we hit the Oklahoma border, I felt something. The country flattened out, and it wasn't anything special, but

I had this sense that I'd seen this before — that I'd been in this part of the country. By the time I got off the bus at Tulsa, I was bone tired, but I felt good. Just before dark, we'd passed a bunch of things in an open field — black metal objects that kept bowing and bowing to the ground, like huge monstrous cranes pecking at snails — and I'd said to myself, *Oil!* I knew those were old rigs pumping the oil out of the ground, and I knew that I'd seen lots of them.

But the bus station didn't ring any bells, nor did the city. I walked around when I got off the bus, finally found a vacancy at a dive called the Elite Motel, and checked in. When I hit the bed I died for about twelve hours, not even bothering to take a shower.

It was after four when I woke up, and by the time I had gotten cleaned up and had a breakfast of ham and eggs and doughy home-style biscuits at Denny's, it was nearly six. I decided to go see the lawyer, even though it was late, so I got directions from a skinny cop who looked too young for the job.

Tulsa was as flat as a Monopoly board. All the streets ran north or east, making it easy to get around.

I got off the elevator and found the door marked in very severe letters: *D. K. Wolfe — Attorney.* The door opened on well-oiled hinges, and the carpet was so thick I hated to put my dirty shoes on it.

The room wasn't as big as the Coliseum, but

then it wasn't much smaller either, and I made a guess it cost about as much per square foot. If the outer office was like this, I couldn't wait to see the real thing! The front desk, about the size of an aircraft carrier, was manned by a guy wearing a young-old face, staring intently at a thin blue book. The waiting area was full of empty yellow leather and stainless steel benches and a hat rack made from deer antlers. Coffee tables made out of whole sliced walnut slabs were scattered everywhere.

I waded through the carpet up to the desk and said, "I'd like to see Mr. Wolfe."

The guy didn't even look up. "You have an appointment?"

"No, but —"

"Then you'll have to make one. What's your name?" He did look up then, and he had color-less eyes that were casually threatening. Eyes that seemed to look right through me as if I was beneath his contempt. "Who recommended you to this office?"

"I'm Adam Smith. Dr. Kimpel from Louisiana sent me."

He certainly wasn't being friendly, and I found myself getting stubborn. "I think your boss will want to see me." I sat down firmly on one of the yellow benches and looked at the pictures on the wall of some horses just crazy to jump fences. "I'll wait."

He might have had objections, but just then a door opened, and a big man that looked like a fat politician barged out. His pudgy face was red as he slammed the door behind him. He stopped and glared at me, then turned to the guy at the desk. "You know," he said slowly, and I could tell he was forcing himself to talk civilly despite his fury. "You know, D. K. Wolfe is a real pain in the neck!"

"Do you want another appointment, Judge?"

The secretary's eyes got brighter, and I could tell he was liking all of this. The big man took a big breath as if preparing to yell, but then he glanced at me and grunted, "I'll . . . call you later."

He rushed out of the room, and the secretary got up and went through the door to the office. I sat there wondering why I was here, why Doc had asked me to come, and I almost walked out. But just then the secretary came back and said, "You can go in now."

He stood blocking the door, and I knew he wanted to throw me out the window just to see how high I'd bounce. He wasn't too big, but I thought I'd better not try to wrestle him to see if I could get in. Finally he whirled and marched back to his desk.

I went through the door, and at first I thought I'd gotten into the wrong room. There was a desk and the walls were lined with books, but I didn't see anyone who looked like a sharp lawyer.

Instead I saw this strikingly beautiful woman with the blackest hair possible wearing a simple pearl gray dress that somehow I knew cost enough to feed a small third-world village for a month. She was standing by the bar built into the wall, holding a glass in one hand and staring out the window at the lights of Tulsa.

Thinking she hadn't heard me come in, I cleared my throat and said, "My name is Smith. I'd like to see Mr. Wolfe."

She just stared out the window and acted as though she hadn't heard me. There was no other desk in the room, but there was a door on the right wall. I thought maybe this was his secretary and Wolfe was lurking in another office. She just stood there. I stared back, waiting for her to get Mr. Wolfe. Then she slammed the glass down on the bar and turned to face me.

"I'm Wolfe. Sit down."

Somehow I had expected D. K. Wolfe to look like some of the movie stars I remembered — Perry Mason or Edward G. Robinson. Or maybe a short, fat, bald, lawyer type with a harsh voice and the manners of a major-league umpire.

If she'd said, "I'm Rebecca of Sunnybrook Farm," I would have been less surprised. She looked like the actress I'd seen in an old movie — Sophia Loren, that was her name — the high cheekbones, large, expressive eyes, wide mouth with a full lower lip. And that body . . . D. K. Wolfe was about to waken all sorts of memories within me.

"When you get through checking me out,

Smith, you can sit down and tell me what you want."

I felt my face burning. I had been staring at her like a teenage boy. She suddenly smiled. "Well, I don't believe it! A blush! Maybe Kimpel was telling me the truth after all!" She motioned at a chair and said, "Sit down. What would you like to drink?"

I plopped into the chair and stammered, "Nothing for me." I'd figured out that I wasn't a big fan of alcohol.

She glanced at me steadily and asked, "Smoke?"

"No, thanks."

"What *do* you do, Mr. Smith?"

I looked right at her, not exactly sure what she was trying to say.

She gave a sudden laugh and said, "Come on. It's quitting time." She picked up a coat and a purse from a rack, and I followed her out the door. She stopped long enough to say to the man at the outer desk, "If Moore calls, tell him to get another lawyer, and pull Dailey off the Minton thing — it's a waste of time."

"Anything else?"

"No. You might as well go home." She turned to me and said, "Let's go, Smith."

I could feel the guy watching us as we went out, and on the way down, I said, "Your secretary doesn't like me — hard to believe, isn't it?"

"No. He doesn't like anybody except me." As we stepped off the elevator, she added, "He's a murderer. I got him off, but he was guilty as Judas."

"You've got to be kidding."

Her silence was enough of an answer.

"I can see why you want him for a receptionist, though," I said. "Spreads sunshine everywhere he goes."

"Don't make any mistake about Maury," she warned quickly. "He's deadly. Black belt in karate. Once in a great while an unpleasant character drops in." She looked me up and down with one complete shift of her eyes. "Maury takes care of them."

"I never knew lawyers had bouncers," I said.

She gave me a frosty look. "You hungry?"

If I wasn't it wouldn't have made much difference. D. K. Wolfe led me to a fancy restaurant on the fifteenth floor of some building with a menu in some language I couldn't read, ordered for both of us, ignored me while she ate like a field hand, then paid the bill by signing her name. Most of the time she seemed to forget I was there, confining her remarks to comments on the quality of the meal or the sorry attempts of the combo to play jazz. Finally she marched out, and I followed her to a cab like a puppy on a leash. When we got to her apartment, she unlocked the door and I followed her inside. The furniture was all harsh angles of black and white. Pointy steel sculptures were scattered around. She led the way to the couch and flung herself on it.

"So, Smith, here I am," she said with a careless wave at a chair opposite. "Are you just going to stand there?"

"Yep," I said, careful not to sit down. I guess she heard something in my voice because she looked up and paused. Our eyes locked.

Silence.

Then, "Suit yourself." She kicked off her black pumps and continued, "After I talked to Kimpel, and he told me your problem, I thought just *once* I'd find a man I could meet on a plane of equality. I mean, if you really can't remember anything, you must have forgotten all your prejudices about women."

"Maybe," I said with a short grin. I looked at her, thinking I couldn't have seen a woman more beautiful than this, not ever. Then I said pleasantly, "But new ones tend to form pretty quickly."

She stared at me again, her body rigid, then said coolly, "Toughen up, Smith. If you can't handle me, you probably should leave now. This is who I am. If it bothers you, too bad. I don't change to make my clients feel better." She looked me up and down again and with a little less harshness said, "Goes with the territory, I suppose."

It seemed she suddenly felt awkward sitting there by herself, and she stood and went behind the couch, sat on the edge, and crossed her arms. "Kimpel called two days ago. I've been looking for you. Tell me why you came."

I instinctively sat down in the chair she'd

pointed to earlier, and I could see it irritated her. The muscles in her face tensed up, so I decided to try to relax the tension a bit. "What does D.K. stand for?"

She walked around the couch and right up to me. She was wearing perfume that smelled like violets. As she stood over me, some sort of complicated signals were coursing between us — a man-woman kind of thing that was apparent even to a guy without a past. I figured she wasn't going to tell me what D.K. meant, but then she said quietly, "Darla Kaye."

With that she backed up and sat on the couch, staring at me, so I started telling her what little I knew, what I hoped to discover. But the whole time I felt distracted. My mind kept wandering to D.K., and I kept wondering who she was. I found her incredibly attractive — despite her tough-lawyer act — and longed to be close to her, to know more about her. Finally I said, "Well, that's it. Not much to go on, is there?"

She leaned forward a little on the couch, placing her elbows on her knees. "Are you sure you actually want to know who you are, Adam? Most of us spend our lives forgetting that very thing."

I smiled at her sincerity. "A policeman told me that," I laughed. "But Kimpel says nothing's worse than being nobody."

"He's wrong," she said definitively, staring across the room at nothing. "Did Kimpel tell you about me?"

"Just that you're a lawyer."

Suddenly she got up and began pacing around the room nervously, though she acted as if she were doing something important. She straightened a few magazines and poured herself a drink. But her hands were unsteady, and her face had lost its hard quality. She turned to me and bluntly said, "I killed my husband." Her eyebrows raised in anticipation of my response. "Kimpel didn't tell you that, did he?"

I shifted nervously in my chair, and she watched me intently. She then said, "I didn't shoot him or anything like that. We'd had an argument . . . and then we left the club. I was driving . . . and I guess we'd both been drinking too much. I never saw the car that hit us. . . ." Her eyes were distant, and it seemed natural to reach out and touch her hand, but she was too far away. "I was thrown out, but Joe . . . he was thrown under the . . . the truck . . . and I tried to wake him up but . . ."

I waited for her to go on, but suddenly she sat back down on the couch, and her earlier demeanor snapped back, that of killer lawyer. She raised an eyebrow at me and said emotionlessly, "Kimpel, he pulled me out of it." She laughed a little. "Maybe I'd have been in a nut-house like you."

The words stung, but I tried to dismiss them. I watched her for a long time, and she just sat on the couch, distant and uninvolved. Finally she turned to me and said, "I guess you're wondering what kind of freaky woman the good doctor sent you to." Her hands trembled as she searched methodically for a cigarette. "I have no idea why I just spilled my guts to you. Maybe because you seem to understand a little. Who knows?" She got up to pour herself another drink, though she hadn't finished her previous one.

"I suppose it's like whispering secrets down a well," I said softly. "To a man who has no past and no future."

She turned suddenly to look at me, and her face shifted into an amused expression, pondering my last statement. She sipped her drink and said, "I can help you, Adam. I have a friend in the government. He can access a computer database that will give us every missing person that even remotely resembles you," she said with confidence.

For the first time I felt a twinge of hope. I also felt something else, something strong for this woman. She was hard core, but underneath there was a lot of pain. Somehow I could easily sense it. I stood and joined her at the bar.

"Are you just going to stand there, or are you going to offer me a drink?"

She laughed a little. "You drink?"

"I drink water," I smiled.

She nodded and quickly poured me a glass. She handed it to me and looked me directly in the eye. "You know what my philosophy has been, Adam? All will go wrong. Maybe I've been too long in court. Maybe I need to see something go right . . . just once more."

"Is that why you're helping me?" I asked. She nodded and played with the rim of her glass. I grinned and said, "And here I thought it was because you found me irresistible!"

Her eyes narrowed a bit, and at first I thought I'd been too forward. But she set her glass down and took another step closer to me. "Why would you think a silly thing like that?"

We locked eyes. "I don't know, D.K. Maybe you're going soft. Next thing you know you'll be hugging trees and trying to save the whales."

D. K. Wolfe laughed, and laughed hard. I hadn't seen her laugh yet, and it was exhilaratingly beautiful.

Then we were both conscious of being close . . . conscious of hungers aroused. "I . . . I guess I'd better go," I stammered.

For a moment her eyes burned with darkness; then she took a step backward, and her body straightened like a soldier's. Her face was as hard as it had been at first.

"I'll call you," I said feebly, trying to interpret her signals again.

"All right," she said, her voice like a razor's edge.

I went to the door, opened it, then turned to say, "I'm . . . um, I'm a little messed up, D.K. You know?"

She smiled slightly, her eyes a little less

fierce. "No kidding."

I laughed and left, with visions of a beautiful too-tough lawyer filling my head. I got back to the hotel without remembering a single step.

What Are Friends For?

FIVE

MAYBE there's something more boring than reading old newspapers, but I doubt it. While waiting to hear from D.K., I spent the better part of the week reading old papers, seeing what I could learn in Tulsa about my past. I'd start my days by getting up and eating a cheap breakfast at the Dew Drop Inn — an establishment that had not established a meaningful relationship with the local health board. My one theory about food had been that nobody can mess up breakfast — after all, what can you do to eggs? The short-order cook had the face of an executioner, and after having his eggs sit in my stomach like a dead armadillo a couple of times, I switched to pancakes. They were worse. But my money was short, and the helpings were massive.

Then for five hours I'd sit in the reading room of the Tulsa Public Library searching five-year-old newspapers. They were as boring as the Congressional Record, but I learned pretty quickly how to run through them. Front page — just to see if anybody important had dropped out of sight. Inside of front page — maybe. I learned to hit the headlines with one glance, then skip on to the next page. The wrap-up of state news was always on page six, and it covered anything big in the rest of the state. After one day I could wring a paper dry in less than two minutes.

But it was depressing. All those screaming headlines. And now who gave a dead rat about any of it? It was like wandering through an old cemetery reading the names of people who once meant something but didn't anymore. I found out that you could skip a month, and nothing was really lost — the same old world messing around in people's lives. Nothing changes; all is vanity under the sun, as somebody said. And today's headline won't be anything but a smear of ink on yellowing paper in a little while.

But I kept it up, even though it looked pretty hopeless. I quit at one o'clock and ate a jumbo hot dog drenched in mustard and onions and fries at the Sonic, right across the street. It was a drive-in, so I sat on a bench and fed the pigeons while I ate. I'd found out one thing about myself. I was an avid reader. When I had no book or magazine or newspaper to read, I read gum wrappers or the backs of cereal boxes.

Later that afternoon, I bought a New Testament small enough to fit in a shirt pocket, and from then on, whenever I had a spare moment, I would eagerly read it. It was all so familiar to me, as if it was woven into the fabric of my being. When I read the third chapter of John's gospel, I knew what Jesus was going to say to Nicodemus before my eyes reached His remark. So I didn't read the Bible for information, but for something else. Exactly *what* I was seeking as I read the Gospels over and over, I couldn't pin down. All I knew was that it touched a part of me that novels and newspapers couldn't. And every time I read the statement of Jesus "Ye must be born again," I found the same question being whispered in my head. *Have I* been born again? I had no answer for that, but it gave me a strange feeling not knowing what kind of personal interaction I'd had with this God that I seemed to know so much about. More than once I put the New Testament away because it stirred something in me too deeply, but I couldn't let it alone, so I kept reading.

My first full day in Tulsa I found a place to work out, so after lunch I wandered over to Long's Gym and spent the afternoon there. Some of Tulsa was new and slick, modern buildings and clean-looking parks, but the east side was a crummy section, like something out of *The Grapes of Wrath* — with decaying buildings and decrepit houses adding to the feeling of despair. I guess they had to have someplace to put the poor folks. The gym was on the second floor of a frame building, and the weight of it seemed to strain the dingy laundromat below.

The gym didn't have any of the class of King's place, and when I went in the first time, "Nighttime" Long almost wore me out with welcome.

He was about the size of Mickey Rooney, and his ears were like overinflated donuts. But they looked better than his nose, which started to jut out, then made an abrupt right turn. He had to breathe through his mouth, and he snorted like old pugs do. "Hey, you wanna work out?" he wheezed and practically dragged me over to a dressing room that hadn't been cleaned since the Flood. He was a good guy, but not too sharp. He obviously had taken a lot of punches over the years.

There was a heavy bag, a speed bag, some weights, and one ring with the canvas patched so often you couldn't put your foot on a surviving original spot. Guys came in all afternoon, and some of them were serious, but it didn't take me long to figure out that the room in back was the real interest. Either gambling or dope — maybe both. Guys would come in, walk right through the gym without a look, and disappear into the room. Then they'd come right out in about three minutes. I didn't plan on doing anything about it, and Nighttime said to me about the third day I was there, "Glad to have you here, Smith. You give the place a look." He snuffled and gave me long, pointless instructions on fighting and how he'd nearly won the welterweight championship from Barney Ross, but his trainer had over-trained him.

I worked out hard and did about fifteen miles on roadwork too. For one thing, it made me sleep better. Most of the night I just sat in the park or walked around town watching people. There was a TV in the room, but I didn't like most of the programs.

A week went by. Then it was Wednesday, and I had to go back on Friday. I was blasting the heavy bag in the gym when I heard somebody call my name. I grabbed the bag and hung on. Turning, I was surprised to see D. K. Wolfe, who had apparently been watching me for a while. She was so clean and sharp she made the whole place look dirtier than it was. The creamy white dress made her eyes look darker, and the two guilty-looking bums who'd just come out of Nighttime's office stopped when they saw her, as if they'd run into a brick wall.

She was waiting for me to say something, and when I got my breath, I said, "Hello, Counselor. Slumming today?"

"Came to see what the common folk are doing." She adjusted her jacket, though she didn't seem bothered by the dirt nor the smell, and it was a treat to see how easily she let her steady gaze slide off the two louts who were staring at her with their mouths open.

"How'd you find me?"

She smiled and said, "I can't spill *all* my secrets, now, can I?" She glanced around the room and said, "I haven't been deluged by your calls, Adam."

"I didn't want to bother you."

"Bother me. My car's waiting outside."

"I'll just go and take a shower . . ." But she

didn't wait for me to finish my sentence. She turned and left the gym with a movement that made the louts quiver from stem to stern.

She was waiting for me after I'd cleaned up and dressed, and I got into the white Volvo.

"How about something to eat?" she asked.

I smiled and nodded. "You're asking now?" She tilted her head a bit and I said, "You like fish?" She nodded, and I told her how to get to Manny's Fish House. It was on the borderline between the haves and the have-nots, located in what had been an old warehouse. I'd found it the first week I was in town and eaten there often enough to meet the owner and be recognized by the middle-aged waitress named Janie. She met us at the door and put us in one of the four booths.

"Hi there, Adam," she smiled.

I said, "Bring us the fish, will you, Janie?"

D.K. watched her leave and leaned back with a look of amusement on her broad lips. "No menu, I take it?"

"You come to Manny's, you eat the fish. That's the way it works."

She slipped her coat off, and I caught myself staring at her. Then I saw that she was enjoying my stare.

"I did a little looking myself in the gym," she said. "Apparently you know what you're doing."

"I'm a fighter."

"I know," she said without blinking. "That's not hard." She laughed and placed the napkin in her lap. "The real question is, Why are you a fighter? I thought Kimpel told me you'd just left the hospital."

"Yeah, well, it's a long story."

"I'd like to hear it," she said as Janie brought us a platter of hush puppies. "These are my favorite." She bit into one and her eyes opened wide. "They're good!" she exclaimed with obvious surprise.

We put quite a few away while I explained about Perry and the unlikely master plan to finance my search for my roots by fighting.

"But a *fighter?*" she asked thoughtfully. "It's sort of brutal . . . it doesn't really fit you. Why a fighter?"

"To keep the world safe for democracy," I joked as Janie brought another platter of fish and some slaw and tartar sauce. "Eat up, Counselor."

She stared at the fish for a moment, and I playfully mocked, "That fish was swimming around in a tank in the back room an hour ago. You can still feel it wiggle if you try."

She glanced up at me with a smile, took her knife, and swiftly cut the fish up into about ten small pieces. "There. Shouldn't be a problem anymore, should it?"

It felt good to laugh heartily, and before long we had both devoured logger-sized portions of fish. Afterward she seemed a little embarrassed about something and eventually said, "I don't usually confess my sins in public, but, about the other night . . . when you came to my place . . ." She shrugged a bit and then said, "I guess I'm apologizing for blabbering on about my . . . the accident . . . when you've had so much worse." She drew a pattern on the blue Formica top, and her voice was so soft I almost missed what she said. "I know what they say about me — the Iron Maiden and all that — and I . . . it's true, I suppose. But I waited for you to call or come back all week, and then when you didn't, I decided to come find you . . ." She looked up at me for a moment with those amazing eyes and then said, "Um . . . just to tell you that I don't have any good word, but I'm trying."

"Thank you."

"My 'friend' in high places tried to give me the brush-off, but when I reminded him of certain pieces of information that I've been good enough to keep quiet about . . . well, let's just say I tightened the noose a wee bit." She smiled wryly and added, "We'll have the result of that computer search in a few days."

I took one of her hands, small like an exotic bird, and said, "Tightened the noose? With these pretty little things?"

She waited for me to add something to that, and when I didn't, she pulled her hand away a little. There was a touch of red on her high cheekbones. "I suppose you don't ever stoop to that kind of low behavior."

"Us saints have to stay above such earthy methods. I try to keep it in the ring."

Her eyes glinted, and with a hint of a smile, she said, "Here you are like a chick just out of the shell, and you've already got this nice little code of ethics made up . . . your own little rules."

She was half joking, but inside I felt it was true. I did have a standard, and I recognized it, but I didn't know where it came from. I looked up at D.K., and by now she was sitting back in the booth, looking at me questioningly.

"I thought the information you wanted was important. This is how you get important information in the real world, Adam."

I nodded a little, but I knew she could see the apprehension. I wondered how far D. K. Wolfe would go to get what she wanted.

She stood, picked up her purse, and said, "Don't be so quick to judge, my darling. You never know, you could be a murderer who escaped death row."

I followed her out to her Volvo, and as we got in, there was an odd silence between us, as if we were lost and didn't know exactly what to do.

Then, after a moment, I impulsively said, "Let's go to the circus." She laughed, dispersing the tension, and I felt better. "I noticed it's in town. The auditorium is over on Elm Street. We can just make it."

"You definitely belong in a nuthouse! All right, I haven't been to the circus since I was six years old."

It was fun. We had popcorn, Cracker Jacks, and cotton candy and yelled and clapped like two little kids. The last act was the Flying Renaldos, and they were *good*. Every time one of the flyers would turn loose of a bar and go sailing through the air to meet the catcher's hands, D.K. would give a gasp and clutch my arm tight.

"How do they *do* that?" she breathed.

"Well, they start when they're about six years old, I think," I said. "Then by the time they're about the age you were when you got out of law school, they're almost over the hill — for the flying, that is."

She looked over at me. "How do you know so much about it?"

I shrugged. "Just some more useless stuff I got filed away. Did you know Alfredo Codona was the first man to perform the triple somersault? Did you know that when he comes out of that triple, he's traveling sixty miles an hour — and that at least four people have been killed trying the triple?"

She shook her head. "I never understood why people risk their lives like that — climbing mountains and all that. What does it prove?"

"What does it prove to work fifty years as a shoe clerk and drop over dead?"

"I don't know." She stared at the flyers and seemed to be hypnotized by the beauty of their fluid passes. "Look at that girl. See how beautiful she is! And in a few years she'll be fat and fifty."

I shrugged and said, "You want to put her in a deep freeze?"

"Yes!" D.K. said instantly. She turned her intent face toward me and said, "You know, Adam, there's a scene that fascinates me on those old *M.A.S.H.* TV reruns. Have you seen it at all?"

"Once or twice."

"Did you notice the scene at the beginning — when they give the credits? There's a bunch of helicopters flying low, bringing in the wounded, and people are running toward the camera."

"Yeah, I saw it."

"There's this one girl a little ahead of the others — a beautiful girl! She's blond with an athletic body, and she has this intent look on her face as if life is worth spending yourself for, you know? But I keep thinking that was filmed *years* ago. She's not young anymore, and her hair isn't blond and —"

"She'd be a freak if all that *was* the same, D.K." I put my arm around her and said, " 'Grow old along with me! The best is yet to be.' "

She gave me a startled look, then relaxed, "I guess so, Adam. I get all tense sometimes . . . when I think that life is passing me by."

"I don't care what your philosophy is or if you drool in your sleep — if you'll just get me another Coke from the concession stand, I'll love you when you're running the bedpan Olympics in Riverview Nursing Home."

"You dingbat!" She hit me sharply on the shoulder. We laughed at the clowns and had a great time. Finally we left and she dropped me off at my hotel.

"I'll be heading back to New Orleans tomorrow," I said. "I've gotta be in Mobile by Saturday. See you when I get back. Maybe we'll go to the barber college and watch a couple of haircuts."

"Sounds good," she smiled. "And, Adam . . . don't worry, I'll go easy on the poor guy with the computers. Why are you going to Mobile anyway?"

"In all probability, to get my brains beat out," I said in my simple eloquence.

When I crawled between the ropes three days later and looked across the ring at Rufus Tyler, I almost turned around and went back to the dressing room. He was about the size of a drive-in movie and reminded me of those nasty fairy-tale trolls lurking under bridges. During the ref's instructions, he glared at me like an alligator looks at a fat pig on the riverbank. All I could think of was the part of that book *How to Win Friends and Influence People* that tells you to find out what a person is interested in and talk about that. Tyler looked as though he was only interested in tearing off one of my drumsticks and eating it.

"Why didn't you tell me he was so big?" I asked Perry when we went back to the corner.

"He weighs 230 pounds, but after all, he's only six six," Perry said.

"That's the good thing about the heavyweight

division," I nodded. "No nonsense about limits on the size of the guys you have to fight." Perry had stripped off my robe, and just before the bell rang I asked, "How do you want me to fight him?"

"Very carefully!"

"I wish you wouldn't confuse me with such detailed instructions, Perry. Mind if I rub your head for luck?"

It wouldn't have done much good. Tyler moved out toward me like a tank, and for the whole round I demonstrated the art of survival. He wasn't fast, but if I ever got in the way of one of those thunderous rights he kept bringing up from the floor, I'd have no face left. After three minutes of dodging on my part, the crowd got restless, and a few boos were starting to filter up to the ring. When the bell rang, I slumped down on the stool.

Perry just stood in front of me and said, "You owe this guy money? You never laid a glove on him."

"I'm afraid he might hurt me."

"Goes with the territory. Now you gotta step inside and belt him! His arms is too long, and you can't stand off and hit him. So next time he draws back to give you a right, just step in and pop him one."

It sounded all right, so I tried it. He drew back his right, and I took one step forward, set my feet, and out of nowhere came a left that nearly tore my head off. I went backward and spread

111

out flat on my back, with bells ringing and bright purple lights flashing everywhere. At the count of five I looked up, and there was Perry motioning for me to get up. I was up before the count ran out, and Tyler was after me like a duck on a June bug. He got me cornered before my head was clear, and I spent the next two minutes getting hit from every point of the compass. He kept me pinned against the ropes, and he could jar every nerve in my body by clubbing me on the back of the neck. Then he managed to cut my lip by ramming my face with his shoulder. That's not to mention rubbing the laces of his glove across my eyes as the mood took him.

Finally the bell rang and I staggered back to slump on the stool. Perry slapped a sponge on my face and said, "My! Don't time fly when you havin' a good time?"

I slurred, "He's beatin' my brains out!"

"Someday you'll look back on this and laugh, Champ."

"If something doesn't happen quickly, I'm dead."

Perry was very calm and quite logical about my wounds. "Naw, Rufus ain't never killed nobody. He ain't *bad,* just sort of ratty mean. Now you see what he's good at. Got no right, but a sneaky left he can catch you with. But when he's give you *that,* he's through. So what you gotta do is let him take that shot. If you can make him miss — or if you can *take* it — he's wide open."

112

The next two rounds went like that. He'd fake with his right, then I'd step in and he'd try to nail me with that left hook. Way it went, either he'd miss and I'd get my shot, or he'd connect and I'd go reeling away. Both of us were pretty skinned up, and when he'd get me against the rope, it was as if I were caught in a giant rotary lawn mower.

Finally just before the last round, the sixth, Perry said, "I want you to nail him. He can't take no punch like you got. When he throws that left, you move your head just four inches to the right. Set your feet and blast him with that right hook right in the mouth. I personally guarantee he go down."

And that was exactly the way it went. I slipped the left, planted my feet, and started my punch. It only traveled about ten inches. That's all a punch takes to be effective. It's the point of impact that counts. Only about ten inches, but it *exploded,* and after a moment Rufus quivered as if he was shivering from the cold.

If a punch lands too soon, you're just *pushing* at the guy. If it's too late, it doesn't connect at all. But if it starts in your heels and whips through your legs, connecting with the muscles of the upper body and lashing out through the arm, and if it strikes with exact timing right on the chin, it's like a bomb. It jars that fragile membrane the brain is packed in and results in a brain concussion.

So I concussed Rufus with that one blow, downing all lines from the brain to the muscles, and the count was a formality.

I tried to watch while his handlers were holding his head up, but Perry tried to hustle me off. "Don't never watch that," he snapped.

I pulled away from him. "Why not, Perry? Should it make me feel any better to not see what I've done to him?"

I felt Perry glare at me. "You a doctor? Gonna patch him up? Or a preacher? Gonna ease his sorrows? Whut you think you doin' in there? You wanna *hurt* him, so stop mopin' around about it."

We went to the dressing room, and while he was stripping the tape off my hands, I could feel his eyes, more concerned now, on me.

"What the matter wit' you?"

I sighed, feeling a heavy burden. "I don't know, Perry. It just seems like such a pointless sport."

"Sport!" Perry slapped me across the chest with his fist. "Yeah, this is a sport! You git that into your head right about *now!* And this 'sport' gots one idea. And that's to give another man a big headache. Hit 'em so hard they ain't never gonna get up." Perry stooped a little lower to look me in the eyes, and I hadn't seen him that serious in a while. "You better get rid of that conscience of yours. 'Cause that's what you done to Rufus. That's what he try to do to you. He ain't gonna think twice 'bout it. And neither should you. Or you is gonna be down like he is." He threw the tape and towels into a bag. "That's

114

what boxing is. You do that to a guy outside the ring, and it's aggravated assault — five to ten with time off for good behavior. But in there, it's 'sport'! You agreed to this and we makin' good money. You want out? Have right at it. But decide 'fore you git back into that ring."

"That ain't the worst advice I ever heard," a familiar voice said from behind us.

We both jumped a little, turned, and there stood Lieutenant Cossey. He had that thick cigar stuck in his face, his eyes were hard, and there was a mean-looking grin on his face.

"Hello, Cossey," I said. "I'm flattered you came all the way from New Orleans just to see me get beat up."

"It was a pleasure, Smith," he grinned. He turned to give Perry a thin smile. "You keep on usin' up your White Hope like this, you'll need another one."

"Plenty dumb white bread in this world," Perry snapped. He didn't like it that Cossey was there. "You ain't supposed to be in here."

"I'm a policeman, Perry. Thought maybe there might be a dangerous criminal lurking in this dressing room. Don't see any, though. Just a crazy amnesia victim who let himself get fast-talked by a ghetto bandit into getting his brains kicked out for a few bucks. No law against being stupid, I guess."

Not many guys looked tougher than Cossey. He must have been a frightening sight to criminals he was after. Big buffalo shoulders, beetling brows, and eyes that were as cold as an iceberg. But I'd learned to read him a little, and I knew he wasn't there for laughs.

"What's up?" I asked him. "You didn't come all the way to Mobile to see a fight."

He grinned and rolled his cigar around, then said in his unusually high-pitched voice, "I guess maybe I did, in a way. Did some fighting myself back a while. Golden Gloves, heavyweight. Just wanted to see what you looked like." He looked at Perry and said, "He ain't bad, but he can get his brains scrambled if he goes too fast."

"I told him that," Perry grunted. "Look, we gotta get cleaned up."

"How about I take you out for a burger or something? I want to talk to you, Smith."

"Sure. I won't be long." I showered as quick as I could, all the while trying to keep from getting my hopes up. But that's hard to do when you've got *nothing*, and somebody may have *something*.

We went to the Outback and had steaks. All the time we were eating, Cossey talked about his fights in the Golden Gloves, and I saw he was doing it to calm Perry down. Aside from his dislike for whites, Perry was leery of policemen in general and Cossey specifically. I think Perry was convinced that Cossey had come to talk me out of fighting, but then he heard him saying, "You take care of this guy, Perry, and you two can do real good. Pick up some nice change. I guess you know better than anybody how rough it gets when you step into the upper division."

116

"Yeah," Perry nodded and smiled for the first time at Cossey. "I sure do, and we ain't got no ideas like that. Just prelims and pick up some coins. I keep him outa anything that could get him hurt."

Cossey nodded, then turned to me, and I knew he was ready. "I been racking my brain about something I wanted to give you. You know how stuff like that is — you try to force it and it's no good. But last Wednesday I was lying around watching some idiotic television show, and it came to me."

"What is it?" I asked.

"Probably nothin' much," he said slowly. He pulled a fresh cigar from his pocket, stripped the cellophane off, licked it, and lit it up. Finally, when it was burning nicely, he said, "When you said you was maybe from Oklahoma, I got this nagging feeling. So here's what it is — the same day you was found in that fire, a big businessman from Oklahoma was killed in a plane crash."

Feeling disappointment begin to creep in, I said, "But if he's dead —"

"Wait a minute, will ya?" he protested. "The thing is, nobody *knows* for sure he's dead. He went down into the sea in a single engine plane, and, get this, he went down after flying a straight line from pretty much the same location where you were found!"

I let that soak in and finally asked, "Who was he?"

117

"Name was Dan Majors. Came from Oklahoma — had a wife and a kid, I think. Pretty well off. Partner in a small oil company."

Perry argued, "But if the man's dead . . ."

Cossey looked at his cigar, then at me. "Like I said, it's probably nothing. But here's what bothers me. Nobody saw Majors die and there's no body. Seems the guy flew too high, had oxygen failure, and passed out. Plane was on automatic pilot and eventually crashed when the fuel ran out. A chase plane was close by and saw the plane go down, but they couldn't see anybody in the cabin. They thought maybe he'd fallen over. One of them thought he could see somebody slumped over the controls, but it was too dark to see much."

"What was a chase plane doing watching the plane?" I asked.

Cossey grunted and his brow ridged. He looked at me and said, "That's the goodie, Smith. He was running from the law." He waited for me to ask, and when I said nothing, he went on. "Seems like this Majors had embezzled a real bundle from his firm — he had two partners, one of them his own brother. Way the report reads, the brother, Frank Majors, caught him with his hand in the till and was gonna turn him in. So Dan shot Frank, took the loot, and went to escape in the company plane."

"Why'd he do that?" I asked.

"Well, he knew the cops would be on to him pretty quick. Plus he wanted to make a stop at the company beach house, which had a safe with a bunch more goodies in it. Anyway, Dan Majors gets to the beach house, the story goes, raids the safe, and is just getting ready to take off. But in the meantime a SunCo bookkeeper, one Will Pentland, finds the body of Frank Majors back in Oklahoma. So he alerts the third SunCo partner, George Renfro, and the two of them charter a flight, catching up with Majors on the air strip at the beach house."

Perry cut in, "He have all the cash?"

"Nobody knows for sure. Renfro said he had a case with him, and the insurance company finally admitted that was it."

"What happened?" I asked. "Why didn't they bring him in?"

" 'Cause he pulled a gun on them, tied them up, and took off. They got loose, called the cops, and sent out a chase plane, which managed to catch up with Majors. But like I say, he went down."

I thought about it and finally took a sip of the cooling coffee. "Let me see if I have this right, Cossey. You think that somehow Dan Majors *wasn't* in that plane? That somehow he got out of it, got in the middle of a forest fire while the plane went on without him — and that I'm him?"

"It sounds worse when you tell it," Cossey admitted. "Only thing that got me was the four constants — the *time* is right, you're both from Oklahoma, the plane comes from the spot where you was found —" He puffed and looked at the ceiling.

"Well," I snapped, "what's the other?" He suddenly looked at me, and his eyes were icy.

"The other thing is this pain in the middle of my neck I get sometimes when I read a report. It ain't never failed, and something about this Majors jazz is phony. I got no proof, you understand? And it's probably got nothing at all to do with you, but something stinks about that business."

"But look at the good side of it," Perry grinned mirthlessly. "If it does turn out that you are this Dan Majors dude, why, you get to start life all over again. You can get right at it by facing charges of embezzlement and murder one. Ain't that right, Lieutenant?"

"Yeah." Cossey grinned. "Ain't that a wonderful plan?" He reached down into his pocket and handed me a thick manila envelope. "Here's the report — as much of it as I could find. I think you'd be foolish to do anything with it, but it ain't my problem."

I sat there holding the envelope, and I could feel the looks from Perry and Cossey. Finally I said, "You're probably right, Cossey. I'll do a little looking into it when I go back to Tulsa. Thanks for going to all the trouble."

"My pleasure. Hey, you done anything yet with the scraps of melted metal found on you?"

"Not yet."

"Give 'em to me. I'll let the FBI lab see what they can find."

"Well, thanks, Cossey."

Cossey stretched and yawned horribly. "What are friends for," he said, "if not to push you into a little murder indictment?"

The High Hat

SIX

TWO days after the fight, Perry and I were back at the Elite Motel in Tulsa. He'd said we could train there for the next bout. The next morning we slept until noon, then got something to eat at the Sonic. I showed him the library, and we spent a little time there, but he said it was a waste of time, so we went over to the gym. He didn't say much, but I could see he noticed Nighttime's back room almost at once, and while I was pecking away at the speed bag, he disappeared for about thirty minutes. When he came back he seemed to have perked up a bit.

"What 'bout this lawyer babe you tellin' me 'bout?" he asked. "Let's us go pay her a call."

I thought it was funny, the idea of taking Perry to D.K.'s fancy office, so I showered and we went over. Maury was there, and he seemed to loathe Perry almost as much as he did me. When I asked him about seeing D.K., he said, "She's in court. Won't be back today." He hated to tell me where the court was, but I guess he figured I'd find it anyway, so he grunted that it was at the

Federal Building over on Sixth and Maple.

The courtroom was surprisingly crowded, so we edged into seats in the back corner. It was nearly four o'clock, and there was a nice-looking middle-aged lady on the stand, with this smooth talking black-haired guy asking her questions. We didn't have any idea what was going on, of course, but after a few minutes Perry leaned over and whispered, "That mama's *lyin'!*"

I listened closer, but I couldn't see anything but a nice lady. Then the black-haired guy said, "I have no more questions," and the judge nodded at somebody I couldn't see at first. It was D.K., and she looked plenty good when she got up and walked over to the witness. She was wearing a kind of coat dress, brilliant red with padded shoulders and a white collar with a navy blue stripe.

"Wheee-oooooo!" Perry murmured. "That lady is *somethin'!*"

I ignored Perry and listened hard. It seemed that D.K. was very smoothly running this woman over her testimony, and she sounded so sweet and pure nobody would have been surprised to hear that they were best friends. Perry guessed what was coming because he took a sharp breath and whispered, "Uh-oh! It's all over now, Mama!" And then D.K. went for the jugular. She'd found some lie in the woman's testimony and tore into her like a piranha! It took her about three minutes to reduce that woman to a bundle of nerves, and everybody in the room was absolutely convinced that her entire testimony was worthless.

The judge ended up dismissing the case and setting the defendant free. A short squatty man in a tight-fitting pinstriped suit and a red face jumped up and went to hug D.K., but she impaled him with a glance, stuffed some papers into a briefcase, and started down the crowded aisle. When she got to the doors, we met her and I said, "Good show."

She glanced up at once and gave me a startled look. She then smiled, took in my discolored eye, and as she proceeded to pass me said, "Forget to duck?"

We followed her out, and I awkwardly tried to introduce Perry as we dodged the crowd in the hall. "This is my manager and trainer, Perry Jester. He's made me what I am today. Perry, this is Darla Kaye." I knew it would make her mad to use that name and it did, but when I just laughed at her, she shoved her briefcase into my hands, took my arm with one firm hand and Perry's with the other, and towed us through the door.

"Let's go to my place and eat," she said as we made our way down the steps of the courthouse.

"Shy little thang, ain't ya?" Perry laughed. "You done a neat bit of work on that lady. Don't know as I ever seen anyone sliced up so quick and so complete! Next time I go before a judge, you wanna lawyer for me?"

I hesitated and held my breath, ready for that

razor-sharp tongue to slice and dice Perry with ease, but she simply smiled and winked at him, and I could see they somehow took to each other. We got to her apartment and she went to change, leaving Perry and me to peel potatoes. She came back wearing a white linen ensemble that caught my attention so completely that I nearly cut my thumb off with a butcher knife.

"Anybody got anything against rib eyes?" she said, her eyes sparkling.

Two hours later we were staring down at the lights of Tulsa, stuffed and helpless, on comfortable lounges out on the balcony. D.K. had grilled the steaks, and Perry had shown a surprising talent for whipping up salads. I hadn't done anything much except eat.

"Miss Darla, that wasn't no soul food, but it do suffice!" Perry murmured.

"You wouldn't know chitlins if you saw them, Perry," she laughed softly.

"You wrong about that. And I guess the worst food I ever ate was pretty good. I even liked army food! But I was raised on moon pies and Kool Aid — guess you'd call that ghetto soul."

D.K. turned to look at me and said, "Your face looks like a piece of raw meat. What happened?"

"He hit me right in the face, D.K., and I was too proud to run."

"What price machismo?" she smiled. "I suppose you'll do it again — fight, that is?"

"In four weeks, about," Perry said. "But he

125

won't get cut up none. I see to that."

"Isn't there an easier way of earning enough money to live on?"

"Nope," Perry said. "I know it looks bad to you, but Adam is *good,* white lady! And we ain't gonna git involved with *contenders* 'cause they out for blood. But this boy can handle prelims just like you handle the lady in the witness box today. You didn't get hurt, now, did you?"

She changed the subject, and I thought she wasn't too proud of her performance. "So tell me what you've been able to find out since we last talked."

"Well, Cossey came to the fight in Mobile, and he gave me the report. I read it over, plus a couple of things in the library today. The Majors story, it bothers me. They seem different up close. Not what they look like from the newspaper stories."

"They almost never do," she mused. "Life would be so easy if everybody looked like what they were inside.

"Wait a minute," she said suddenly and got up. "I've got something for you." She went inside and was back almost at once with a large cardboard file. "This is the printout I asked for," she said, and her face was a little pink as she looked at me.

I only said, "Thanks, D.K. Did you look it over?"

"Sure. But it's going to take more than a look."

"Lots of names?"

"You wouldn't believe! Of course, you can eliminate most of them. They've been found, or they're obviously much different from you — smaller, older, like that. But you'll have your hands full."

Perry looked at the bulky list and said idly, "Lots of folks getting beamed up on the *Enterprise*. How much a chance would you say Adam has of finding his tracks?"

She hesitated, then shrugged again. "Not too good." She patted my shoulder and said, "Of course, he still hasn't been told about the tooth fairy, so he'll just ram his pointy little head into places hoping to meet himself like Zoroaster."

"Zoroaster?" I asked.

"Legend has it that Zoroaster met himself one morning while he was walking in his garden."

It tickled Perry's fancy. "Now wouldn't that be a shock for most folks! Here we spend most of our time tryin' not to let on who we are, even to our own selves, and then to up and meet your own self — why, it'd be enough to scare Mike Tyson!"

I said quietly, "Guess maybe I'd like it, though." Neither of them said anything. I saw them exchange a long look, and D.K. shook her head just once. "Life of the party — that's me!" I said quickly, "I'm going to Oklahoma City tomorrow."

"What for?" D.K. asked.

"That's where SunCo is located — the Majors

firm — or it used to be. The third partner owns it now."

"What you figure to turn up there?" Perry asked.

"Probably nothing," I laughed shortly. "But I'll have a look and get it out of my system. Probably find out that Dan Majors was black or something I'd never be able to equal. What are you going to do?"

"Well, I think I spread myself around and find out who is the best poker player in Tulsa — then I take his place. You be back day after tomorrow, though. This guy you meetin' in a month — Dave Mowen — he's just average, but I want you to come out without a hair turned."

We stayed for another hour, then left and went to the hotel. After we were settled down in the twin beds, Perry said with a grin, "She's all right, Adam Smith. No, sir, not bad at all — for a white lady, that is!"

Oklahoma City had less character than Tulsa. It lacked the rowdy, wide-open attitude that still saturated Tulsa. I looked in the yellow pages for SunCo under *Oil*, and the list of oil companies took three pages. Oklahoma had oil companies like a Walker hound had fleas, I guess.

SunCo was located in a five-story building along with lawyers, architects, and other professional people. The office wasn't as impressive as D.K.'s, but they had a good-looking receptionist with hair an unlikely raspberry color and about a dozen nice chairs. I'd made up my story back in Tulsa, so when the receptionist asked me what I was there for, I said, "I'm trying to locate a man named Ron Ferrell. He worked for you about four or five years ago."

"Are you from the police?"

"Oh no. I'm just a friend of Ron's. Think I've got a job for him."

"Was he an administrator?" she asked.

"No, just a driller."

That was evidently beneath her notice. She sniffed and said, "The best way would be for you to talk to Spud McAfferty. He's been with the company since it started. If anyone could help you, he could."

"Do you know where I might find him?"

She grinned suddenly and said, "As a matter of fact, I do. He'll be at the High Hat — drunk, in all probability." She added before I could ask, "It's over on Davis Street — about the eight hundred block if I remember."

"Thanks a lot." I ducked out just as a big man in a three-piece suit came out of the inner office. I heard the receptionist say, "Oh, Mr. Renfro, you'll miss your appointment if . . ." Then the door shut and I went on outside. I didn't want to meet Renfro right away, but I didn't know why. What I wanted was to talk to somebody who'd known Dan Majors well and would talk about him. Renfro didn't seem to fit the bill.

But Spud McAfferty did.

The High Hat was one of those concrete block

beer joints that seemed to spawn on the city limits of most cities. The windows had been painted black, and there was only one of those glittering sort of spinning lights overhead to see by. I groped around until I found a stool at the bar and waited until my eyes got accustomed to the cavelike murkiness. The place was fairly well crowded even though it was still early — only about seven. There were three young women wearing brief costumes and spike heels who kept the booze flowing from the bar to the booths, and it was pretty noisy. The smoke burned my eyes, and the blaring jukebox hurt my ears.

The clientele was pretty low rent: working men with big hands, red faces, and loud slurring voices. They lurched across the room, swaying from side to side, trying to walk like John Wayne. None of them were close to being the Duke. For the first half hour I sat there, I saw three almost-brawls. Sooner or later there'd be one, of course, and somebody would get hurt.

"Hey, Spud. I thought you was going out on that Arizona job?" somebody said loudly.

I turned to see a tall skinny guy wearing a big white Stetson and high-heeled cowboy boots with sharp silver-pointed toes stop in front of a table where a little guy was sitting alone with a bottle and a glass in front of him. He was about fifty or maybe closer to sixty, but he looked like one of those wiry leather types who just get tougher as they get older. He answered the tall guy in a voice that was slurred by the whiskey.

"Naw. I didn't want it. Manny Gonzales, he went."

The tall guy said a little more, but the older man didn't want to talk. He slouched lower in his chair and sloshed another inch of Jack Daniels into his glass. I sat there trying to think of some natural way to get acquainted, but who can get acquainted in a bar? That's not what they're for. They're there to get drunk in, and apparently McAfferty was well on his way. I waited for ten minutes, but nothing came to me, so I got up intending to go over and strike up some sort of conversation, though that didn't seem too easy.

Three guys had been making about fifty percent of the noise in the place, and I'd seen at one glance that they were looking for trouble. All three of them were big, all wore the required Western garb, and they'd started toward the back, maybe the men's room, just as I moved away from the bar. They got to McAfferty's table, and I saw the leader glance down at the drinker, then stop. He had a broad face, with small eyes set too close together under bleached eyebrows. His small nose turned up, making him look piggish, to put it in the kindest way.

"Well, lookee here what we got — Old Spud!" He laughed loudly as if he'd said something clever, then turned to glance at the other two. "Lookee here, fellers, Old Spud is out by his own self. Ain't you, now? What you doin', Spud, out by your own self?"

131

McAfferty looked up slowly, and there was a gleam in his frosty blue eyes. He ran his glance up and down the tall length of the man who towered over him and said loudly enough for everyone in the room to hear, "Countin' maggots, Beeler. You make six."

The man called Beeler flushed under the spinning lights, his pig eyes gleaming with malice, then forced himself to laugh harshly. "Always the kidder, ain't you, Spud? I guess you'll go to your grave kidding, right?"

McAfferty took one look at Beeler, then poured himself another drink, ignoring him.

The big man grabbed McAfferty's shirt and yelled, "Think you're too good to talk to me? Look at me, McAfferty!"

The older man didn't even look up, and Beeler's face twisted with hatred. He reached out a hand like a dragline and grabbed the older man by the collar, yanking him out of his seat. McAfferty was caught off guard, and when he tried to grab the fifth of Wild Turkey to give Beeler a shot between the eyes, he missed. Beeler then drew back his fist and hit McAfferty right in the face. The blow made a meaty sound in the silence of the bar, and McAfferty went back as though he'd been shot out of a cannon, hitting the wall with a crash. He didn't go down, though. His eyes were glazed, but some instinct kept him propped against the wall waiting until he got his senses back.

Beeler said to his buddies, "This is the guy

that got me fired from the best job I ever had! I'm gonna kick his face in fer that!"

He started for McAfferty, and I saw the bartender, a little guy who looked like Don Knotts, standing there with a pasty face and trembling hands. "You got a bouncer?" I asked him, and he just looked at me and shook his head.

Beeler was almost up to the old man, and I saw that McAfferty's head had cleared enough to take the situation in. He was pretty sharp, Beeler was. His two friends had come up and blocked out any heroes who might want to lend a hand, and McAfferty knew that even if by some miracle he managed to whip the monstrous Beeler, he'd still get creamed by the other two. But he wasn't scared. His mouth was bleeding and his legs weren't too steady, but his frost blue eyes were clear, and there wasn't a trace of fear in him.

I liked that. I moved across the room, angrily shoved aside Beeler's buddies, and got to Beeler just as he drew back to let McAfferty have another crushing right. I reached out and grabbed his wrist, clamping down on it pretty good. Beeler gave a little grunt, then tried to pull loose as he whirled around, but I hung on and gave a twist that put a choked holler in his throat. We stood there, and he gave a big lunge trying to pull loose. He was a big man, and he'd worked hard all his life, so he had a good arm. But I just held on, not letting any strain show on my face as I held him. It was quiet in the room, real quiet. Finally I turned his wrist loose and he stepped back, his small eyes getting wider.

"Who do'ya think you are? What do you think you're doing?" he said loudly, trying to look tough.

"I didn't come to write a sonnet about your Easter bonnet," I said. "Let's part friends, okay?"

He glared at me; then I saw his eyes cut around the room and knew he'd never back down. He was on stage — he had to prove his manhood. He turned to say something to the crowd, and I knew he was hoping to get me off guard. I got him instead. Just as he whipped back to try to catch me with a sucker punch, I belted him a wicked blow at *least* six inches below the belt, with a right that had every one of my two hundred and eight pounds behind it. It drove more than the wind out of him, as I'd known it would. It wasn't a punch I was proud of, but it did the job.

Beeler fell to the floor in a fetal position, keening in a high-pitched voice that had no words. Just a long moan as he lay there rocking himself.

"What . . . why'd you do that?" one of his pals said. He was every bit as big as Beeler, but there was shock on his face, as if he'd just seen a real bad accident on the highway.

"I don't like to lose."

The two looked at each other, and the other one said, "You mebby hurt him bad."

I looked down at Beeler, and to tell the truth, it

was so bad I wanted to grab my stomach and hold on, as if some of the pain that had turned him into a mewling baby had touched me. But I didn't let any of that show.

"He'll be all right. Now, you two pick him up, or I'll break your thumbs, and you'll never play pool again."

I must have heard someone say that in some movie. But I was getting used to things like that jumping out at me from my past. The two guys took it seriously. They pulled Beeler up and carried him out like a huge squealing ball.

I glanced at McAfferty. "You all right?"

"Yeah," he said. He came off the wall and stuck his hand out. "I guess I owe you a drink."

Waving my hand and shaking my head, I just said, "Keep the change, Jack. You'd do it for me," and began to move away.

He caught me by the arm and pulled me over to the table. "Now, wait a minute. You gotta have a drink. That monkey would have busted me up bad if you hadn't fixed him. Sit down, will ya, and let me buy you a drink. You'd do me an honor."

I let him persuade me, and before long Don Knotts popped up with a fresh bottle. He set it in front of me and said, "On the house, mister. That guy is nothing but a headache."

"Won't be his head that's achin' now, I guess," McAfferty grinned. He uncapped the fresh bottle and poured a stream of Jack Daniels out for me, then himself. "I'm Spud McAfferty

135

— foreman at SunCo."

"Adam Smith. Just passing through town," I said. "About the drink, I'll have a 7-Up. I don't drink the hard stuff."

"Hey, is that right? Okay — Mitch, bring a 7-Up and a glass of ice."

The guy was lonesome, he was grateful, and he was well on his way to becoming seriously drunk. I sat there for half an hour while he took long swallows, and it wasn't hard to get him started talking about the old days. I didn't even have to bring up Dan Majors. He did it himself.

". . . before all these computers and stuff came along, I started drillin' with a wore-out old rig I wouldn't give ten bucks for today. But we had good men — you ever hear of the Majors family?" He peered at me hazily across the table, then shook his head before I answered. "Naw, you wouldn't remember them. But Dan Majors was a good guy, Smith, a good guy! That's what he was — a good guy."

"He died, did he, Spud?" I egged him a little. He stared at me, then nodded, and a bitterness filled his blue eyes, long lines running down the sides of his face.

"Yeah, he's dead."

All I had to do was sit there, and before long he was telling the whole thing — going back to the beginning of SunCo. How Dan Majors had kept things going when the wells played out, when there wasn't any hope. He drew me into it, because he was a good storyteller. Some guys can do that, and he made the whole thing jump into focus. I forgot about the High Hat and Beeler and even Adam Smith for a while. He went through the hard times, then the high-rolling times as SunCo hit one good producer after another. About Frank, Dan's brother, who was just about as good a man, and then about George Renfro, who'd come in to run the office. Finally as he kept drinking, he got slower and slower in his speech, but when he told about the part of the story I knew — the death of Majors — he had moisture in his frosty blue eyes, and I knew it wasn't whiskey crying.

I let him run down, then gently suggested, "Sounds like he was a good guy, Dan Majors. Can't see how he ever did such a thing."

McAfferty stared at me through the whiskey fumes, then shook his head. "It stinks, Smith. Stinks real bad!"

"Well, from what you told me, I guess Renfro pulled the company from the brink of disaster after Dan ran off with the cash. Guess people are pretty grateful to him for that?"

"Yeah. I guess he done that all right. He started in after Dan . . . died. I gotta say he worked like crazy to pull it off. 'Course he *had* to — or go bust." Then he frowned and poured another drink with a wandering hand. "If it wasn't for the Majors — I could like him better."

"Dan and Frank?"

"Naw, their folks," he nodded. "They ain't

never believed that Dan done it — killed Frank nor stole nothing."

"They must be pretty well off — I mean they got two thirds of the company."

He slapped his hand down on the table, tinkling the glass. "They got *nothing!*"

"How can that be?"

"I don't know about stuff like that. Best I understand it, the three partners had it wrote up that if any one of them died, the other partners split his share. So when Dan and Frank died, Renfro got the whole thing."

I thought about that. "But . . . didn't he do anything for the parents? And didn't Majors have a family?"

"Both of them did, but they didn't get a penny. Guess that's why I can't look myself in the mirror when I'm shaving. SunCo used to be the biggest pride I had. Now it's nothing."

"Where'd you say Dan's parents lived?"

"On a little horse ranch just outside Broken Bow. Well, Mrs. Majors does. The old man died some time back. I go over there often as I can, but she won't take no help. Proud as anything that woman! The boys was the same."

His eyes were getting heavy, and I kept him talking as long as possible, probing him for everything I could get. But he finally struggled to his feet and said in a slurred speech, "Thanks . . . fer bustin' that . . . guy. I'll see you . . . again."

He lurched off, and I went to the bus station and caught a late one back to Tulsa. When I let

138

myself into the room, Perry woke up.

"You dig up anything?" he asked.

"Tell you tomorrow," I said. He rolled over, and I lay awake until almost dawn thinking about it all.

Perry was gone when I woke up, so I figured he was out ratting around. All day I looked through the report Cossey had given me, then ran the stories down in the papers. Finally I called D.K. at her office. When His Majesty finally let me talk to her, I asked her to meet me. She agreed at once and suggested her apartment.

When I knocked on the door at seven that night, she opened it and said, "You'd better get a key if you're going to make the trip so often."

I never knew how much she meant by remarks like that. Sometimes I thought she was serious, but usually I figured it was just a hard-shell cover-up. We sat down on the balcony again, sipping sodas, and I told her about SunCo and about McAfferty. Finally I asked her, "You think there might be something in all this?"

She was quiet for a long time, then finally said, "You don't say much, Adam, but I know how hard it is — not knowing who you are."

"Yeah, well, I don't see much sense in talking with a tremor in my voice."

"What if you never get it back?"

"Way the cookie crumbles."

"No, seriously."

For a while I sat listening to the traffic far

down the street. A plane blinked its way across the black sky — red, white, over and over. She wasn't asking out of idle curiosity, and finally I tried to tell her about it.

"I know Car Hubbell struck out Cronin, Ruth, Simmons, and Jimmy Fox in the 1934 all-star game. I know *that* trivial fact, D.K., but I don't know the color of my mother's hair. I know how to overhaul a diesel engine, but I don't know if I have any kids. Maybe somewhere there's somebody who needs me. Somebody who's going down the drain because I'm not there. I know that sounds noble, and maybe I'm kidding myself."

"I guess not," she said softly.

I looked at her in surprise, then said, "Anyway, if nobody needs me, I guess *I* need . . . somebody. I feel like I'm floating around on some huge sea in a little raft or something. All around me there are people in boats — always two or more in every boat — and they're all laughing and having a good time. So I keep calling out for someone to let me in the boat with them, but when I do they all just . . . just vanish. So I just float around by myself in that big old sea."

"You dream that much?"

"All the time . . ." Then I shook my head. "Caught me." I gave her my best smile under the circumstances and said, "Guess I'm president of the Poor Me Club."

I got up and went to stand at the railing,

looking down at the lights of the cars making patterns on the square blocks of the city. She came to stand beside me, and I felt her touch my arm gently, so I looked down at her. She was wearing a different perfume, and it was just about as potent as the other kind. She didn't say anything, but I felt her sympathy. Finally I said, "If I were a poet — and maybe I am — do you know how I'd describe you? 'Voluptuous, with coy mischievousness lurking in the sparkle of your eyes.'"

"You've been reading True Romances again?" she said. Then she reached up and pulled my head down and kissed me. It was a nice kiss. As if she was saying, *You'll be all right.*

Then she drew back and said shakily, "I could get used to kissing you, Smith."

I just stood there for a minute, then said, "I'm going to go over to Broken Bow and see Dan Major's mother."

"I knew you would. I've got a '97 Bronco you can use — a 4-wheel drive. I went through a back-to-the-land period once. Wanted to be a pioneer or something. Haven't driven the thing in a year. It's just collecting dust. I'll get you the key."

She turned, and I followed her into the living room as she fished a set of keys out of a drawer and told me the address where the vehicle was stored.

"I'll look at the SunCo business," she said at the door. "There's a guy in Oklahoma City who owes me a favor. Maybe we can dig up something." I guess she thought about my reaction to the pressure she put on the government guy, because she grinned as she closed the door, saying, "I'd like to promise I won't push him around — but as an old spinach eater says, 'I yam what I yam'!"

Out of the Past

SEVEN

THEY call it déjà vu, and I had a real taste of it when I parked the Bronco and walked into the café called Mary's Place. It was just like fifty others I'd passed on the way from Tulsa — a long concrete block building anchored by three eighteen-wheelers on one side and a strip of concrete sprouting one-armed gas pumps in front. It was flanked by a sad-looking tourist trap that was failing to attract any attention with its grim display of brown pottery lined up across the sagging front porch like weary soldiers.

A big-boned woman with a face that had seen too much was slamming a plate down in front of a customer. She glared at me as if I had affronted her by coming in. Since Broken Bow probably didn't have another truck stop, I decided to be nice and sat down in one of the five red plastic booths — sad affairs with large tears patched with silver duct tape. There was a large glass sugar container, the outside heavily grained with loose sugar, a napkin holder stuffed to the max with white paper napkins, and a salt-and-pepper set, both shakers empty. The Formica on the table was chipped, and someone had carved a poem into the surface. I had to turn my head sideways to read it:

The Horror!
Oh, the Horror
Of Grilled Cheese!

A small, shapely waitress with beautiful violet eyes and dirty fingernails chewed to the quick slammed a fly-specked menu in front of me and asked around her Juicy Fruit, "Yeah, what you having?"

"Not the grilled cheese, I guess." I gave her a sincere smile, and she yawned. "Well, maybe a hamburger — no, a double cheeseburger, fries, and a big Coke." She turned, and in my best imitation of Bogart — which came so easily I must have used it way too much in my former life — I said, "Maybe we'll get together after you get off, kid."

She never even looked up, and I heard a low, meaty laugh, then turned to see a big guy with his belly spilling over his belt. He had on a pale gray Stetson and wore a star on his chest that said *Sheriff.* Shoving back a slick platter, he explored the crevices of his teeth with a round toothpick, then said, "You ain't gonna do yourself no good with Jenny."

"She spoken for?" I asked idly.

"Might say so," he sighed and heaved his bulk

off the cane-bottomed chair. "Waylon Davis's woman. Mean man, Waylon. Already beat up the local talent." He gave me close inspection, then remarked slyly, "Though you look like you might give him a little trouble."

"Not me, Sheriff." I held up my hand. "I'm a peace-loving citizen."

"You just passing through?"

"Well, I'm just about busted. Looking for a job. You know of anything?"

He grunted and heaved his .45 higher up on his hip. "Naw, ain't much doin' around this burg. You mebby oughta try down in Dallas or Fort Worth."

I nodded and said, "Yeah, thought I might. Got to get there first, though."

He put his hand on the blunt .45 at his hip, caressed it lovingly, then nodded. "Employment Office is down on Main. Might try it, but doubt you'll do any good."

"May have to take what I can get, you know? Know of a good cheap room I can get, if I do find something?"

"Talk to Mary there. She knows everything in this town." He gave me another sharp look and went out. I watched him get into a black-and-white car marked *SHERIFF* and drive slowly off.

I had the feeling I'd been in places like this lots of times, but nothing clear came to me. I ate the meal Waylon's girl brought and was amazed at how good it was. Then I stood up, went over to the cash register, and paid the check. Mary looked pretty grim close up, but I made a try. "You know where I might get a cheap room for a few days, Mary?"

"You looking for work?" She listened while I told my story, and then she reeled off the possibilities of survival in Broken Bow like an auctioneer. "Exxon needs a part-time grease monkey; pipeline outfit needs a guy to handle a Mexican dragline; Mrs. Majors lost her hired hand; State Highway Department was lookin' for a guy; two farms around here could use a little grunt-type work . . ."

She ran the list on, and I finally said, "Sounds like lots of golden opportunities around Broken Bow, Mary." I talked about a couple of the jobs to keep her off the track; then I said, "What about the Majors' place. What they need?"

"Oh, nothing big, just a hired hand for the heavy work," she said and swatted a fly with a practiced backhand. "She runs a few pretty good horses, few cows — like that." Then she gave me a look and said, "Does furnish room and board — guess you'd be interested in that?"

"Yeah," I said. I'd worn some old faded jeans and my favorite short-sleeved shirt that should have long been retired, and the dust from the country roads had settled on my face.

"Well, you go straight down this highway for about six miles — you'll see a big grain dryer to your left. Turn right at the next gravel road, go another two miles, and ask at the first house you get to how to find the Majors' place."

"Hey, thanks a lot, Mary — that was a good burger." I gave her a wave and drove through Broken Bow without being terribly impressed. An off-the-beaten-track Oklahoma town. What can you say? Probably a better quality of folk than in New York or London.

Twenty minutes later, I drove up to the place and shut the engine off. The house was set back off the road about a hundred yards and was sheltered by tall pines. It was a good layout. Over to the right was a large barn with several corrals — far enough from the house to keep the smell away. On the flat land behind the house was a pasture, and over to the left was a series of outbuildings, large and small, with two tractors and several pieces of harvesting equipment scattered around. The house was a long, low ranch style, but with gray stone and cypress instead of the usual brick.

A good place once, but it's gone to seed, I thought, taking in the rusty equipment, the sagging fences, the strip of galvanized roofing missing from the barn, the broken gate as I walked up the weedy brick path to the front door. Here and there someone had tried to keep things up — like with the freshly painted white windows that made the flaking paint on the rest of the trim look shabby. But it was a losing battle, and I was a little sad to see the Dr. Pepper bottle of fresh wild flowers somebody had stuck up on a shelf just beside the front door — some

147

small grasp at color and beauty in the middle of gray disaster.

"Yes? What is it?"

I took off my cap and nodded at the large woman with silver hair and dark eyebrows who had stepped outside the screen door. She had a sort of direct stare that lots of southerners have. A tough, merciless breed who had scared the soup out of the Union troops they had faced during the Civil War. Not that this woman was mean, just real steady.

"Name's Adam Smith. Are you Mrs. Majors?"

"Yes." No words wasted.

"Mary at the truck stop said you might need a hand."

"That's right. Come on in." I followed her into the house, and she led me through a carpeted living room and into a large kitchen. "Sit right there." She pointed to a tall stool at a little breakfast bar while she moved to the icebox, took out a tall pitcher and a glass, and set it in front of me. She poured the tea, and I liked the way she didn't ask if I wanted some. Any fool would have wanted tea on a hot day like this.

"You wanted by the police?" she asked without batting an eye.

"What?"

"Hard of hearing, are you?" She took a glass and poured herself a glass of the tea, then sat down on the stool next to mine and sipped it.

"No, I'm not wanted." Not by anybody, I thought.

"You figured to come out to this broken-down horse ranch to make your fortune?" she asked mildly.

Her eyes were bright as a bird's, and she took in every muscle that worked in my face. It wouldn't be wise to try to deceive this lady!

"No, not hardly, Mrs. Majors. I'm broke, and I need to work at something long enough to get some traveling money." She didn't even nod, and I decided to cut it pretty fine. "What I am, Mrs. Majors, is a fighter — a prizefighter. Got me a fight in about a month, but I need some place to stay till then. When Mary told me about you, I thought maybe we could work out something."

"Like what?" she asked.

"Like maybe I could work a good half day for you — just for room and board and maybe a little spending money. Then I could train the rest of the day."

She looked at me and I just waited. Finally she nodded and said, "I guess you're about as honest as is necessary. You know anything about horses?"

"They have four legs, don't they?"

She smiled then, and it changed her whole appearance. I saw that the hard lines had been superimposed over a gentle face. The hard manner wasn't natural, but something she'd had to develop.

"All right, you can make yourself useful, I guess. You're big enough. I've been needin' someone for quite some time. The place has started to go to seed."

She got up and led me through the back door to a square building about thirty yards from the house. It was built of cedar and had lots of windows. Shoving the door open, she led me inside, saying, "You can stay here, Smith. I don't intend to clean up after you, you understand?" She nodded at the litter scattered around the room. "My grandson's been using it for a clubhouse, but I'll tell him to take his things out."

"It's fine," I said. There were two half beds, several small tables, a space heater, one over-stuffed chair flanked by an old brass reading lamp, and two large closets. A small bath was visible through an open door. "I'll get my stuff."

"You can park your vehicle over there," she said, then went back to the house.

I moved the Bronco, unloaded my suitcase, and hung up my one suit. I opened the top drawer of one of the chests to store my socks and underwear, but it was filled with old copies of sports magazines, most of them going back five years or more. As I ran my thumb across the stack, I noticed a *Playboy* magazine about half-way down. The boy's, of course. I dropped the stack back down and closed the drawer.

There was another chest right across the room, and I discovered I knew a thing or two about handguns as I examined the small weapon in its top drawer: a fourteen-ounce Colt .38 Special, trade name "Agent," drop forged aluminum frame, full checkered walnut stocks, Colt bluing, equipped with hammer shroud. Six rounds in the cylinder, and a full box of ammo in a plastic bag next to it. If you had a sincere desire to kill somebody, this item would simplify the process quite efficiently.

I put my stuff in the drawer, shoving the piece to one side, then covered it with my shorts.

It was only a little after three, so I walked around the place, soaking in a few things, mostly noting things that needed fixing. Behind the barn I found a barbed-wire fence holding in two strong-looking quarter horses, but someone had cut the wire in two or three places, and it sagged, threatening to drop off at any minute. Over by the barn I had seen a roll of wire, some staples, and a staple hammer. I got the Bronco, loaded up the wire, and started to work on the fence.

How did I know how to build a barbed-wire fence? How did I know how to use the vehicle to stretch the wire taut, sink the staples in? And why did I *like* it? It was hot, and the sweat started running down my face, and before an hour I was dripping. My hands were bleeding from those little nips the barbs always give you, and it should have been a hateful chore.

But I enjoyed it! Maybe I was just a natural-born drudge. There was something about seeing those bright new wires stretched tight as a violin string, straight and true as a ruler. I just *liked* it, that's all. Some guys like fruitcake at Christmas. I liked to string wire.

151

It bothered me, of course. Stuff like that always did, when it came drifting up out of my past like some sort of debris washed onto the beach by a careless tide. I never knew *why* I knew anything, and whenever a face jumped out at me from a crowd, there was nothing to tell me if it was someone I'd loved or hated.

I guess maybe putting that wire up, getting it all straight and true, kept me from thinking. That's why I didn't stop with the short strip behind the barn but kept on until I'd done a stretch that went nearly a quarter mile from the house. I was lost in it until I threw the pliers into the Bronco and noticed a kid watching me. He was just standing there, his hands shoved deep into the pockets of his Levis, staring at me from under a long-billed cap with *Ford* on the front. He was a skinny kid, all legs and arms, maybe twelve or thirteen. Brown hair poked out from under the cap, and his eyes were dark brown or maybe black. His mouth was turned down, and a sullen look on his thin face went with the dislike in the eyes.

"How you doing?" I asked him.

He just shrugged and grunted, "Grandma told me I had to help you with the fence." He spat on the ground and cussed a little, watching me sharply to see how much it shocked me.

"You don't want to help?"

He gave me what he thought was a hard look and spoke scornfully out of the side of his mouth. "Who wants to do *that?*"

152

"Don't do it, then," I said and crawled into the Bronco. I drove off leaving him standing there, then stopped and was busy stretching the top strand when he again came straggling up to me. I pulled the wire taut, then picked up the pliers and staples, starting on the first post without looking at him.

He watched until I had done three posts, then said, "Grandma says you're a fighter. I think that's *gross*."

"It's worse than that, kid," I agreed pleasantly. He so obviously wanted to come up with an insult that would bring adult persecution that I stubbornly decided not to let it happen.

He watched me do three more posts, following me slowly, then said, "You *like* doing that?"

"Compared to what?"

He looked confused and said, "What's *that* mean?"

"Means I'd rather be fishing for red snappers off the coast of Belize. Compared to *that* — this is an awful job. But compared to being in the hospital with hepatitis, this is *great!*"

He thought that over and said, "Grandma'll probably ask if I helped you. You gonna tell her I did?"

"No."

He shifted around and blurted, "But if you tell her I didn't, she'll whup me."

"Tough."

"It wouldn't *hurt* you to say that," he said coldly. I noticed his hands were trembling and

153

his face was twisted in raw anger. "What are you? Some sort of priest?"

I turned to look right at him, and scratching my neck with the pliers, I said, "Kid, I let people do what they want to do. You didn't want to help — that's okay by me. You got your way. Now you pay the price." He stared at me and I shrugged and said, "Way it goes, kid."

I finished that section, then got into the Bronco and asked him, "You wanna ride?"

"I wouldn't ride with you!"

I grinned at him, gunned the Bronco in a circle, and left him standing there. Just as I left I shouted at him, "Like John Wayne says, 'A man's gotta do what a man's gotta do!' "

Mrs. Majors was pulling some clothes off the line when I pulled the Bronco up and started into the bunkhouse. She looked for the kid, and when she didn't see him, she asked, "Where's Matthew?"

I stopped and looked her in the eyes. "He decided not to ride with me."

She pulled a pair of jeans off the line, then asked, "You two didn't get along?"

"He thinks prizefighters are gross."

"He thinks *everything* is gross. Boy can't finish a sentence without that word! He help you with the fence?"

I looked across the level pasture. He was just breaking the horizon, the stubborn set of his back visible even from there. "We did okay," I said, then added, "Guess I'll take a shower."

"I'll call you when supper is ready," she said.

The needles of fine spray felt good, and I stayed in the hot water for a long time. It didn't take me long to pick out what to wear for dinner, since I only had one choice: clean jeans and a fresh shirt with a horrible Hawaiian design that Perry had selected. I had bought a new pair of Nikes, so I put them on, settled down in the La-Z-Boy, and thumbed through a worn copy of *Field and Stream*.

"Time to eat."

I looked up and there was Matthew, standing in the door, wearing the same stubborn look I'd already seen. Apparently he didn't change for dinner. He let his glance shift over to the drawer with the dirty magazine.

"I been using this place. Still got some stuff in here."

"I know," I said and let it drop.

He stared at me, trying to figure out if I had found the magazine, but I didn't bat an eye — just stared it out with the kid. He dropped his face and said, "Grandma says supper's ready."

Somehow staring down a kid wasn't much of a victory. He looked so small standing there, with about twenty tons of guilt pulling him down, I had to say, "No sweat, Matt. Let's go eat."

I put my hand on his thin shoulder, but he pulled away at once and gave me a look of pure hatred.

"Big deal! A crummy old magazine! You

155

gonna tell on me?" He shrugged as if he didn't care.

But that's not what I read in his eyes. He'd been shrugging at me all afternoon, so I gave him one of my own. "Not me, Matt. Remember? I let people do what they want to do." Pausing, I said, "Though you might want to give some thought to whether you should be looking at stuff like that."

He stared at me and then finally he turned. I followed him into the house.

As I walked into the kitchen, the smell of spicy Mexican-style food filled the air. Mrs. Majors was pouring something into a large white bowl. "Go on in, Smith. It's all on the table except the cheese dip."

Matthew had gone on through the double doors, and I went in after him. The round table was covered with a red-and-white tablecloth, and goodies were spread everywhere. I realized I knew the names of most of them: enchiladas, tacos, tortillas, frijoles . . . Whatever else I'd eaten in my dim past, Mexican food must have been big.

"Sit down."

A voice caught me off guard, and I started a little. Matt had sat down on one of the heavy oak chairs, and I thought we were alone. But there was a large built-in section of walnut cabinets, filled with dishes and stuff, running halfway between the family room and the kitchen, and a woman had been standing around the corner of it. She stepped into my view and smiled.

"Food's ready."

And I'd seen her before!

She was a small woman, maybe five two or so, but put together beautifully. Small bones, perfectly symmetrical. She had a neat cap of fine, silky golden brown hair, which framed her oval-shaped face, somehow giving the almond-shaped blue eyes an oriental flavor. Full lips, the bee sting effect — always compelling. Not prim either. She was watching me, and I guess she was used to being stared at, because there was no trace of nervousness in her face.

But I'd seen her before.

It was the first time that had happened. Oh, faces had looked familiar, but probably just because they had the same chin, the same shape in the ears, of someone I'd once known. But this time I was positive that I'd touched on at least some part of whatever my past was!

I guess I was gawking, because she smiled suddenly and said, "I'm Dawn Majors. You're Adam Smith, is that right?"

"That's . . . right," I said, my throat catching. This is Dan Majors' wife? If so, this may be my wife — and this my son — and this could be my mother!

My head was suddenly swimming, as if I'd taken a hard right to the jaw, and I was trying to act *normal* at the same time everything was whirling around. I was staggered by the thought. If this woman was my wife, wouldn't we have

157

entered into that relationship reserved for lovers — so intimate that no stranger could ever know its fullness? And this boy, staring at me with eyes full of dark resentment? Had I held him when he weighed only a few pounds, his face red with the struggle of entering this inhospitable world? And had Mrs. Majors, this woman with a straight spine and silver hair, held *me* in that same way?

I wanted to get away, to think it out calmly, but Mrs. Majors came in with a tray covered by small bowls of cheese dip.

"All right, everybody sit down. We eat before it gets cold."

I sat down across from Dawn, with Matthew on my right. Mrs. Majors sat down and without warning bowed her head and said a blessing, beautiful and sincere.

"Lord, we thank you for this food. We thank you for health and all the good blessings you have given us. We thank you for Adam who has come to help . . ."

I was moved by the mention of my name, and for some reason I opened my eyes and looked up. Dawn Majors' gaze took me in, and glancing to my right, I saw that Matthew was glaring at me with his usual hatred. The almond-shaped eyes of Dan Majors' widow were a strange color — sort of a cross between hazy gray and light blue. She held me with those smoky eyes until finally I dropped my head, glad to have the lengthy prayer as an excuse for looking away.

". . . in the name of Jesus. Amen," Mrs.

Majors said firmly. She gave me a glance that had a wry humor almost hidden behind her stern features and said, "I like long prayers, Smith. Makes the food taste better if you wait for it."

"Hunger is the best sauce," I said. I took the dishes and filled my plate, conscious of being the feature attraction. The food was great, and I complimented my boss. "This is great, Mrs. Majors!"

"Just *Cora* will be all right, Smith. And I'm glad you like the food." She herself didn't eat much, but pushed a few bits around with her fork. "You must have done a lot of fencing. That's one of the best jobs of work been done around here in a coon's age."

"I've done a little bit of everything, I guess, Cora." I poured some of the delicious hot sauce on a taco and snapped at it hungrily.

"You're a fighter, Mom tells me," Dawn said. She wasn't eating much either, I noticed, and I wondered if she had to diet to keep that petite figure. "Have you been one long?"

"Not too long."

"You must not be much good — way your face is beat up," Matthew piped up.

"Matthew, that's not polite!" Dawn said, giving him a sharp look. Then she gave me a small smile, and it rang bells in my limping memory. "Maybe we can go to one of your fights. I used to go some, when —" Suddenly she broke off. We all heard the sound of a car pulling up outside, and she threw a harried glance at

Cora and stood up, saying, "This is good, Mom, but I'm going to get something later."

She put her napkin down and said, "I'll be in late. I've got a date. See you tomorrow."

She left, and I saw Cora Majors sweep her with a quick glance, then dart a look at Matthew. The kid's face was down, but anger was written all over the stiff set of his back and the white-knuckled grip he had on his fork.

The front door slammed and then a car started up — sounded like one of those muscle cars — and went roaring off. The tension was pretty thick, so I just put my head down and kept on eating. Cora asked Matthew how school was, and it was, predictably, gross. The ball team was gross also, as was the new history teacher. He skipped off as soon as he could; then Cora and I talked about the ranch.

After we finished I helped Cora with the dishes. I liked the way she didn't fuss about it. While I was drying one of the big bowls and listening to her speak of a new horse she'd just bought, my eyes lit on a big framed picture I hadn't noticed just to the right of the fireplace.

She saw me looking at it and said slowly, "That's my menfolk. Made about three years ago." She didn't add anything to that, and I looked at the three big men, especially the young guy on the left. The man in the middle was white haired, and the one on the right was obviously his older son. And the one on the left . . .

"Good-looking guys," I said, then made

myself add, "Where are they now?"

"Dead," Cora said and looked at me with such pain in her fine eyes that I felt like cutting my throat, but I had to know some things.

"Sorry." I didn't know what else to say.

"You might as well hear about it from me. You'll find out soon enough."

Then she told the entire thing, slowing down from time to time to hold a dripping dish over the sink. One thing was clear, the law might say different, but Cora Majors *knew* that her son never stole anything — and he had never killed anyone, much less his brother, Frank!

"Look at him, Smith," she said. And as I walked closer to the picture and stared at it, she continued softly, "Does that look to you like a man who would do those awful things?"

I stared at the picture, taking in the full-lipped grin, the square jaw, thick brown hair blowing in the wind. His honest eyes stared back at me.

"I don't think he could do it." Then I took a big chance. "You know, Cora, your son — Dan, I mean — don't you think . . ." I broke off and stared at the picture.

"Don't I think *what?*" she asked and came to stand beside me, looking at her dead family.

"Well, don't you think he looks like *me?* A little bit?"

She looked at the picture, then at me. I felt her gaze going over me and waited to see a light of recognition in her gray eyes. Finally she nodded and said, "Yes. You have the same color eyes and hair. And both of you look rugged. You do remind me of him. 'Course, you're much heavier. Dan was lean like his dad, you see?"

But he wouldn't have been lean if Perry had built him up with weights for almost two years. "He looks like he was tall."

"Just about your height," Cora said. Then she suddenly pulled herself around and left the room, saying, "I'll have breakfast early. You sleep well, now. It's good to have you here."

I walked slowly back to my room and went to bed. For a long time I thought about Dawn, Cora, and Matthew. What else did I have to think about? Finally I picked up the Bible I'd put on the table. I read a number of the psalms and as always wondered about the old men who wrote them. They had a freedom that seemed remarkable to me. I mean, the psalmist cried like a baby, complained that God never listened to him, went into fits of anger asking God to kill all his enemies. No restraint whatsoever! I liked that, but I knew I was so tied up in knots I could never pray like that. But I wanted to. I wanted to cry out to God and weep and tell Him He was my God and to come down and straighten me up.

But I didn't do it. I tried to pray, but I seemed to be talking to myself. Finally I dropped off to sleep, thinking at the last moment of a pair of smoky, almond-shaped eyes. . . .

Sunday Morning

EIGHT

MAYBE it was because I couldn't remember any time when I'd fallen into a routine. Maybe it was because I was desperate for some connection with my past — I don't know. But after a few days at the ranch, it was like I *fit* there. That wouldn't mean a thing to anybody who'd always had a place, had people, had a job to do, but it got to me somehow.

I guess it was partly the *order* of it all. Get up at six-thirty, be at the kitchen at seven for one of Cora's big breakfasts. Always eggs and bacon on Mondays, Wednesdays, and Fridays — pancakes on the other days, except for Sunday, which was blueberry waffles. Always the same without fail, and I knew that if I stayed ten years, it wouldn't change.

Church was on Sunday morning and evening and Wednesday night, regular as the sun coming up. I went with them on the second Sunday at the urging of Cora. I felt out of place in my Levis and Nikes, but when I'd offered this up as an excuse, Cora put me at ease.

163

"We are not going to a fashion show, Adam. It's what's inside that counts, not what you wear. God looks at the heart."

Dawn didn't even get up for breakfast, but Cora, Matthew, and I piled into her Ford pickup and rattled off. Matthew was wearing a pair of twill pants and a white shirt, but he argued all the way to church about the necktie Cora had made him wear. He'd dragged me into the middle of the argument when he asked, "Did you have to wear a tie to church when you were a kid?"

I winked over his head at Cora. "I was never a kid." Cora laughed a little in amusement at my joke, but truthfully I wasn't joking. I had no memory of being a kid. As far as I knew, I'd come into the world six feet tall with facial hair.

Matthew twisted around, eyeing me skeptically. "You're not wearing a tie. Why do I have to? What good do they do?"

"They make you look cool," I said. "Cal Ripkin Jr. wears a tie nearly all the time." I had no idea if this was true, but Ripkin was Matthew's baseball idol, and I figured he wouldn't mind if I used him a little in a good cause. The mention of Ripkin sent Matthew off into a long discourse about the pennant race, loaded with stats about the players.

"You learn all that about ball players, but you won't learn math!" Cora had her eyes fixed on the road but took them away long enough to sizzle Matthew with a sharp glance. "I'd like to know why that is."

Matthew pulled his head down between his shoulders and then straightened up to add, "Who cares what x plus z equals? It's no good for anything."

"And what good is baseball going to do you?" Cora countered. "I hope you're not thinking of being a baseball player. That's not a job for a grown man!"

"Ken Griffey Jr. made four and a half million dollars last year," Matthew said. "He gets twenty-one thousand dollars every time he comes to the plate — whether he gets a hit or not."

"Money isn't everything! You've got to learn that, Matthew."

"Well, *not* having money isn't all that great!"

It was a family argument, and I had no right to speak. I listened idly, watching the prairie roll by, and then somehow it came to me out of the past into my mind — a weather-beaten man with light blue eyes and hair the color of dark honey. It seemed to form a little at a time — like the Cheshire cat that shook Alice up, the eyes appearing first, then the wide mouth — until finally I had it all. And he said in a gravelly voice, *"You ain't got no dogs in this fight!"*

Then the Ford hit a pothole that jarred my teeth — and the face was gone. It scared me a little, for I *knew* that I'd seen someone out of my past and that he'd said that same thing to me more than once. My father? A friend? Grandfather, maybe? It was just a fragment that had flashed into my mind, and I couldn't pull it back, no matter how hard I tried. Somehow this wasn't just a human sort of memory, but a *personal* one, part of what I'd been before I'd lost it all. As we jolted along over the ripples in the asphalt, I felt like a man in a foreign country, thousands of miles from everything he's ever known, who suddenly comes face-to-face with a friend he's known all his life. I sat there trying to pull the face back into focus, but it was no good. It gave me a frantic feeling, as if I'd lost something precious and would never get it back.

Cora pulled up at the church five minutes later, and we piled out. As I waited for Cora to get her purse and her Bible, I glanced over the parking lot. No Jags or Mercedes. Mostly vintage pickups, dusty Chevys, and Ford sedans. The cream of the crop was a brand-new Dodge Ram with an extended cab, bright red, gleaming in the morning sunlight like a ruby. A broad silver band ran along the lower parts of the body, and a foxtail on the antenna moved in the slight breeze. Two high-powered rifles lay mutely in the gun-rack across the wide back window, and a bold bumper sticker announced in large red letters: *I'd Rather Be Hunting!*

The church was very old — so old that it seemed to lean slightly to one side, staying upright with an effort. It was a white frame rectangle with a steeple capping the ridge and two narrow windows six feet high that flanked the double doors, which stood open. Six enormous walnut trees shaded the structure, three on each side in neat rows, standing like sentinels keeping watch. The service had started, for the sound of a tinny piano underlying the voices singing a hymn layered the air:

Rock of Ages, cleft for me,
Let me hide myself in thee;
Let the water and the blood
From thy wounded side which flowed,
Be of sin the double cure,
Save from wrath
And make me pure.

I knew the song, could have sung it with the hidden singers. I'd seen it on the pages of a hymnal, could see the shaped musical notes that seemed to bounce along over the words.

But even as the words floated across the yard and I was waiting for Cora, who had shut the door of the pickup and was moving around to join me and Matthew, something happened to me. I was just looking at the old church, humming along with the singers, and then . . . well, I can't describe it very well, but it seemed that time *stopped*. The scene before me *changed* — like in a movie when one setting will sort of dissolve, and as it fades away, another scene will emerge.

The ancient church and the parking lot filled with vehicles lost their sharp definition, going out of focus, but even as they faded into a misty nothingness, another scene began to appear. A church took shape — a very similar one — but *different* somehow. It was a new building, gleaming with fresh white paint, and the roof still gave a faint odor of tar pitch. The church stood in an open field that was waist-high in sawgrass, almost hiding the narrow, recently paved road that led to it.

The first thing I noticed was that the area in front of the church was filled with cars from the '60s and '70s. A couple of faded bumper stickers jumped out at me. *Go Cowboys* read one. *Nixon-Agnew '69* said another. The whole scene was veiled, not sharp and clear, but I knew it was something out of my childhood, something good.

". . . matter with you, Adam?"

I jerked out of whatever sort of spell I was in, to find Matthew poking at my arm, looking at me anxiously. "You're not sick, are you?" he asked.

"No, I'm all right." I tried to grin, but this second shock, coming on the heels of the vision of the face, shook me up. Then I thought that maybe everything was coming back to me, my memories taking their places inside my head.

Cora was staring at me with a peculiar glint in her eyes, but I said, "Guess we're late."

"We'll have to sit up front," Matthew said with resignation. "All the back seats fill up first."

As I followed Cora and Matthew up the

shallow steps, I noted the shiplap lumber sheathing. It was very wide, almost eight inches, and somehow I knew lumber like that hadn't been used in a hundred years or so.

The inside of the church was dark and cool after the bright, hard sunlight. I blinked to adjust my eyes and with one glance took it all in. Simplicity: one large rectangular room with a fourteen-foot ceiling; three windows on each side, all over eight feet high, held open by hidden cords with molded lead window weights; three rows of walnut-stained hand-built pine pews, the middle one fifteen feet long, those on the side about eight; the floors made of heart pine and worn smooth with the passing of many feet over many years.

As we made our way to the front, people took their eyes off their hymnbooks to check out the latecomers — mostly me, I think. We took station in the middle of the second pew, directly in front of a varnished pulpit that dominated the platform, which rose about ten inches from the floor. A chair sat on each side, one of them filled by a strongly built man in a dark blue suit. The other was empty, and a skinny fellow wearing snakeskin Tony Lama boots and a black string tie stood to the right of the pulpit, pumping his arm up and down vigorously, beating the time to the song he was leading.

I felt a nudge and looked down to see that Matthew was thrusting a paperback hymnal toward me. Taking it, I saw on the faded cover the title *Heavenly Highways*. "It's page forty-four," Matthew whispered, and when I found the place, I held it so he could see it. I noted at the top of the page the name *Fanny J. Crosby, 1820–1915*. I knew the words and began to sing:

Blessed assurance, Jesus is mine
Oh, what a foretaste of glory divine!
Heir of salvation, purchase of God,
Born of His Spirit, washed in His blood.

Then the chorus:

This is my story, this is my song,
Praising my Savior all the day long;
This is my story, this is my song,
Praising my Savior all the day long.

My voice felt a bit raspy, as if it had atrophied from lack of use.

"You have a nice voice, Adam," Cora, who was sitting on my right, leaned closer to whisper. She smiled, then turned in her hymnal to the number announced by the song leader. It was one called "Life Is Like a Mountain Railroad," and the lyrics enjoined all to make certain they kept on the right track. It was a simple melody, and I picked it up at once. I noticed that the top of the pew had a six-inch strip of unstained wood exactly in the middle and wondered why. Later I saw that all the pews had that same unstained strip, all in exactly the same spot.

After the song service ended, we sat down and the husky man rose, a worn black Bible in his hand. He was about forty years old, I guess, and had a square face with as steady a pair of dark gray eyes as a man could have — sort of like lasers, I thought. His face was tanned, and he had an out-of-doors look about him. A hunter and a fisherman too.

"That's Brother Leon Anderson," Cora whispered. "Fine man — best pastor we ever had!"

A tugging at my sleeve caught my attention, and I leaned down to catch Matthew's whisper. "Brother Anderson was a soldier — won the Medal of Honor in Vietnam! He never talks about it, though."

I took a closer look at the preacher, who was giving a few announcements, and saw that he was indeed the kind I'd want on my side in a rumble. He had powerful hands, bronzed and thick, and his chest swelled against his white shirt. He had a pleasant tenor voice and spoke deliberately, like a man giving instructions. He made a mild joke about the song leader, and I saw the humor in his face.

Finally he said, "We're happy to have some visitors this morning. Now, we're going to take a collection, but please don't feel constrained to give. You are our guests, and we want you to feel at home. Brother Simms, will you and the elders come to receive the offering?"

I sat there while Anderson prayed a brief prayer; then when the dark wooden plate with the green felt inside came by, I dropped several bills into it. I felt Matthew's eyes on me — Cora's too — but neither of them said anything. The piano, an old upright, was played by a young woman wearing a bright yellow dress. She wasn't too bad, and I enjoyed the trills and runs she made on the old instrument.

After the last notes sounded, the pianist left the upright and took her seat on the front pew. I could almost feel the congregation settling down as Anderson rose and went to stand behind the pulpit. Quickly glancing around, I noted that most of the congregation were over fifty. The men looked stiff in their white shirts and neckties, being more accustomed to open-collared Western shirts. The women by their sides were strong and scorned to dye their hair, though some had gone uptown to visit beauty parlors and get permanents. Five or six young couples with small children dotted the congregation, and several reluctant teenage boys hunkered down, giving the bulk of their attention to the young girls, who tried to appear unaware of this scrutiny but at the same time enjoyed it.

"The subject of my sermon this morning is 'Which God Will You Serve?' " Anderson stood beside the pulpit, rather than behind it, and the Bible looked small in his big hands. "Turn with me to the book of Joshua, the last chapter." He smiled slightly, adding, "If you have trouble finding it, open your Bibles in the middle, then turn left. You'll get there."

I flipped mine open. It seemed to open at just the right place. "It would take too long to read the entire story, so we will focus on one statement found in verse fifteen. 'Choose you this day whom ye will serve; whether the gods which your fathers served that were on the other side of the flood, or the gods of the Amorites, in whose land ye dwell: but as for me and my house, we will serve the Lord.'"

Anderson paused and I looked up at him. He was easy enough in his manner, but as he spoke, I sensed some sort of power in him.

"Most of you know the story of Joshua," he began, "but for those of you who may have forgotten, let me remind you that when Moses led the Israelites out of slavery, out of Egypt, they came to a spot where they met what seemed to be terrible enemies. All wanted to turn back to Egypt — all except two men, Caleb and Joshua. It was Caleb who scoffed at their fears, saying, 'Why, they'll be bread for us!' I guess put in today's language, he was saying, 'They'll be duck soup for us.' But tragically the Israelites did not listen to these two, and they were forced to wander in the desert for forty years. . . ."

I leaned forward listening intently, for I'd read the story before. It was fresh and clear in my mind. As Anderson repeated the story, how Moses had died and the leadership had fallen on Joshua, it was familiar ground for me. I had a fleeting thought of how, when I picked up a book, sometimes I knew I'd read it, sometimes not. But the Bible — I knew it better than any other book.

"So Joshua had led the army of Israel to victory. They had conquered the land. Now Joshua is an old man, ready to die. That's the scene we have in the last chapter. All of Israel is gathered to hear the last words of their leader. And what does he say? He tells them they must *choose*. Either they must serve the idols of their fathers, or the Lord God of Israel.

"And this morning I want to show you that every one of us comes to this moment of choice, and the choice never varies. The names of the idols have changed, but the choice is still the same: Will you serve the gods of this world — no matter what their names — or will you serve the true God?"

For a moment the preacher stood there, his steady gray eyes on all of us, his lips firm. Finally he said, "We move now from the day of Joshua to our own time, and from the Old Testament to the New Testament. Turn in your Bibles to the gospel of John, chapter one."

A rustling sound punctuated Anderson's words as pages were turned. I glanced over at Cora's Bible and saw that the page was heavily marked, some verses underlined and most of the margin filled in with notes made with a fine pen. I followed the words as the preacher read slowly and carefully.

In the beginning was the Word, and the

Word was with God, and the Word was God. The same was in the beginning with God. All things were made by him; and without him was not any thing made that was made. In him was life; and the life was the light of men. And the light shineth in the darkness, and the darkness comprehendeth it not. That was the true Light, which lighteth every man that cometh into the world.

Anderson paused and lifted his head to put his glance on his hearers. "The next verse," he said quietly, "is to me the saddest verse in the entire Bible. I never read it without having to fight back the tears." He closed his eyes then and recited the verse. " 'He was in the world, and the world was made by him, and the world knew him not.' "

A silence gripped the room, heavy and almost palpable. Anderson prayed a brief prayer, then began to speak. Somehow when Cora asked me to come to her church, I had expected a harsh-voiced thumper, maybe a shouter, for I somehow knew that this style was popular in this part of the country. I'd heard late-night samples on the Christian radio station that came all the way from Del Rio, Texas — men who shouted until they were hoarse.

But Leon Anderson kept his strong voice under control, speaking almost as if he were addressing a single friend. And that was it, the thing I'd missed in some of the preachers I'd listened to on the radio — call it *love,* I guess. Some of the radio preachers had seemed totally lacking in this quality, and I wondered how they thought they'd win any converts by ramming accusations down the throats of their hearers. If they *had* any.

"The words of this gospel," Anderson was saying, "are not popular. For example, John insists that the world was created by God. All of you well know that this is not an acceptable position in most of America. Our children are taught that the world and the universe are a cosmic accident — made by no one. It takes more faith than I have to believe that!"

A smile turned up the corners of Anderson's lips, and he held up his arm pointing to his wristwatch. "How can you account for a watch without a watchmaker? Did the metal of this watch just flow out of the earth? Can you believe that it formed itself? I *know* that this watch was *made,* and when I look up at the stars, I *know* they were created by a starmaker. . . ."

He spoke with fierce intensity, quoting from the Old Testament and the New, then moved on to another idea.

"Not only is it unpopular to believe in a Creator, but few people believe in the next verse, which says, 'In him was life.' Now, all of us have houses that are wired for electricity. Tell me, when you throw the switch on your wall, what happens? Why, the lights go on, of course! But *how* does that happen? Does your house contain the source of power? No, it does not. That power comes from a generating plant many miles from here. If the lines go down — as they have many times — you don't have lights, and your washing machines are dead."

Pausing for a moment, Anderson said slowly, "There is only *one* power source for man, and that source is Jesus Christ. If our lives are not connected to Him, as this verse states, why, we're *dead*. He is *life,* and Jesus claimed that for himself, for in this same gospel, chapter six and verse thirty-six, He said, 'He that believeth on the Son hath everlasting life: and he that believeth not on the Son, shall not see life, but the wrath of God abideth on him.' "

A fly buzzed in front of my face, and without thinking, I reached out and trapped it in my fist. It wasn't until Matthew uttered a strangled "Wow!" that I realized what I'd done. Couldn't kill the thing, so I opened my hand and let it fly away.

I listened to the sermon, admiring the way that Pastor Leon Anderson wove together Scripture and other sources. He'd read a great deal, and I heard names that were familiar to me: C. S. Lewis, Augustine, Dietrich Bonhoeffer, and many others. He built his sermon as a man builds a house: First, lay out a good foundation; then erect the structure, binding it firmly together; and finish it with the fine touches.

Toward the end, Anderson suddenly halted, his head held at a peculiar angle as if listening to an unheard voice. Then he shook his shoulders together, straightened his back, and looked full at his congregation. "I've never spoken of that part of my life I spent in Nam. But it's always with me. Some of you men here this morning remember how it was. . . ."

And as he spoke, I suddenly knew that sometime in my past, I had known the heated fury of battle! It was not that I had a memory of a battle, but I just *knew!* It shook me, and I had to clench my fists together to keep them steady.

And then he spoke of the horror of that war, the senseless deaths of soldiers dying in agony. His eyes were haunted as he related in stark terms the massacre of women and children, and his voice broke as he whispered of the loss of his fellow soldiers.

Total silence had fallen over the building, and I saw that Cora's hands were white with strain as she gripped her Bible. We all felt the pain of the big man who stood there, his face twisted with searing memories.

"Why do I tell you all this? Because *that* is what the world is like! That war is over, but we live in a world of terrible anguish. Our land is filled with blood, no less than the jungles of Nam! When I was there, I thought it was like an insane asylum, and I tell you, the world is no better. Oklahoma is no better!

"How can there be a God of love when the world is so terrible?" he asked, his voice rising. "We Christians are living in enemy-occupied territory! The world we have now is *not* the same world God made!" He went on to trace the fall of man and finally said, "There are those who say that Jesus is a great teacher but who refuse to serve Him. They don't understand His claim to be the Son of God! And it comes to this: Jesus was either who He claimed to be, or else He was as insane as a man who claims to be a poached egg!"

This sent a shock through all of us — at least through *me!* It sounded hard and demanding. But Anderson then began to plead, and I was aware that he believed what he was saying with all his heart.

He continued, "Mankind needs to know the answer to three questions: Where did I come from? Who am I? Where am I going? None of the 'great' religions of the world offers a decent answer to any of these! Only the Bible answers them all. Man was created by God, he is made like God with the power of choice, and he is going to an everlasting destiny! You must either choose Jesus Christ or reject Him!"

I lost track of time, his words echoing in my mind: *Where did I come from? Who am I? Where am I going?* The very certainty of his answer disturbed me. Only *one* choice?

He closed by saying, "How can Jesus Christ make such claims on all of us? First, He died for us. Read the Gospels, and when you get to the end where you read of His death, I think you'll sense this was no ordinary death. It was God in

179

the flesh, the Lamb of God, dying for the sins of the world. Second, Jesus is alive. He came out of the tomb and was seen by many witnesses. Go to the tombs of the founders of other religions, and they'll all be occupied. But if you found the tomb Jesus was buried in, it'd be empty. He's alive! And He comes to each of us, saying, 'Choose ye this day whom you will serve — me or the gods of this world!' "

A silence lay over the room, and Anderson's gaze moved from face to face. I thought he was through, but he said, "You may think the choice is too hard, but men and women and young people always have hard choices. If any of you here this morning is Texan, you remember how a battered band of soldiers was once trapped in an old fort, surrounded by an overwhelming force. Colonel Travis, the commander, called them all together and drew a line in the dirt with his sword. He said, 'Let those go to safety who choose. Let those who will stay and die for Texas step over this line.' And every man made his choice. Jim Bowie lay on a cot, too badly wounded to walk. But he cried out, 'Carry me across the line!' They did, and Bowie and every man at the Alamo *chose* to die for what they felt was their duty.

"Now will you please stand, and I'm going to ask you to make your choice. Will you serve Jesus Christ, or will you serve another? We're going to sing hymn number 118. If you have heard God speak to you this morning, if your choice is to follow Jesus Christ, I urge you to come forward. We will pray with you and you'll find peace."

The pianist began to play and we sang:

Just as I am, without one plea,
But that thy blood was shed for me,
And that thou biddest me come to thee,
O lamb of God, I come! I come!

On the third verse, a woman moved forward, weeping. She was met at the front by Leon Anderson, and we sang several verses as the two talked. Finally the pastor held up his hand, and when the singing stopped, he said, "Marian Lockwood has been seeking God for some time. This morning, she comes to say that she's chosen to accept Jesus as her Savior, and we all rejoice with you, Marian."

A chorus of cries went up — "Praise the Lord!" "Amen!" — and then Anderson asked one of the men to pray. After the prayer was finished, Cora went at once to embrace the young woman who was weeping steadily. Matthew and I waited, and several people stopped to shake hands and welcome me.

Then we were leaving, and I moved along the line of people waiting to shake the preacher's hand. He smiled at Cora, then turned to me. "Good to have you in the service," he said.

His grip was firm and his gray eyes locked onto mine. I nodded and muttered something but found his steady gaze somehow hard to meet. He said only, "Come back when you can, Mr. Smith."

Then we were outside and the clear sunlight seared my eyes. Blinking against the glare, I walked to the pickup behind Cora, with Matthew trailing alongside. We got in, and as we were driving slowly away, I turned suddenly and stared at the church.

"What's the matter, Adam?" Matthew asked, craning his neck to look back. "What are you looking at?"

"Oh, nothing really . . ." I mumbled as I studied the humble church. The spire pointed a slender finger upward. There were Fords and Dodges and Chevys jostling as they left the old building. Some of the older ones left smudges of black smoke, and I saw the new Dodge Ram pickup power out, digging chunks of earth, throwing them high in the air.

"How did you like the sermon, Adam?" Cora asked, keeping her eyes on the road.

"Fine." She glanced at me and I spoke up quickly, changing the subject. "Cora, I noticed an unstained section on the backs of all the pews. Why is that?"

"Back in the old days, the men sat on one side of the church, and the women sat on the other. A six-inch board was nailed down the center to set them off."

She glanced at me, and I knew she somehow sensed that the service had hit me harder than I wanted to admit. I didn't know what it was, and I didn't like it. I shoved my back against the seat and stared out the window, noting the herd of Black Angus that flashed by, dark heavy blots against the pale sky. The tires hummed on the blacktop, and when the words of the sermon came like a thin echo in my mind, I shook my head and began talking too loud to Matthew about baseball. But even as I spoke, the words *Choose ye this day* came to me like an insistent low whisper, and I knew I'd have trouble forgetting Rev. Leon Anderson's sermon.

The image of that weeping young woman making her way to the front of the church moved me deeply and stayed with me all day. Had I ever stepped across the line as she did and given my life to Jesus Christ? If I hadn't, could I do so now? I couldn't even confess my sins, for I couldn't remember them. What happens to a person's faith if he can't remember it?

That night I lay awake, thinking of God, and when I finally fell asleep, I had the dream again. The flames and the voices were so real to me. I woke up panicked, crying and begging God to protect me from this torment. I got up, went to the window, and looked up at the stars. They glittered like diamonds, and I remembered the Bible said that God knew all their names. Finally I turned away and whispered, "What kind of man am I? A man of God . . . or perhaps a murderer?" The thought kept me awake much of the night.

At the Lake

NINE

AS the days passed, I never quite shook off the "vision" of the man's face. The sermon stuck with me too. But I kept on with my life, clinging almost desperately to the order I'd found. After breakfast every morning, I talked with Cora about the work: fixing the fence below the south thirty, propping up the feed stalls in the big barn, graining the horses extra that day. I began to know the stock. Rattler, the best quarter horse, who loved candy. Belle, the best milker, who'd give you a dreamy look, then bite a plug out of your rear when you least expected it. Dan Tucker, the bull terrier who looked sleepy and harmless but who would take on a pride of Nubian lions if they suddenly appeared and threatened the Majors' place.

And the people — I guess I clung to them too.

Dawn went out every night. I never asked, but Matthew watched with sullen eyes, and Cora wouldn't look at her at all. She'd come roaring in at two or three in the morning and sleep until two or three in the afternoon.

184

Matthew, mixed up and rebellious, tried to be hard like a young James Dean, yet at the same time was desperate for approval.

Cora always worked. She canned beans, mopped floors, made a quilt with little Dutch figures in it, or fixed food for some family the church had taken in. A hard look marred the gentle contours of her face. As she talked with a neighbor about the most elemental and earthy necessities of stock breeding, or looked at a spectacular sunset with a poet's gaze, she always carried some burden she could never share with anyone. I went with her to church on Sunday morning and evening and prayer meeting on Wednesday night, which pleased her a lot. No matter how often I went, though, I stayed pretty tense. I liked Leon Anderson — if only because he didn't climb over a pew to grab me and pull me into his way of believing. Something to be said for that.

Perry had listened to me without a word when I'd called him and tried to explain why I was staying. After I'd stumbled around for a while, he snorted and said, "I guess you're as well off there as here. You keep up the roadwork, and keep that speedbag poppin', you hear me?"

"Yeah, sure. You doing all right?"

"Whoooeeee! These here Oklahoma gamblers is a piece of cake, buddy!" he chortled. "I 'bout got my stake back, and maybe in a week or so I come down and put the fine touches on you for the bout."

"Good! See you then, Perry." I hung up the phone and dialed D.K.'s office. After the usual joust with Maury, I got through to her. "Hey, this is your big bad boxer calling — Bruiser Smith."

"I prefer sailors," she said, and I could almost see her generous mouth curving into a smile. "Are you back in town?"

"Well, actually, I'm still in Broken Bow." I explained that there was just cause for staying at the Majors' place, and when I finished there was a little halt in the conversation.

"I've been looking at some stories in the papers about the case, including pictures of the family. The widow looks pretty sad and pathetic."

"Dawn? Well, she's —"

"Pretty, though. If you like the type. Anyway, I'm still doing some research. So tell me again why you feel the need to stay there?"

Her voice was tinged with a slight chill, so I decided to keep things on a high plane. "The money. The salary's a gold mine," I joked.

She didn't seem amused. "Well, I'm turning over a few rocks here, and it's not unlikely that something will come crawling out." She paused and then said, "That's my philosophy — everybody has something nasty hidden under their own private little rock."

An odd silence swept over the phone, and I wasn't sure how to react to D.K. at that moment.

She continued in a brittle tone, "Well, take care of the widow and the kid, Adam, and I'll keep turning rocks. Maybe we'll find something."

"Thanks, D.K. I really mean it."

"I owe Doc Kimpel a favor. This is it."

She hung up the phone, and I felt terribly guilty for no reason I could come up with.

Most people have a string of people they can tie to, so if they lose one or two — there's somebody to step into their place. Like Jim said in *Huckleberry Finn*, Solomon had so many children he could gamble with the baby the two women brought to him. He was *careless* with young'uns! But if a man only had one child, he's likely to be more careful. So when D.K. cut me out with that fatal drop of the phone, I was shaken. I had D.K., Kimpel, Perry, a little bit of Cossey — that was about it. Just the thought of losing any ground with one of the few ties I had on this frail planet frightened me, and I spent most of that day working hard and not saying much. That evening I took out my frustrations during my workout at the local gym. The mind-numbing rhythm of the punching bag soothed my confused emotions.

Cora had told me to try to do something to keep the feed out of the wet. The old barn was leaking in a dozen places and sagging like an old drunk, so I had suggested it might be easier to build a new small storage building than to patch it up.

She nodded and said, "Got plenty of material to do that. Matter of fact, one of the hired hands *threatened* to do it, but he never did."

And so I built a new barn, although *barn* is a bit generous. I found a lot of studs and two-by-sixes stacked under some tar paper, and early one morning I got after it. Matthew was out of school for some holiday, and Cora put him to helping me. He was as sullen about that as usual, but I just went at it ignoring him.

There was enough lumber for a storage building about eighteen by twenty-four feet, so I laid out the slab first. It was cool, but no sign of rain, and there was something good about setting up the strings, picturing the finished structure in my mind. I knew I'd done things like this before, and as the sun rose, I got a kick out of it, laying out the foundation straight and true.

Matthew had joined me, standing off to one side, not offering to help. He was watching with a trace of contempt in his brown eyes as I took my time, getting the corner square, the measurements accurate.

Finally he snorted and asked impatiently, "What you want to mess around with all that for? Why don'cha just guess at it and start in?"

I was putting the line level on one of the nylon strings, and waited till it stopped swaying and was absolutely still before I answered him. "Well, Matt, I guess I'm being so careful because building something like this reminds me of the importance of doing things right. If you don't follow the rules, the walls will fall down, or the roof will leak."

He thought that over and said, "I *hate* rules."

"Yeah? Well, I do too. Some of 'em. But, you know, it's nice to have rules sometimes. Something that won't change. Something you can count on."

He got a puzzled look on his face, then, coming up closer, asked, "What's *that* supposed to mean?"

"Seems like nobody has any answers these days. Like you can't find anybody who takes a stand on anything. You have three choices: (*a*) good, (*b*) bad, (*c*) something else. And just about everybody these days won't come right out and admit that something's good or bad. Depends on your perspective, they say. Someone who plants his feet and says something is *right* — and that every other answer is *wrong* — well, he's usually charged with being a fanatic."

He thought that over and asked with a nod of his head at the strings, "Maybe, but what's that got to do with this?"

I took a measurement from one corner of the stringed rectangle, then the other. "This tells me if the area is square — if the right angles are true."

"Who cares?" he shrugged. "So what if it's crooked?"

I pulled in the tape and stopped to look down at him. "*I* care, Matt. Like I said, you start letting a few mistakes slip by, and before you know it you're standing in a pile of rubble. Accuracy matters, Matt, and even more so truth and integrity." I squinted down the string and added, "People can talk about sex and almost anything else these days — but not about truth or decency."

I picked up a shovel and began digging a footing around the stringed area. He took the other shovel and began scraping at the earth. "What are you, some crazy old philosopher or something?"

I laughed at that, and for the first time a grin came over his somber face. "Yeah, I guess so," I answered. It was a start for us.

The construction became the center of attention. Cora couldn't stay away for long. I guess she'd have been digging the footings if I hadn't taken the shovel away from her. She'd had so much sorry help that she just couldn't believe anyone was actually getting something *done*.

Matthew was off and on. He'd get interested in how to cut rafters, and I couldn't tell him where I'd learned, but I showed him how to do it. He got a real thrill when we raised the first stud wall, and even Dawn was on hand to lift it up. All three of them held it while I nailed a brace on to keep it in place, and we all gave a cheer at the single wall. Dawn ran in to get a picture, and Matt let me drop my hand on his shoulder while we smiled into the camera. "Big deal!" he said under his breath, but I knew he was a little proud.

It was the end of the week by the time we'd got the rafters nailed into place and the corrugated roofing nailed on. There was still a long way to go, but we had a celebration that night. Cora cooked up a feed of barbecued ribs, cabbage, fried okra, and Texas toast, and after supper we sat around in the living room and played Monopoly until midnight. Dawn stayed home for the first time that week, and she joined in the game with such energy I thought she'd pop. I saw a new side to her that night: a simple and very winning woman, gentle and warm. Matthew thawed, and I saw Cora's face relax as she looked at her daughter-in-law with a hopeful gaze.

Finally as we were putting the board up, Matthew said, "Do you think we could go somewhere tomorrow? It's Saturday — I don't have school!"

Dawn ruffled his hair and smiled at him. "Go where?"

"I don't know. Somewhere."

"Maybe you could go fishing," Cora said. "You haven't been to the lake since —" She broke off quickly, and Matt's face grew still.

I said quickly, "I'd like to go. Not much of a fisherman, but it would be good for a change."

Dawn tapped her chin with her finger. "Let's all go! I've got a new suit, and I can get a tan while you two fish."

Matt's reaction was almost magical. One minute he was dark and gloomy, the next, smiles and sunshine. "Sure, Mom, if you want to." She must have been blind not to have seen how the boy hung on her, longing for attention. I met Cora's eyes, but neither of us said anything.

I got up in the predawn night — nearly four o'clock — and Cora stuffed us with eggs, sausage, grits, white gravy, huge biscuits, orange juice, and coffee.

Dawn was groping around like a zombie, but Matt was everywhere. He directed Cora as she put a lunch together, collected all the fishing gear, got the night crawlers he'd collected for bait, and was like a drill sergeant heading us into the Bronco.

"I know the way," he said as we pulled out of the yard, waving good-bye to Cora in the breaking morning light. "It's not too far."

Dawn leaned her head against the window and went right to sleep, but Matthew talked all the way to the lake. He told me about huge fish he'd *almost* caught, about close calls from falling out of boats, about the nights spent out at the lake. But he never once mentioned with *whom* he'd done all this. It was as though he'd blocked his father out of his mind, and when I probed at him once, he dodged the issue.

Lake Kennedy had been named after the president at that time when they were naming anything and everything after him — lakes, highways, streets, buildings, telephone poles. It was a huge man-made lake held in place by a massive earth dam that caught the waters of a valley basin, forcing them up into fingerlike inlets on the borders of the main body.

"We're going to Indian Head Landing," Matthew said. He pointed at a gravel road, and I turned off into a thick forest of evergreens. "There won't be anybody there," Matthew went on. "Not so many people go there, so we'll be by ourselves. That's why we . . . I like to go there."

He'd almost slipped up, but I only said, "You come here a lot?"

He paused, then nodded, "Used to, but not for quite a while." He was quiet for a time, staring out the window silently, but when we got to the landing he was alive with excitement. Piling out of the Bronco, he pulled Dawn around to the back, pushing fishing gear into her hands as she yawned hugely and gave me a small smile behind his back.

The banks were clear of brush, and Matt gave up on us as being much too slow. He was down by the water threading a night crawler on a hook as Dawn and I were slowly unloading the Bronco. She was wearing white shorts and a sky-blue sleeveless T-shirt, her hair was tied back with a silver and turquoise pin into some kind of ponytail, and even in that casual garb she was quite fetching.

Since it was too cold to swim that early, I joined Matt, and we drowned a lot of his wiggly worms, catching baby perch for about an hour. It was fun, but Matt was after bigger game. We went back to the table where Dawn had arranged

all the gear and drank the steaming hot choco-
late Cora had sent along.

"I wish we had a boat," Matt said mournfully.
"If we could just get out in the middle of the
lake, we'd really catch the fish!"

"I don't think that's right," I said. "Look at
the people out there in the boats — they're getting right in close to the bank."

"Yeah, well, we gotta do *something!*"

We stooged around for about an hour, and
when it got warmer, Dawn slipped behind some
trees and put on a bikini that was definitely an
eye-pleaser. She caught my look and smoothly
said, "I'll just go lie in the sun while you boys
catch fish." She found a spot on a large grassy
plot near the bank and lay down on a blanket
with a bottle of oil. She began to put the oil on
her long, smooth legs, and I averted my eyes,
afraid to watch anymore.

I worked hard on turning my full attention on
the fishing and Matt's conversation.

Something came bubbling up in my mind, as it
did when I was trying to think of ways to do
something, and finally I said to Matt, "We're not
doing any good like this. We have to *find* the
fish."

He shot me a scornful look. "And how we
gonna do that?"

An old memory floated up, and I began to
strip off my shirt. I kicked off my shoes and then
my watch. I handed it to the boy and said, "If I
don't come back I want you to have this."

His eyes got big and I laughed at him. "Just kidding. Look, it's the time of the year when the fish are spawning. They won't be out far. They'll be bedding down close to the bank, maybe in about five or six feet of water. I'll swim along the bank and find them. When I find a bed, I'll come out on the bank. We'll catch that bunch, then move on to another one."

He stared at me, then asked, "How do you know that?"

"I just do," I said, putting him off. "Now, can you carry the rods, the bait, and the stringer?"

"Sure."

"Let's do it." I slipped into the water, gasping at the cold, then began to swim slowly along the shoreline. I kept my face down and swept from side to side, covering all the area from about five to fifteen feet parallel to the bank. I had to lift my face for air pretty often, and the water was murky, but it was one of those things I'd done before, somewhere, sometime.

Then I spotted a bed of bream about five feet down. The nests were shaped like doughnuts, about a foot across, and over every doughnut was one or two large fish. I took a big breath of air and nosed down toward the nests. The fish skittered away but came right back. I put out my hand, and one old granddad of a bream came right at it, then scooted away when I gave him a poke. I counted about thirty doughnut-shaped nests before I ran out of air. I surfaced and marked the location by a pine that had been blasted by lightning.

"You find any, Adam?" Matt asked.

"You bet! See right out where I'm pointing? Drop a worm there, and if you don't get a whopper, I'll buy your lunch."

He put on a massive crawler and dropped it right on the beds. The cork didn't even pause but disappeared with a satisfying *PLOP!* Matthew gave a yelp and began struggling to bring his fish in, which on the light tackle we were using was quite a job. Finally he got it in and held it up for me to admire. "That's a *good* bream, Matt. Maybe three quarters of a pound."

"It's the biggest one I ever caught!" he breathed. "What kind is it?"

"Punkinseed perch." How did I know that? "We can get a mess right here."

When you find a bed, it's just like finding a store. You just throw your bait in, pull a fish out. We caught nine large fish, mostly bluegill, bream, and punkinseeds; then I swam along and found another bed and we caught eight more. I thought Matthew would have a heart attack. Every fish was like the first one to him, and the stringer got so packed, I had to make a new one out of a stick and a piece of nylon leader.

At noon, I said, "We've got plenty, Matt. Let's go on back."

"No," he said, and a stubborn look crossed his face. "I want to catch more."

"What for? We have more than we can eat."

"I want to, that's all."

I picked up both stringers, which by now were too heavy for him, and the flopping fish flashed golden in the sun. "Come on. Your mother must be worried about you."

"I don't care what she's doing!" he said, his lip trembling.

"Yes, you do," I said, looking right at him.

He hesitated and then muttered sullenly, "You know everything, don't you?"

"I know you don't hate your mother."

He shot out with a tortured expression on his face, "Why shouldn't I hate her? The way she sleeps around with all those men!"

I just looked at him, and he suddenly dropped the fishing rod and turned his back. His thin shoulders were shaking, and I put the flopping fish down and walked over to stand beside him. I didn't touch him, but he knew I was there. Finally I put one hand on his shoulder and said, "It's okay to cry. I do it myself sometimes."

He eventually gave one last sob, then turned and faced me. "I didn't mean that — all that stuff I said."

"I know," I said. "Let's go see what your mom's doing."

I was glad to see that Dawn had dressed and was trying to get a fire started in one of the steel charcoal cookers set in concrete. She looked up and said, "Goodness! What a lot of fish you . . ." Then she took a closer look at Matt and didn't finish her sentence. His face was streaked where he had wiped the tears away, but she only gave me a wondering look and said, "I can't get this fire going. Were you ever a boy scout, Adam?"

"Never made eagle — just a lowly tenderfoot," I answered and got a fire going using twigs and newspaper from the lunch.

We stayed at the lake until nearly four o'clock, eating, napping in the sun, tossing a few more lines into the water off the point, watching Dawn make a face over threading a worm onto a number-seven hook. We had a good laugh when she lost her cool after a bluegill grabbed her line and tried to run off with it. She was jumping up and down trying to reel that fish in.

She screamed when she finally landed it, all atwitter with excitement. She asked while admiring the gorgeous colors of the fish, "Is it a him or a her?"

It tickled me that she would ask that particular question, and I said, "It's a her. The mama lays the eggs, and then the papa bops along and fertilizes them. Then he scoots off to play around. The mama has to stay over the nest and keep the baddies from gobbling up junior. They can't leave the nest until the eggs hatch, and that's why they bite the worms so good. All they can do is eat whatever comes into their area. If they leave, the little fish will be gobbled up by an ol' egg-eater of some kind."

A strange look crossed Dawn's face and she couldn't meet my eyes. She looked over at Matt, who wasn't listening, and added, "It's always the mama who is supposed to watch out for the small fry."

It was quiet on the lake and she was standing close to me, so I could smell the clean scent of her tanning oil. I could see the tiny freckles that were almost invisible from two feet away, and flecks of gold that tinged the tips of her hair. When she suddenly turned and looked at me, some sort of sadness touched her eyes, a sadness that she had kept well-concealed up until then.

Far away some sort of waterfowl was making a plaintive cry that gave a ghostly echo across the lake, and the cumulus clouds that decorated the deep blue of the summer sky drifted silently toward the west. She suddenly leaned toward me, and I knew that all I had to do was touch her and she'd respond. But I didn't. I don't know what was holding me back! Maybe it was the sight of Matt trying to put his line in the center of a brush pile where he couldn't possibly land a fish. Maybe it was the mystery of her evening outings. Maybe there was some genetic trait from my great-great grandfather who might have been a fiery Baptist preacher who'd pluck out his eye rather than look at a pretty woman. Maybe I was just nuts!

"Say, I guess we ought to be getting back, you think?" I said. Dawn pulled herself upright with an abrupt movement, and it was as if she'd suddenly hung a sign across her chest that said in bold letters: *No Admittance! Keep Out! No Trespassing!*

"I guess so," she said stiffly and called down to Matt, "We have to go, Matthew."

He protested, but I guess he saw that she meant business, so we loaded all the gear and the fish into the Bronco and headed back to the ranch. I kept up a conversation with Matt on the way. He was still excited and wanted to talk about scuba gear and if we could get some tanks and clean out the lake. I discovered I knew a few things about that too, so we filled the silence up, and he never noticed that his mother wasn't saying a word. Or maybe he was just used to it.

When we got to the house, the first thing I saw was D.K.'s car in front, covered with summer dust. "Whose car is that?" Matt asked.

"I think I have company," I said. We got out of the Bronco and went into the house to find D.K. and Perry sitting in the den, drinking hot tea and talking with Cora.

"Hey, Champ!" Perry grinned and waved his big hand at me. "Didn't know you were here on a vacation. Catch any catfish?"

"Hi, Perry," I said and looked over across the room to where D.K. was sitting. She was wearing a periwinkle dress that came down to within about four inches of her knees. Her coat had some sort of opalescent buttons, wide lapels, and flaps that followed her tiny waist, flaring out over smooth hips. A satiny blouse the color of cranberries showed at her throat. Simple. She was one of those women who'd look good in anything.

I saw her eyes go right to Dawn. It was like a security scanner, the way she took in Dawn's figure, her hair, her walk. She had her cessed in one split second, and there was a glint in her dark eyes as she said, "Hello, Adam."

"Hi. This is Dawn and Matt. You've met Cora, I see."

"We've been having a good talk," Cora said. Then she said to Matt, "Take those fish outside, Matthew. You're dripping all over the carpet."

"Ah, Grandma . . ." he complained.

"Guess we'd better do it," I said quickly. "It's gonna be a chore cleaning that many. You know how?"

"Sure I do!" he said and turned to leave, burdened down by the overloaded stringers. "I can do it."

"Be out and help you in a minute," I said. He left and I turned to Perry, saying, "Well, you staying?"

"Sure am, if Mrs. Majors can take another boarder."

"That'll be fine," Cora said. She looked at Perry and added, "You'll have to pay or work."

"Oh, I'll pay, Mrs. Majors," Perry grinned. "Adam here, he's the worker. I'm just a simple old darkie trying to get by with white folks."

Cora looked hard at him, and there was a gleam of humor in her eyes as she said, "I see that." She got up and said, "I'll put some more beans in the pot. You'll stay for supper, Miss Wolfe?"

"No, thank you. I have to go back right away. Can I have a word with you, Adam?"

"Sure," I said. I glanced over at Dawn, who was leaning against the wall, not saying a word. Her arms were locked behind her in a pose of forced casualness. Her gaze took in the three of us. She was also exchanging a long look with D.K.

This is like the Shootout at the O.K. Corral. D.K. and Dawn took to each other like dogs to cats. Not that it showed; both of them were pleasant, agreeable, and charming. But the weapons were drawn.

"Let's go over to my room," I said. I led Perry and D.K. outside and across the yard to the bunkhouse. They stepped inside, and I waved them toward the two chairs. "Be it ever so humble . . ." I said.

"This ain't too bad," Perry said. "I been in lots worse."

"Two beds in an empty room," I grinned. "Sounds like the title of a country song."

D.K. was taking the room in, not looking at me; then she turned her eyes in my direction. There was a funny set to her lips, and I knew that she had something on her mind.

"You got anything, Darla Kaye?" I asked.

She turned to me with a glare. "I spent twenty years answering to that stupid Scarlet O'Hara name, Adam, and I'm a bit tired of it."

"Sorry. I sort of like it."

D.K. turned, pretending to take in the room once more, and said coldly, "Yeah. You seem to like a lot of things these days."

I stared at her and said, "Nicely put, Wolfe. Anything you want to tell me?" She looked over at me and I added, raising my palms to her, "Strictly business, of course." We were glaring at each other across Perry, and I didn't know what we were fighting about — but again, maybe I did. After a moment we both seemed to relax a bit.

"I've got to get back right away," she said, a little softer, "but I just came to bring Perry down and to tell you that I've got something on Renfro. Well . . . maybe I have."

"What is it?"

She looked at me, cocked her head in that way she had, and said, "Something doesn't fit, Adam — about the Majors case. I've done some looking, and what it amounts to is that Dan Majors is clean. Nobody ever heard of him taking a dime from anybody."

"Yeah, well, maybe —" I started to say, but she broke in.

"But George Renfro — now *there's* a boy for you!"

"How's that?"

"Well, he's a playboy, for one thing. A *sportsman*." She made it sound a little obscene. "Plays the horses, the numbers, the stock market."

"It's not against the law," I argued.

"No, not as a rule. But he did a lot of business with Dane Taggert."

"Whoa, now!" Perry straightened up in his chair and stared at D.K. He shook his massive head and said, "Anybody who does business with Taggert is either a mark or an accomplice. That dude is poison!"

"What do you know about him?" I asked.

"He ain't never gonna win the Citizen of the Year plaque." Perry shook his head. "He's a two-time loser, well-known pimp, and all-around dingbat with loving ties to the Mafia. Shrinks have him down as a paranoiac, possibly homicidal. Your common everyday garden-variety maniac."

"That's him," D.K. nodded, "and he was bosom buddies with George Renfro."

I walked around the room and then came back to look at D.K. "You think he may have been mixed up with all this?"

She shrugged those beautifully knit shoulders and said, "He's a candidate, I'd say." She got up and said, "I better get back. Maybe you can get somebody from around here to say something about Renfro."

"I don't know. They might be afraid to talk. I mean, if there's anything in what you say."

Perry snorted and gave a short laugh. "This place ain't no different from any other. There's guys here that would tell on Dracula for a couple of bucks!"

"Find them, then," D.K. said as she went to the door. "We have to get somebody talking if anything ever gets clear. Adam, walk me to the car."

I touched my forelock and made a quick, short bow. "Yass-um, I sho will," I said humbly.

She gave me a startled look, then broke out into a tinkling laugh. "Sorry about that — Mr. Smith, would you be so kind as to see me to my car, if you have the time?"

Perry was breaking up and I said, "Be glad to, D.K."

I walked with her to her car, and she stepped in when I opened the door, then turned to me, saying through the window, "Call me, Adam. Soon!"

"Sure. And thanks for coming."

She started the engine and gave me one quick look and a mischievous grin. "Watch out for strangers bearing gifts. Specifically the widow Majors."

"I don't know about that," I said lightly. "I'm careful about any enterprise that requires the purchase of new clothes."

"Emerson," she nodded with a quick look of surprise on her face. "How'd you know that?"

"I don't know, D.K. Just another chip of my fascinating personality, I guess."

I stepped back and she said again, "Call me, Adam. I'll be waiting."

She launched out of the yard like a rocket, and I watched her go, then turned back to clean fish with Matt.

At the Blue Duck

TEN

WILL PENTLAND came the third Monday I was at the ranch. He drove up to the front door in a muddy Chevy pickup, saw me clearing the weeds away from the house, then gave me a long look before going inside. He didn't knock, and I wondered who he could be to barge in like that. Cora stuck her head out the window a few minutes later and hollered, "Adam! Come in the house!"

I put the swing blade down, and when I went into the house, Cora said, "This is Will Pentland, Adam. Adam Smith, Will."

He was one of those big men who had shrunk with age and disease until his skin fit him like a suit three sizes too large. He had a bad color, sort of gray with liver spots here and there, and his face was red with whiskey and lined like road maps. He put his hand out, and it was like a bag of very fragile bones, although once it must have been a powerful grip. It was a ghost of a hand, and I was careful not to squeeze it too hard.

"I want you to witness this, Adam," Cora said

after we shook. She pointed to some papers on the table and picked up a pen to sign them. "Will was with SunCo from the very first. He still helps me out with business, such as it is."

"You sign right there as witness," the old man said in a tenor voice. He watched as I signed, then said, "That's fine. That ought to do it." He looked at me with a sideways tilt to his head and added, "Cora tells me you've been a real help on the place."

"Haven't done a whole lot."

"Don't listen to him, Will," Cora nodded. "He's a *mule* for work, just like Owen and the boys. Never knows when to stop. You say you want to get some things out of the bunkhouse?"

"Sure do. Then I have to get on home."

"No, you're going to stay here for a day or two. That place of yours won't go anywhere, and you need some good food." She pulled at his arm, and he gave her a fleeting smile that revealed the good looks and humor that had been there before time and excess had broken him.

"All right. Maybe I will." He looked at me and added, "I'll get some of those boxes out of your way, Smith."

I followed him to the bunkhouse, and he began pulling at several dusty cardboard boxes that were stacked under a table. He looked around when we had them stacked beside the door and said softly, "Lots of memories in here."

I glanced at him and decided to see what I could get. "You were real close to the Majors family, I guess?"

"Sure. I knew Owen Majors when he was a young man. Knew the boys. Helped raise them." He sat down on one of the chairs and looked at me. There was a still, hopeless sadness engraved on his worn face. "Terrible thing! You know the story, I guess?"

"Just what I heard."

He snorted and spat on the floor. "I can guess!" He got up and began to walk around the room, pulling at a set of books that were stacked over a chest in a rough wooden shelf. He looked at one of them, handed it to me, saying, "Look at that."

It was an old composition book with *Red Horse* written on the cover. Under that was written in a big sprawling hand: *DAN MAJORS — HIS JOURNAL*. I opened it and saw page after page filled with that big handwriting.

"Dan kept that ever since he was a kid. Must be twenty of them on that shelf. Guess I ought to see they're put in a safe place." He shook his head sadly. "Matthew is angry with his dad now, but someday he'll want to read these."

"Cora doesn't know they're here?"

"No. It would hurt her to see them. Look, here's something else." He reached up on a higher shelf and pulled an old photo album down, then handed it to me. It was packed with old snapshots — some of Cora and a man that had to be her husband, and many pictures of two boys growing to manhood. I saw near the end one of Dawn dressed in a wedding gown.

"She doesn't know about this either?"

"Guess not. Maybe doesn't *want* to know." He sagged and flopped into his chair. Pulling a battered silver flask from his inside pocket, he took a long swallow, then waved it at me. "Have one?"

"No, thanks." I flipped through the pictures, saying casually, "From what I've heard, Dan Majors was not the kind of guy to kill his own brother."

The works shut down right then. Pentland suddenly turned a putty color and got up, saying abruptly, "I'll get this stuff out of your way." He grabbed one of the boxes, and I helped him put the rest in the spare bedroom inside, where he was sleeping.

He stayed in the house for the next few days, most of the time talking with Cora. But I managed to get him alone a few times, and after he'd mellowed down with enough pain-killer out of his silver flask, he'd talk about the early days with SunCo. A pattern kept coming up. He'd talk about the early days, and his face would come alive, but when I tried to steer his conversation to the last days just before the tragedy, he'd clam up or change the subject. He left the ranch before I'd obtained any useful information, and I resolved that before long, I'd be paying another visit to Mr. William Pentland.

I went through those journals from cover to cover. Perry spent his evenings at a pool hall in town, and I almost memorized those books. I stared at the pictures in the album so long and so hard they were etched in my mind. Most of the diary was written during the youth of Majors and was interesting enough. He wasn't given to emotional outbursts, to say the least. Most of it was simple records of activities. The most poetic thing in it was the description of Maggie, his first horse. There were large gaps, as if he had put the journal idea aside for years, and then started up again.

The last two journals were written after his marriage, and they were the sections I pored over. He mentioned Dawn quite matter-of-factly — except for one phrase he put in just a few months before his death: *Worried about Dawn. She'll never learn!* That bothered me, and there was a reference to Matt that said: *Hope Matt never knows everything.*

But the most baffling thing was his references to Frank, his brother. He didn't say a lot, but from his scattered remarks it was clear he loved the man!

About George Renfro there were only references to matters of business — except for one line: *George takes too many shortcuts!*

The photographs were intriguing. They were made with an inexpensive thirty-five-millimeter camera, but the quality was good enough to capture the spirit of the Majors family. The earliest shots went back to the boyhood days of the brothers — hunting, birthdays, vacation at

Grand Canyon, Christmas tree with presents piled high under it. The usual things.

But it was the *honesty* of the faces of all the Majors that said the most. No matter which one I looked at, from the parents to the boys, all of them had that square jaw, that look in the eye that said, "Do right!" Not that I thought you could spot a killer by his expression. But there was a natural wholesomeness about them that didn't go with murder — especially the murder of one of their own!

I got so engrossed in the material that I started daydreaming about them, and when I looked at Cora, Dawn, or Matthew, it got all mixed up with the faces of Owen, Frank, and Dan. I had strange dreams that night about all of them, and it was a bad scene — some kind of confused picture with Dan Majors as a murderer and Dawn and Matt crying! So different from my dreams of fire, but real enough nonetheless.

I was thankful for the distractions of work and Perry. He didn't do anything but stay up all night gambling at the pool hall, sleep till noon, then put me to punching a bag and doing roadwork all afternoon. I got up early, went over the work with Cora, and did what I could until after lunch when Perry got after me.

About ten days before the bout, Perry said after lunch, "You lookin' sharp, Champ. But it's time for a break. Don't want to get *too* fine! Let's us go to town and celebrate you winnin' the fight."

"You think it's in the bag?"

He frowned and snorted, "Never doubt Jester, Champ. Last man who doubted Jester wound up in the pen!"

Maybe if we had gone into another joint the thing wouldn't have happened, but he took me to a place called the Blue Duck, which wasn't blue and had no duck. "I been here a few times," he said, leading me inside.

It was no better nor worse than any of the other dives in Broken Bow, I guess. Same dark interior, same meaningless laughter, same smell of stale beer, stale tobacco smoke, and un-washed bodies. Perry led me to the bar, and I noticed that the bartender, a thick-necked char-acter with a pair of anchors tattooed on his forearm, gave us the briefest of nods. "Two Blue Ribbons," Perry ordered, then turned to survey the room.

"Just a Coke for me," I said quickly. "Don't like the hard stuff."

"Best that way," Perry muttered. We got our drinks and I looked the room over, not too impressed. Perry and I sat back and made idle talk.

Perry began making offhanded remarks about the "bar clientele," that it was a gaggle of red-necks in their natural habitat. In my other life I must've known the breed pretty well, because as I looked around the Blue Duck, I realized I could write a book on the guys in there. I knew they were "good ol' boys," and as we sat there with our drinks, we began to have our-selves a real good time bantering back and forth about the nature of the beast.

I suddenly got real involved and sat up straight in my chair. I adjusted make-believe glasses and ruffled my hair in an unruly sort of way. In my best professor voice and attempt at a British accent, I said, "The typical red-neck can be identified by several distinctive characteristics. They start life on a hardscrabble eight-acre farm south of St. Louis and have large hands from driving tractors, running chain saws, driving eighteen-wheelers, and running traplines. He will have two brothers, named Bubba and Junior, and several sisters, all with two first names — Mary Sue, 'Lizabeth Ann, Sally June."

I must've caught Perry off guard for a second, because he had this sort of bewildered look on his face as he watched me. Then suddenly he burst into such a loud laughter, several people around us gave us questioning glances.

"That is the funnies' thang I ever did hear, Smith!" he said as tears of laughter rolled down his face.

I continued without breaking character. "He will probably drive a pickup with a pair of fuzzy dice dangling from the rearview mirror, three high-powered rifles in a gun rack across the back window . . ."

". . . an' a bumper sticker that say 'Goat Ropers Need Love Too!' " Perry chimed in, his loud voice sprinkled with laughter.

We both kept laughing and I continued, still trying to be the professor. "The pickup will be a four-wheel drive with a chrome bar topped with several halogen lights, and it will be jacked up so high with risers you can drive a Volkswagen under it. You can expect to see him pulling an Ouachita Bass Boat, which will be a sparkly metallic blue color. It will have a Black Max Mere in the rear, a trolling motor in the bow, and a live well used for cooling beer more often than fish."

"Sure enough, Smith!" Perry cackled. "And the truck and boat'll be washed more frequently than the owner."

We took a second to catch our breath and try to control ourselves, and as we looked at the company around us, we felt sure we were being completely accurate!

Perry started up this time, and I hadn't remembered when I'd seen Perry have such a good time. "And they be hangin' out at beer joints all the time, a'ways on the edge o' town . . ."

". . . by the wrecking yard," I added wistfully.

"Yeah. By the wrecking yard! And the name's somethin' like Lola's, and it got blacked out windows. And the sign, it in red neon lights," he said, moving his hand in front of him like he could actually see the sign.

"But," I said holding up a professor-like finger, "in more recent years they can be found in large crowded bars with an artificial bull and

214

the most powerful Klipsch speakers available belting out the ballads of Willie and ol' Waylon."

"Whooooeeeee!" Perry exhaled, and it primed me for more.

"Good ol' boys like red Walker hounds, CBs, going to the deer woods, early Clint Eastwood . . ."

"Them early pre-Bronco Billy variety."

"Loni Anderson."

"Yessirrreee!"

"And .44 magnums, overdone steaks, and Skoal."

Perry almost leaped out of his seat in excitement. "And they hate them cats! And that fancy Viiiidal Sassooooon shampoo and conditioner! I sus'ect they ain't likin' no John Denver an' his high rollin' Rocky Mountains!"

I laughed and then pretended to be very serious. I looked Perry right in the eye and said somberly, "And they dislike African-Americans, particularly large male-types driving black Cadillacs with red interiors and fender feelers."

Perry laughed hysterically and pounded his fist on the table. "That's right, Champ! That's right! I guess I is lucky I don't drive one of them fancy Caddys!"

I continued with a brief, knowing nod. "The uniform is rigidly standard, consisting of faded blue jeans with the Skoal print on the back pocket, a red-checked shirt in winter, and in summer a T-shirt with the arms cut off, Tony Lama ostrich-hide boots, and cowboy hats with a band made from rattlesnakes . . ."

". . . they killed themselves!"

I emphasized my British accent and said, "He will read *Argosy* and *Sports Afield*, but there have been cases of intellectuals among them that would come right out and admit they had read a Louis L'Amour Western all the way through."

I really had Perry rolling now, and I kept going. "Their language is profane beyond belief, but it's not just profanity. They have a gift for metaphor, never calling a thing by its dictionary name. A true red-neck would die of shame if he called the thing he drives a truck. It's a rig. And his statements are never simple phrases. When one of them wants to tell you how he felt uncomfortable in a certain situation, he might say . . ." I eyed Perry and said, "Would you do the honors, good friend? Can you do justice to the red-neck metaphor?"

Between chuckles and swigs of beer he managed to get out, "I felt as outa place as a bullfrog on the freeway with one o' his hoppers busted!"

"Marvelous, marvelous, dear Perry!" I cheered. "He wasn't nervous but . . ." I waved a hand in his direction.

"As anxious as a long-tailed cat in room fulla rockin' chairs!"

"Not, it was *bad,* but . . ."

"It wuz worse dan slidin' down a fifty-foot razor blade into a vat of alcohol! Whoooeee!"

We laughed even harder. Perry wiped tears from his eyes, wiggled his finger at me, and said,

"The way you goin' on, you might've been some college professor in your past life, maybe some sooooociologist or somethin'!"

I nodded and smiled, wondering if it might not be true. I felt good inside. I hadn't laughed that hard since I could remember. But I soon noticed that the bunch at the next table were watching us. One of them, a big guy in a yellow shirt and a worn black Stetson with the inevitable snakeskin band, kept saying something and then nodding over at Perry and me. He must have been the star, because he raised quite a few laughs from the audience, and he kept getting louder all the time.

"I think we're about to be named Queen of the May," I said to Perry.

"Yeah, I see 'em." He took the last swallow of beer and nodded, "Le's get ourselves out. Law says your fists is a deadly weapon, and we don't need no scrimmage." He set the glass down and got up to go, but it was too late.

Snakeskin got up and moved between us and the door. He didn't look at the crowd at the table, but he was on stage. "Ah, you guys ain't leavin' already, are you? I wuz just gonna buy you a beer."

He was big, about 220, with a lean waist and knotted shoulder muscles that meant bad news to anyone he belted. Maybe about thirty or a little less, and tough as leather. His eyes glinted with eagerness. He was looking for trouble.

217

"Thank you kindly," Perry said with a careful smile. "We both had our limit. Maybe next time."

It wasn't going to work. I saw it, and Perry did too. A couple of the guys at the table got up and stood behind Snakeskin, and a couple more slid their chairs back so they could get into the action quickly. Perry leaned back and let his shoulder touch mine as a warning, but his voice was silky as he said, "Now, let's not have any trouble. I do purely *hate* trouble! We'll just pass on out if that's okay with you, Boss."

Snakeskin laughed, and when he spoke, he had a voice like rancid lard. "What's wrong, Smokey? You don't like our company?" He turned to grin at his audience and added, "Now, I want you dudes to be nice to Smokey, you hear? He's got his civil rights, ain't he?" A laugh went around, and three more of the crowd got up, two of them moving to my right and the other one flanking Perry. We were surrounded like Custer, and I knew there wasn't going to be a nice ending to this.

Snakeskin stared at me, and I knew I was his target, not Perry, but I'd never seen him, so far as I knew. "You the big *fighter* livin' out at the Majors' place, ain't you?" He gave me a tough smile and turned to the big guy just behind him. "He don't look so tough to me. Does he look tough to you, Jiggs?"

"Naw, Waylon, he don't look tough to me." Jiggs was a thick-bodied hairy hulk with a protruding jaw and a dim light in his eyes. "He don't look tough at all."

He'd called the leader "Waylon," and I realized at once that this must be Waylon Davis, the boyfriend of the waitress at Mary's Café. He'd already whipped the local talent, the sheriff had said, and now he was ready to take me on to keep his reputation intact.

"What you think, Roy? He look tough to you?" Davis said.

A stringy type with eyes too close together spit on the floor and said, "Naw, he don't look tough to me."

I saw I had to push it. Even Davis might be a handful in a barroom brawl, but he wasn't alone. Maybe if I got him mad enough we could get out the door.

I looked him straight in the eyes and said, "You do realize, don't you, that you're not doing the 'tough guy' part right. You're supposed to have a cigarette dangling from your lips and squint your eyes together more."

It got quiet as a church in the Blue Duck. The overhead lights framed us in the glare, making me think of the ring, but this was different. There'd be no ref here to pull Waylon and his outlaws off if we went down!

"Squint? I'll squint you!" he gritted out between his teeth and was about to say something else when I cut him off.

"What's your name?" I asked.

He stared at me and settled back on his heels,

flexing his thick arms. "Button your lip, boy!" he spat out.

"Okay, Button Your Lip Boy. That was a pretty rotten name for a mama to pin on a helpless baby, but your mama probably saw what kind of mess you were before the cord was cut."

Perry leaned against me, and I figured he knew what I was doing — even if I wasn't so confident. We had to get them off balance long enough to put him away quick so we could make the door. It was still daylight outside, and I didn't *think* they'd shoot us there — but you couldn't be real sure with a bunch like this.

Maybe we'd have gotten away with it easy, but Waylon gave me a tough grin and mouthed, "I hear you been stayin' at the Majors' place." He gave a wink at the crowd and grinned broadly. "Now, that Dawn — she ain't too bad. I guess I ought to know! You know what I mean, prizefighter?"

A sudden gust of rage filled my mind, and a roaring sounded in my ears. I was hot, but at the same time cold as ice. He was off guard, looking over at his buddies, still grinning at his line, when I let him have it. He had a big nose, and I planted my feet and tried to drive that nose right through the back of his skull. His feet were set, and the force of my fist smeared his nose from cheekbone to cheekbone and drove him back into the arms of the guy behind him as if a charge had gone off in his face. The two of them went to the floor, and one look at Waylon's eyes rolling up to show the whites told me that he wasn't going to continue the argument. One of the guys next to Perry said in a shocked voice, "Hey! What the —" just as Perry reached out and put a solid right under his ear that cartwheeled him into a table, scattering glasses and people everywhere.

All this took about five seconds, and two of their little army had packed it up, but there were at least six or seven more, and all of them jumped right at it. I managed to kick the feet out from under one, and while he was scrambling around, I got the one called Jiggs with a solid left right in the Adam's apple, sending him down gurgling and totally defeated. Perry, though, had caught the worst of it. At least four guys were coming at him, and just as I started to pitch in, somebody caught me from behind with a chair. It drove me down, slightly stunning me, but my shoulder took the worst of it. My left arm felt weak, but I managed to roll over just as a little guy with a huge mustache raised the chair to finish the job. He hit the floor where I had been, and I got up with a fury and put a fist under his chin. He staggered back and tripped over another overturned chair.

It wasn't like a fight in the ring, where everything was rather neat and orderly with rules and refs. This was like a pack of wolves, with death in every eye. I knew these guys weren't worried about putting Perry and me down for keeps, so for about sixty seconds it was like a prolonged explosion, with yelling, breaking glass, falling bodies, and bloody wrecks. The women were screaming, and the heavy, meaty sounds of blows falling on flesh could be clearly heard over the curses spilling out of raw throats.

It couldn't last long. They would have buried us if the cops hadn't come. I found out later the police used the Blue Duck as a home away from home, dropping in for coffee and talk several times a day. I was going down for the last time, and Perry was buried under a pile of legs when there was a new set of voices, and I caught a quick glimpse of a big hand with a nightstick wading into the fray.

Law and order is a wonderful thing!

My joy dissipated when the cops piled Perry and me into the car and took *us* to jail — just us, none of the others. I looked over at Perry as we were hauled out of the car and shoved into the little cell that smelled strongly of urine and stale vomit. His face was bleeding, and he was trying not to make a face as he moved, but he grinned at me and said, "God's in His heaven. All's right with the world."

"Guess so." I looked down at my knuckles and saw that someone's teeth had plowed little ridges along the knuckles, and as the shock wore off, my muscles began to tremble and I started to sweat. I rubbed the lump on the back of my head and carefully rotated my left shoulder a few times. I had a small cut over my right eye, but not too bad, and as we compared wounds, we were amazed at how lightly we had gotten off.

"They was too many of 'em," Perry nodded. "Couldn't get at us. If they had just some of 'em stood back, it would have been murder one." Then he gave me a sideways grin and said, "You surely got touchy 'bout that widow woman."

I didn't want to think about that. The blind rage that had jumped out of me when Davis had spoken of Dawn was a frightening thing. "You think we'll have to stay here long?" I asked to change the subject.

"Oh, we get out when we pay the fines."

"*They* started it!" I protested.

"But *they* is home folks and we ain't," he explained. "On top o' that, my friend, I jus' ain't the right color for this kind o' deal." Then he lay down carefully on the ratty bunk and added, "They sho ain't gonna be in no hurry."

He was right. We stayed in the jail all day and night. The next morning we came up before a judge with a face as hard as corrugated roofing. He laid a fine of two hundred dollars on each of us, and when I started to argue, Perry gave me a shot in the ribs with his elbow and said, "Thank you kindly, Judge."

"You two give me any more trouble and you'll find yourself doing road work for ninety days." The judge stared at me and asked, nodding at Perry, "You a *friend* of his?"

I knew I ought to keep my mouth shut, but I stared straight at him and said, "He likes me, Judge . . . but he won't let me marry his sister."

The judge drew a sharp breath and his lips got white. I looked into his flinty eyes and knew I'd better not come up before him again. Perry dragged me out, paid the fine, and we left town.

"Why'd you say that to the judge?" he asked as we eased down the main street, being shadowed by a car plainly marked *SHERIFF*.

"I said it because it wasn't fair."

I could feel Perry staring at me. He whistled softly, gave his head a shake, and finally said, "Baby, you is *something!*"

"Perry, judges are supposed to be fair! That's what law is all about, isn't it — fair play for all?"

He patted my arm as he would have that of a willful child and said gently, "You is about a million light years away from whut is happenin', man. You gotta grow up quick!"

"Maybe I'd rather keep on being dumb." I gave him a sort of grin and added, "Guess those fines put us down to the bottom of the well."

He frowned. "Sure did. I guess maybe I better put in some night work with the cards to catch us up."

"Better not do it at the Blue Duck."

"You right about that. You all right? We can get outa that bout if you don't feel like it."

"I'll murder the bum," I said with a gangster accent and a smile.

We talked about the fight until we pulled up to the bunkhouse, but the door to the main house opened and Matt came skittering out, calling at me before I got out of the Bronco. "Adam! You got out of jail!" He ran right up to me, and I thought he was going to grab me, but then he pulled back and tried to look cool. "We thought you'd have to stay in jail for a week at least."

"Come on in the house."

I looked up and Dawn was standing there, and her face was different. She looked . . . I don't know . . . *triumphant* is the word that came to me. She met my gaze, then walked up to me and pulled at my arm. "Come inside."

I glanced at Perry, but he just gave me a shake of his head, and we both went inside, where Cora was waiting.

"We heard about it," she said at once. "No means of communication will ever equal the gossip of a small town." She got up and put both her hands on my shoulders, and her face was still. She seemed to be searching my face for something; then she took one hand and put it on my cheek very softly. Her finger tenderly traced the small cut above my eye, her face unusually gentle, welcoming. "I'm proud of you, Adam. And I thank you for defending the family."

I don't know. It got to me. The room was absolutely quiet, and my face was burning, but she kept her hand on my cheek for a brief space, then turned abruptly and made her voice brisk.

"Well, I know you must be starved, both of you. How do bacon and eggs sound?"

We went to the bunkhouse and washed the stale smell of the jail off, and when we finally sat down at the table, Cora said a very brief grace, which caught me off guard.

"Lord God, thank you for the food and for the courage to do the right thing."

Perry and I were starving, so we told the story between huge bites and swallows. Dawn listened, but she just picked at her food, giving me a heavy-lidded look I couldn't read.

Finally Perry shoved back and said, "Adam, I've been thinkin'. How about I go into Tulsa for a week? Take care of some business. I be back by Tuesday, and we do a little more light work, then go for the bout. That sound good?"

I knew he was headed for the big game, so I nodded. He said his good-byes and left to pack his stuff. We sat around the table, and in about ten minutes we heard the Bronco head out. I looked at Cora and said, "Hate that the fuss started. We shouldn't have gone to that bar."

Cora shook her head firmly. "No, it's the town. The name of Majors was once honored there. Now riffraff like Waylon Davis feel free to drag it into the saloons."

"You know him?" I asked.

Dawn suddenly said with a rosy tint on her fair cheeks, "He's always tried to get me to go out with him. I wouldn't, and he's . . . talked about me ever since."

"Did you really *bust* him good, Adam?" Matt asked intently, leaning across the table, his dark eyes gleaming.

"I can answer that!" Cora said with evident satisfaction. "Old Doc Whitby called me last night. He said the nose was broken very nicely and would never look much like a nose again without painful and expensive surgery."

"Good!" Matt said happily. "I wish you'd killed him!"

"Now, that would have been a bit extreme, so I'm glad I didn't," I said. He looked at me and I just gave him a smile. He seemed satisfied.

After that, Matt was a different kid and stuck by me pretty close. Missed having a man around, I guess. I insisted on doing a few things around the place, even though Cora wanted me to rest. Matt followed me, actually got in my way asking questions and trying to help, but I didn't mind.

We went for a swim late that afternoon in a small stream only about three miles from the house, and I showed him how to do the Australian crawl. He swallowed a lot of water trying to learn, but he loved it.

After supper we sat up, and he taught me a game called Clue. All four of us sat around the table, and there was a lot of laughing and hollering until nearly midnight. Matt put up quite a fight to have just *one* more game. He lost, but there was a contented look on his young face as he kissed the women good-night and gave me a small wave as he left.

We all said good-night and I went to bed. For a time I read Dan Majors' journal; then I read the first few chapters of Genesis. I was just about to close the Bible and turn in, when I heard a tapping at the door. Then Dawn came in.

She was wearing a pale blue robe, silk I guess, and it flowed with every movement as she started into the room. I got up quickly, and she sort of paused at the door, looking as if she were unsure if she should come any farther.

I stepped forward a bit and so did she. She finally walked right up to me and held her hands out. I took them, and they were trembling. I caught the heady fragrance of a perfume.

"Thank you, Adam. I know you did it for me," she whispered in a voice I'd never heard from her.

She leaned forward. My head was swimming and I cleared my throat, which had suddenly gotten thick. "Dawn, I wish . . ."

Then I couldn't go on. There was no sound in the room, so I could hear her breathing. The pounding of my own blood seemed heavy and powerful as my mouth went dry. I took her shoulders in both hands and she looked up at me.

"What do you want, Adam?" she whispered. "What do you *want*?"

I couldn't think, and suddenly I was aware of every nerve in my body. This was the strongest sensation I'd felt since I came back to the world. I reached out and pulled her closer.

"What do you want?" she whispered again.

Sometimes we think — use reason and our minds, facts and figures. But sometimes the emotions and the body take over.

I pulled her head up to mine and kissed her, and then suddenly felt like a man poised on the brink of a cliff about to fall, but holding on by one frail branch. I knew once I let go of that one tiny twig, I would plunge down to the depths and no power on earth could stop me.

For just a moment, I struggled to keep my grip on something, anything. All I had to do was pull her toward me.

Then, unexpectedly, something came into me even stronger than my desire. I didn't understand it, but I suddenly just knew that going to bed with this woman would ruin something deep inside my spirit. Shaking my head, I released her and stepped back.

"What is it?" she asked softly.

I couldn't answer. Everything inside myself was a contradiction. I had no idea what I really wanted at that moment.

She took a step back herself and said, "Do you want me to go?"

"I, um . . . it's just that . . ." I stammered around, but that was apparently plenty of a signal for her. She dodged my stare and with an elegant turn headed to the door. "Dawn, I'm sorry, I just —"

She cut me off with an abrupt reply. "I just wanted to thank you," she said with a courteous smile.

Before I could say anything else, she was gone. I just stood there staring at the wall, my knees weak and my stomach tremoring. I walked over to the bed, sat down on it, and put my head in my hands. For a long time I couldn't even think clearly. Strange thoughts were coming into my mind, and faint memories flickered dimly — always just out of focus.

Finally I lay down without undressing and for a long time tried to make sense out of the scene. But I couldn't do it. The only thing I was sure of was that I'd come close to destroying something very precious, and for the first time since I came out of the coma, I felt the presence of God, or so I thought. I closed my eyes, and it was as though I were being bathed in some sort of warm, inner light. Like — well, like I'd done something that pleased God very much.

"I don't know what's happening, God," I finally whispered, "but if this is you, I hope you'll help me find my way. If you don't . . . I'm afraid I'll just make a mess of things."

Renfro

ELEVEN

I HAD hoped that Dawn would see that something strong kept me from her, but it didn't work that way. I knew she'd felt rejected that night, and as much as I tried to convince her that was not the case, she kept a cold distance from me, though not without an occasional sultry glance to remind me what I'd missed.

I had no memories of ever engaging in any sexual encounters, yet Dawn's simple presence left me defenseless.

Sooner or later I knew I'd take a fall. Few healthy men can stand temptation for long; living in such close quarters with a desirable, willing woman had only one end. Part of me begged for satisfaction — that was the body. It was like a man living in a burning desert surrounded by forbidden bottles of cool, frosty water. I would wake up at night aching with desire and knowing all I had to do was give Dawn one word.

But there was another, more complicated side. I knew full well what the Bible said about forni-

231

cation and adultery. The story of David's sexual sin with Bathsheba had burned itself into my mind, and as the days passed, I knew that if I gave in to my body's demands, somehow I would regret it. Just *how* I wasn't sure, but day by day I became more and more confused.

I guess it was at that point that I began praying.

Oh, I'd prayed before, of course, for something in me said that it was the thing to do. But this was different. Before, I *thought* I was serious, but now I prayed for help with a desperation that was greater than anything I'd faced since I woke up. A man can have a broken arm and pray about that, but when the man in the white coat tells him, "You've only got six months to live," that's another story.

At least it was for me. Things got so bad that I found myself praying practically *all* the time. I'd been pretty single-minded before — determined to find out who I was — but now life became even more intense, a focused struggle from the time I got up until I went to sleep. And even then, I had dreams about her that brought me awake and drove me out of my room to walk for hours in the darkness.

And there was always a voice of some kind whispering inside my head: *Look, you might as well take the easy way. Dawn knows what she wants, and so do you, if you'd admit it. And doesn't the Bible say that if you lust in your heart after a woman, you've already committed adultery? You know you're guilty of that, so just go on and take her. You're not a saint, Adam Smith. You don't even know if you're a saved man. You may never know.*

One of the more plausible arguments that came into my mind was: *Marry her and it will all be legal. In fact, she may well already be your wife. Your memory's not coming back, and you can't live like a monk. Besides, Matthew needs a father.* This rationalization began to sound better and better to me, but I knew it wouldn't solve my problems. A man can always come up with a good reason for doing what he's aching to do!

Every day I'd work on the place, do my road-work, punch the bag, and feel guilty as Judas about Dawn! I'd find myself making excuses to see her, and she would make a few herself, often ending up in my room late at night.

I managed, barely, to resist the temptation by remembering the story of Joseph, who, when Potiphar's wife took hold of his robe and tried to seduce him, simply ran away, his garment still in her hand. But I was no Joseph; he knew God. And what did I know? In my former life, I might have been the weakest man in the world.

Late one night, I found some silly excuse to invite Dawn to my room. Before I knew it, her arms were wrapped around me, and I felt myself losing the struggle.

She pulled my head down, and her lips were soft as she whispered, "I think this is the only thing in my whole life that's right, Adam."

But I somehow wrenched myself from her,

and without a word ran out into the night. As I stood on the side of the road, a bright moon overhead, I tried to convince myself it was all right. She was *good* for me! I needed someone to hold on to, and why not Dawn?

Cora never knew what was happening, nor Matthew. But when Perry came back on Tuesday, it took him all of five minutes to get the picture. A sober light touched his deep-set eyes as he said, "May I speak to you on a rather delicate matter, Champ?" I nodded and he continued, "You know, I think I'm gettin' *literary* hanging around with you. I kind of like it — 'a delicate matter'!"

I fell into the bunk and tried to think of some reply but couldn't. I felt like a ten-year-old caught smoking.

"You been up to some extracurricular activities with the widow Majors, ain't you, now?" When I didn't answer he went on in the same tone, "Now, you know I ain't one to preach, but you making yourself a big mess."

"What's *that* mean?"

"It means you come here to find out if you got anything in common with Dan Majors. Now here's his wife puttin' out a welcome sign. So answer me this, Champ. How you gonna think straight about the whole thing?"

I didn't tell him that I'd pretty well stopped thinking since I'd started up with Dawn. But I had to say something! "Look, Perry, it's more complicated than you think." I fumbled around trying to come up with an answer, and finally said, "I'm remembering things, Perry! For the first time, remembering!"

"Remembering what?"

"Lots of things! Like I remember a name for Dawn that only Dan Majors could have known — a secret name, you know? I almost called her by it, but I figured it wasn't time yet. And I remember a trip to the Rocky Mountains that Dan Majors went on when he was ten — and the first buck he shot when he was twelve! And I remember going to Mexico with Dad and Frank . . ."

"Wait a minute!" The light came on, and Perry sat up in bed, rubbing his skull. "You really remembering all that stuff, Champ?"

"Where else could it come from?"

He got up off his bunk, picked something up, then tossed it at me. "*That's* what you re-member, Champ."

I looked down and saw that he had thrown Dan Majors' *Red Horse* notebook — the one I had been reading just before we put the lights out.

"There's your 'memory,' " Perry said softly. "Maybe I'm wrong, but you can check it out."

"How?" I was angry at him, and bitter with myself.

"I guess you can find pretty near anything you think you been remembering right in one of them books or in the pictures."

He lay back, and I knew he was right. As I

scrabbled around trying to find *one* thing I could clearly label a real memory, I had to admit that it had all come from the journals and the album.

"Yeah, I guess you're right, Perry. It's just that . . ."

He waited until I stopped short, then murmured, "Sure, I know. You wanna be somebody. But it ain't no use to try to force it."

"Yeah, sure."

"Look, man, if you really wanna know for sure, why don't you just go to Dan Majors' dentist and check out the dental records?"

I thought about it for a moment, and the sensation began a trembling in my legs. "I don't want to find out that way, Perry. I've got to remember it up here," pointing at my head. "I mean, I could have the facts, but I *still* wouldn't know who I am."

"Yeah, I suppose you is right," said Perry. "Just a suggestion is all. For all we know, the guy had perfect teeth and never went to the dentist."

Maybe what happened the next day shouldn't have been too much of a shock. Cora had told me that George Renfro had been half in love with Dawn and had taken it pretty hard when she'd married Dan instead of him. I'd asked Dawn about it, but she just shrugged.

"George always liked me. If I hadn't married Dan, we might have gotten together. He's a lot of fun."

When Renfro drove in the next day, it was

pretty clear that his attraction to Dawn was still under warranty. He got there about four in the afternoon, parking his red Dodge Viper in the shadow of the Bronco. I was washing up inside the bunkhouse, but Perry looked out the window and said, "Oh, ho! We got rich visitors, Champ. Look at that machine!"

I peered out the window and there he was — George Renfro. I'd only gotten a glimpse of him at his office, but I knew him. "That's Renfro."

"What he want, you reckon?"

"I reckon he wants Dawn Majors."

"Then you two got something in common, Champ."

"Cute. What a way you have with words!"

He sobered and said, "You think he's tied in with all this?"

"I don't *think* anymore, Perry. I just keep bobbing and weaving!"

When I went in to supper, Cora was waiting to say, "This is George Renfro, Adam. Adam Smith, George. He's working for us now, like I told you."

"Yes, so you said. Where you from, Adam?"

I dodged the question, and as Cora went on to explain how I really wasn't simply a hired hand, I discreetly checked him out. He seemed cared for. He was a pretty big guy, and his expensive suit almost covered up the paunch that easy living had plastered around his middle. He looked as if he'd spent half his life under a sun lamp, his hair was immovably coiffed, and somebody had obviously selected his outfit so that the colors blended into a unified, trendy whole. He'd been "produced," you might say.

His capped-tooth smile was the color of Vermont granite and had about the same warmth as he carefully watched me while pretending to listen to Cora. I had little doubt about what was going through his blow-dried head. *Small time. Cannot help me climb any higher in my world. Lack of material motivation and no inclination to achieve higher status. A financial liability.*

I saw all this in those granite eyes, but there was something else there too, in his eyes, which I couldn't quite nail down. Was it fear? It could just as well have been aristocratic discomfort in the presence of a serf.

Still, Renfro was clearly picking up on the way Dawn's eyes kept following me. He wasn't stupid, even if he was synthetic. After Cora had told my story, he said, "So you're a fighter? Well, some do pretty well in that way. Nothing wrong with ambition, is there?"

"I wouldn't know. I never had any," I said slowly. "Fellow named MacBeth had some. It got him killed, if I remember right."

That stopped him, and he nodded and said, "Something to be said for that, but not much."

We all sat down to eat, but it was a strange meal. Some sort of tense electricity was flowing between Dawn, Renfro, and me. Every time Dawn and I looked at each other, Renfro smoothly launched some subject or other, dominating our attentions. He *knew* about Dawn and me somehow. Call it animal instinct, and I had clearly entered his territory. I knew he wasn't going to be a gentleman about it.

After supper I excused myself and went to my room, while Renfro took Dawn out. I lay awake for a long time, and finally at about two in the morning, I heard the engine of his Viper come to a stop outside. There was a long pause; then a door opened and closed and he left the driveway with a roar.

At breakfast the next morning, Dawn was up — something that signaled she wasn't happy. She tried to catch my eye over the table, but I concentrated on the eggs. She caught up with me, though, later that day. I was clearing a fallen water oak on the back side of the lower pasture when she stepped out and called my name. I shut off the chain saw and asked with a deadpan face, "Have a swell time last night?"

She leaned against me and said, "I didn't want to go with him. He's always been after me."

"You didn't want to go? I don't recall him forcing you."

Her eyes were snapping, and she straightened up, saying, "It's not that easy!"

"Why not?"

"Oh, I don't know, Adam. It's all . . . mixed up. It's hard to say no."

"Sure, takes a whole syllable."

I don't know why I was being so cold. She turned and left, and I watched her leave, totally confused and angry.

When I got back from my workout late that afternoon, D.K.'s Volvo was next to Dawn's Dart. I went right into the house, prepared for World War III.

Dawn and D.K. were sitting across the room from each other. Every time their glances met, blue sparks flew around the living room.

"Hi, D.K.," I said nonchalantly.

"Hello, Adam."

Her lips caressed my name as if it were dripping with honey. She got up, and I saw that she was wearing her "serious" clothes — a simple outfit that would have put most households out of budget for at least two months. Not to mention the pearl nestled sweetly in the hollow of her neck, hanging from a gold chain.

"I've come to take you away." She smiled smoothly — sincere but determined.

"What?" I asked stupidly.

"A little business in the big city, just for a few days," she said.

Her seductive tone was not lost on Dawn, who fixed D.K. with an icy glare, asking in a honeyed voice, "You're in business, I take it, Ms. Wolfe?"

"Surely am!" D.K. smiled like a barracuda at Dawn. The two of them now assumed a fragile politeness that could explode into a screaming brawl at the wrong word. "I'll have Adam back in no time . . . in good condition." Made me sound like a rental car.

After a brief silence, Dawn said in a brittle

tone, "That's fine. A country girl like me just has to put up with this when a fine lady from the big city comes along."

D.K. stretched like a puma, smooth, sleek, and dangerous, then turned to me and said, "Adam, you have this fight day after tomorrow, so I thought you and Perry could ride back with me to Tulsa. Then I could go with you to Oklahoma City."

Something was wrong with all that. I couldn't imagine D.K. wanting to go to a fight, but she was giving me a look that said, "Come on," so I nodded and said, "I'll tell Perry, and we'll get our stuff together."

Perry was asleep in his bunk, but he grinned like a shark when I told him that D.K. had come to get us. We got our equipment and clothes together and met her at the car. Dawn wasn't there, but Matt was. He hung around while we loaded our stuff.

"I wish I could go with you. I ain't never been to a real fight," he said just before we pulled out.

He looked very small just then, and I gave him a gentle punch on the arm, saying, "You haven't missed much, Matt. I'll be back soon, and we'll get some more of those slab-sided bream, okay?"

"Yeah!" he breathed, and his eyes got bright as he stepped back from the car.

As we pulled out of the drive, I saw Dawn looking out of her bedroom window, her face pulled into a frown. I knew she was sore, but there was nothing I could do about it. A stabbing thought hit me — *She'll go to Renfro* — but I shook it off.

Perry curled up in the tiny backseat like a huge possum, and D.K. talked most of the way back to Tulsa about trivial things, witty talk that meant nothing. But she was worried, and sooner or later I knew she'd come out with whatever it was. As she rattled on, I kept looking at her. She was so lovely! *Lovely* — that's a woman's word, and I'd never say it out loud, but that's what fit her. The clean sweep of her profile, set off by that smooth neck and the hair darker than night, made me ache a little. I knew from what little I'd picked up that she'd had plenty of chances to get a guy — some of them top-drawer. But here she was running around the country with a washed-up gambler and a nobody man possessing no past and maybe as little future. I couldn't figure it out.

She dropped us off at the old hotel and merely said, "I'll be ready when you are. Give me a call when you want to go to Oklahoma City. We'll talk after the fight."

I worked out hard the day before the fight. Perry didn't seem interested in gambling, so he stayed with me pretty close. He never mentioned Dawn — not directly. But he skirted around it a lot, and I finally got to wishing he *would* say something.

We went out to eat that night, and afterward we strolled around the streets of Tulsa. I was thinking about Dawn and Matthew and Cora, not too interested in much else. Suddenly Perry dug his elbow into me sharply.

"Good thing you with me, Champ."

I glanced around and saw that we were in a bad part of the city. We were walking past a group of tough-looking young punks who were eyeing us. "Whut you doin' with the cracker?" one of them asked, winking at the others.

"He's my bodyguard," Perry grinned back. "I can't afford a piece, but he's got a real fine one! I carry the cash, he carry the iron."

When we were past the gang and turned the corner, I looked at Perry. "What if they hadn't believed you?"

"Then you would have been in serious trouble."

"What about you?"

"Me? Why, I'm a brother!"

We walked two more blocks, and when we turned down Jefferson Avenue, I heard music. Looking down the street, I saw a small crowd and asked, "What's that, Perry?"

"Street preacher."

Perry's voice was clipped and short. I glanced at him and saw that his lips were drawn tight. He was displeased, and I wondered why.

When we were even with the crowd, I saw the small black man wearing dark slacks, a white shirt, and a broad tie, playing an accordion and singing a hymn. A young woman, his wife I guessed, stood beside him, holding tracts in her hand and singing with him. She was thin and had a frightened look on her face. And she had good reason to be scared. This was a tough crowd — gang members, dealers, pimps, most in their early twenties.

We would have passed on, but as we stepped out into the street to avoid the crowd, a tall, thin individual with a nose ring reached out and grabbed the young woman's wrist. She cried out, and the preacher stopped playing. "Let her go, please," he said quietly.

"Why, Preacher, we ain't goin' to hurt no pretty little thang like this! Why, I might even make her my woman!"

A laugh went up from the gang, and they closed in tighter. They reminded me of a pack of hyenas closing in on a wounded zebra. Their eyes glittered, and the fear in the faces of the young couple gave them pleasure.

I was still moving, but Perry stopped dead still. I stopped and waited to see what he was going to do. One of the gang spotted us and said, "Nickel, we got company."

The tall black man called Nickel didn't release his hold on the woman's arm, but he wheeled to face us. He had scars on his right cheek and tattoos on his forearms of writhing snakes with forked tongues and fangs. He studied us carefully, first me, then Perry. Glancing around at his audience, he said, "You want to join in? Hear the preacher's sermon?"

Perry moved closer, his eyes locked on Nickel.

I stayed back a little, studying the rest of the gang. When Perry was close enough to touch the tall black man, he stopped. He said nothing, and the silence got to Nickel.

"Back off, man!" he said and reached inside his vest with his free hand.

Perry suddenly grabbed the man's wrist and twisted. Nickel cried out, but with his free hand Perry suddenly held a gleaming blade. I'd heard the faint *click* of the switchblade, but it had appeared in his hand like magic.

"I'd like to hear the reverend," Perry said, his voice soft as silk. He must have tightened his grip, for Nickel's face became contorted with pain. "Now, we'd be pleased to have you stay, but I like peace and quiet when I'm listening to preaching."

Perry released the arm of the leader, then stood watching him carefully.

Nickel said between clenched teeth, "Who he with?" He motioned to me.

"He's with me. Now, either move on or stand and listen to the man."

It was a touchy moment. There were enough of them to bury us, and Nickel was weighing the odds. I was wearing a windbreaker and slipped my right hand inside, closing my fingers on a gun that didn't exist. The motion startled Nickel, and he glanced around at his followers. They were waiting for his word, and he gave it.

"Let's split," he said, his eyes narrow and mean. He shouldered his way through the center of the gang, and they turned to follow him down the street.

"You gentlemen better not hang around long." The preacher's face was strained, and he turned to put his arm around his wife. "Those boys won't forget."

"Get off the street, preacher!" Perry snapped. "You ain't gonna do no good with trash like that."

"I have to try," the preacher said. "All they need is Jesus."

Perry stared at him, then wheeled and walked away, his back stiff as an iron bar. I smiled at the pair, then turned and followed him. He was going so fast I had to almost gallop to catch up with him. Finally I said, "What made you so mad?"

"Him, that preacher!" Perry stopped and turned to glance back, anger in his dark eyes. "Gonna get himself killed! And lettin' his wife come in for all that. . . ."

"I guess he thinks he has to do it, Perry. I don't understand it."

Perry shook his head, then turned and walked along the sidewalk. I kept pace with him, glancing at him from time to time. He was thinking hard, and I'd never seen him so tense.

He said roughly, "My daddy wuz a street preacher."

"He was?"

"Yes, and he didn't have no more sense than that one!"

I didn't say anything, and finally Perry stopped walking so fast. I adjusted my pace to his, and soon he began to speak, his voice low, the pain obvious.

"He was a big man, always laughing, Champ. There was nine of us kids, and he didn't have no skills. He worked in construction, and we moved a lot. My ma, she never complained, though she had plenty of reason. We lived in one-room shacks, and once in an old tent for nearly a year."

Cars moved by and we passed by a strip of restaurants. Perry paid no heed, but continued, a dark brooding in his eyes. "I made out all right, even if we didn't have much. But it was his preaching that I couldn't stand. Never in a church. Always out on the street, just like that one back there."

"You went with him?"

"All of us went! I never went one time that Ma didn't make me go. I hated it, Champ, worse than anything in the world. When I was fifteen I couldn't stand it no more. I took off."

"What'd you do?"

"Nothing to be proud of."

His statement slammed the door on other questions, and I just walked along beside him, not saying anything.

Finally he stopped and turned to face me. His features were . . . broken, I guess. Perry had a hard face, but now he didn't look so tough.

"I went back for his funeral, gave Ma some money. But it was bad. I . . . I still remember things about my daddy, Champ. Good things."

"Do you, Perry?"

"He never lied to me, not once. He did his best for us. And he believed what he preached. Maybe I don't have no religion, but he did. He had nothing, but he was happy. He'd be so tired and sick he could hardly stand up, but he'd smile and say, 'Thank you, Jesus, for my fine family!'"

I couldn't think of a thing to say, but I understood why Perry had gone to bat for the little street preacher.

"Know what, Perry?"

"What?"

"I think your daddy is proud of you for standing up for the preacher back there."

Perry blinked, and an odd expression came to his eyes. "You really believe that, Champ?"

"Sure."

Perry took a deep breath, then let it go. He ducked his head and stared at his feet. When he looked up, he had tears in his eyes. "I hope you're right, Champ! I surely do hope you're right. . . ."

The fight was different from the others. Dave Mowen was the guy's name, and he was *good!* It was Saturday night, and the Convention Center Arena was packed because the main event was between the two top-rated welterweights in the world. We were just there to warm up the crowd.

Mowen was sharp — better than anyone I'd seen. He was a perfect size for a heavyweight —

204 pounds, about six-feet, and quick as a snake. He kept peppering me with left hands I never even saw. I blocked some, but they were relentless, coming like rain on a tin roof. They didn't hurt, but they meant points, and since he was backing up all the time, I couldn't get a solid shot at him.

At the end of the third, I said, "Perry! You told me this guy was 'just average.' I can't even *see* him! He's fast as lightning!"

Perry sponged my face off, saying, "Yeah, that's right. He done won twenty-seven fights backing up and flicking that stupid left of his. But I guess you see by now he ain't gonna hurt you with it. And he ain't got no right at all." He pulled my head up to his face and said, "You just gotta wipe this dude out, Adam. You gonna lose this match for sure on points alone. Just lay into him like you did that guy at the Blue Duck. Bust him up!"

The bell rang, and I went at Mowen like a wild ape. He didn't stand a chance. I wrapped my arms around him and pinned him in a corner, then tore him in two with blasting rights to his kidneys and left hooks that just about decapitated him when he straightened up to avoid the body blows. He took it for about ninety seconds. Then I stepped back and turned the lights out with a solid right cross, which knocked his mouthpiece out of the ring and turned his eyes up. The ref counted him out, but he didn't need to.

After we made our way through the usual crowd of screaming idiots, we got dressed and Perry talked to a couple of guys about another bout. Then we met D.K., who was waiting outside in the Volvo.

"Hail, the conquering hero!" she said with a smile.

"Let's *eat!*" I grunted, and she took us to a quiet steak house.

We ate well; then while we were drinking coffee, D.K. suddenly said, "I guess I just don't like fighting."

"Shows you got class," Perry grinned.

She was pushing her lettuce around with a fork, but she looked up at me suddenly. Those eyes of hers could always catch me wide open. "I've only seen fights on TV, and I sort of liked them. So smooth and really beautiful. A tiny square with two muscular athletes moving around almost dancing." She paused, then, "But, you know, when you're there, the violence is pretty grim. Is that why people go?"

"Sure, and that's why most people go to the Indianapolis 500," Perry said. "All that stuff about sport ain't nothin'! They just want to see some poor guy get cremated when he rams into another slob."

She nodded slowly. "I think you're right. In fact, I've noticed the same thing with ballet. On TV, it's so ethereal — superhuman bodies floating in space. But when I went the first time, I was shocked at how *physical* it was! I got seats right on the front row, and it was an eye-opener! I mean, I could see the hair under the arms. And instead of floating, the dancers came *clomping* in!" She gave me a smile and added, "The ballerina had freckles on her neck and stringy muscles."

"I think muscles go with the territory," I grinned.

"Yes, but I liked it the other way — all smooth and no clomping."

Perry said, "Lady, don't get too close to nothing! That's my rule. Ballet, boxing, people, whatever — you get too close, you gonna see the ugly stuff."

That didn't sit right with me. "You can't stay far off from everything, Perry. You got to close in on *something*."

"Then you gotta put up with blood, sweat, and ugly stuff." Perry's face was a study in disillusionment. "I say keep the bad out."

"You didn't keep me out," I reminded him.

"And I told you, it's gonna catch up with me sooner or later."

D.K. said suddenly, "You know, I can see what Perry's saying. Maybe I —" She stopped abruptly and didn't look at us.

Perry glanced across the room and said, "Speaking of ugly stuff, there's somebody I needs to talk to. Brother Dane Taggert, a man with some pull in this city, not to mention a little money to lose to ol' Perry."

Across the room was a party that was pretty

hard to ignore, especially the black man who looked a little like Quasimodo, only not as good-looking. To his right and left, like bookends, were two guys who looked like gestapo types. And on either side of them were several young women — the type you don't take home to Mom.

"I guess I go find out what Brother Taggert knows about the Majors family."

"Be careful," I said. "That bunch don't look too friendly."

"Don't worry. I'll dazzle them with my wit and sophistication," Perry assured me, and we watched him go over and greet the guy in the middle.

D.K. and I looked at each other in silence. Then after about thirty seconds, her face turned a little mean and she suddenly quipped, "You're just consoling her, right?"

Don't ask me how, but she *knew*. Just like Renfro had known, and Perry. She knew what was going on between me and Dawn.

I stiffened a bit. "I feel sorry for her!"

"I bet you do." D.K.'s lips thinned a little; then she forced herself to relax. "Be careful, Adam," she said with a shrug.

Maybe it was because I knew she was right, but the anger swelled up inside me and I blurted out, "You don't get it, D.K.! Dawn's got nothing! Look, I may be her *husband*. You understand that?"

"I bet you're having a good time trying to

drum up some old memories!" she shot back wickedly.

"You won't believe this, but I haven't gone that far."

D.K. stared at me with disbelief, then sighed. Her face grew soft as she whispered, "You are a piece of work, Adam! It's that streak in you. I had a taste of it myself." She eyed me and asked, "What *is* it with you?"

"I . . . just know it would be wrong."

She stared at me and started to answer, but Perry came back, sat down, and said, "Taggert don't know *nothin'*. I never see a man who knew so little. He never even *heard* of anybody named Majors or Renfro."

"That's easy to rearrange," D.K. said. There was a red spot on each cheek, and she carefully avoided looking at me. "If there was ever a connection to Renfro, it shouldn't be hard to find."

"He knows somethin'," Perry said thoughtfully. "I seen it in his eyes when I mentioned Majors."

"Let me take a crack at it, using some of my local connections," D.K. said. She smiled at me, then put her hand on mine as if to say, "I'm sorry."

That was about it. We finished up, spent the night in the hotel, and then Perry and I went back to Broken Bow the next day. D.K. was preoccupied as soon as we got to Tulsa, but she stopped long enough to give me a sisterly kiss. "Be sweet," she said softly. "I'll see you soon."

When we got back to the ranch, I expected Dawn to tear a strip off me about leaving with D.K., but she didn't say a word. She said that Renfro had gone back to the city, and the first time we were alone she caught me in her arms and said, "Glad you're back." Then she was gone, and I knew that I'd reached the end of my resistance.

I looked up as if I could see God through the ceiling and said, "I can't handle this, God. If you don't help me, I'm going down for the count. I can't help it! What do you want from me?"

All day I braced myself for the moment when Dawn might appear when I was alone, and inside I'd given up. I knew that I'd lasted as long as I could.

But it never happened.

Perry left to go into town late that afternoon, and it was only about seven o'clock when the phone rang. Cora answered it, and I half listened to what she was saying.

"What? . . . Yes . . . Yes, he's staying here." A long pause; then she said slowly, "All right, Al, I'll see to it."

She hung up the phone and turned to face me, her face tight with strain. "Perry's in the hospital — intensive care."

The blood was beating in my ears, and I think I knew right then what it was. "Was he in a car wreck?"

"No. He was found in an alley, beaten almost

to death. His skull was cracked. I think we better hurry."

I was numb, and all I could think of was what Perry had said: *"Sooner or later it's gonna catch up with me."*

Now he was dying because of me, and in spite of the numbness that seemed to paralyze my mind, I knew that somebody would pay for this!

Revenge

TWELVE

THE doctor in charge of Perry was so young he'd have trouble buying a drink without showing his ID. He barred my way with all his 135 pounds, insisting in a squeaky voice, "You can see him for five minutes, four times a day. And the next time will be in two hours."

I followed him outside to the courtyard and watched him sit down on a plastic chair. He stared at me for a moment.

"You a close friend?" he finally asked.

"Yeah. Look, he's gonna be all right, isn't he, Doc?"

"He have any family?"

"Not close. Look —"

"He's not good, but he's not dying either." He peered at me as if he was trying to make up his mind about something. Finally he gave a shrug and said, "He's pretty well punched out. Concussion, cheekbone cracked, some ribs either broken or almost. That stuff's manageable, but if he has internal injuries, well . . ." He looked at me sharply and said,

"You know who did this to him?"

"Not yet. I intend to find out."

He stared at my face, taking in my size and the steady gaze I laid on him, then shrugged again. "Yeah, I suppose so. He'll be all right, with good care."

"How long will he be here?"

"Oh, maybe a week. Depends on internal injuries. If there's no problem there, he'll be in good shape soon. But he looks pretty bad right now. I left word for you to see him when it's time. He may not be awake, though. We've got him pretty well sedated."

"Thanks a lot, Doc."

I went back in and sat down to wait. Perry ran with a pretty rough crowd, but I knew this wasn't something he'd brought on himself. It was too much of a coincidence — seeing Dane Taggert one day and getting crunched in an alley the next. I knew Brother Taggert and I were due for a little chat.

Dawn came in a few minutes before I got to see Perry. She appeared all shook up as she leaned against me and moaned about how sorry she was, patting and caressing my arm. But when the nurse stuck her head out the door and motioned me inside, she whispered, "Tonight," with a sly smile. I knew it was an inappropriate comment, considering the circumstances.

I went in alone and stood beside Perry. He wasn't as bad as I had feared. His face was swollen, and there was a bad gray color to him, but I could see he wasn't ruined. Tubes ran out of his nose, and he had a bottle over his head feeding something into his veins. He was breathing steadily, and I just stood there for the five minutes looking at him. When I felt the nurse touch my elbow signaling me to leave, I made myself one of those little promises. Somebody will go down for this!

Dawn was already gone when I went back into the waiting room, so I found a phone in the hall and called Doc Kimpel. He greeted me cheerfully, but when I cut him off with the news about Perry, he sobered at once.

"He's going to be all right?"

"Yeah, no thanks to the guys that got him. I think they wanted to kill him. And I'm convinced it's because he's getting close to the truth about me."

He chewed on that, then asked in an odd voice, "You all right, Adam?"

At that the floodgates burst open, and for nearly an hour I spilled all that was going on inside me. I told him the whole thing: what I was up to with Dawn, my relationship with Matt, how I couldn't tell if I was remembering or not, the memories of the man's face and the old church . . . Finally I said, "Doc, it's so *hard!* I feel like I'm some kind of snail . . . with the shell stripped off. I'm running scared."

"You'd be a fool if you weren't!" he snapped right back. "Many people who have *great* memories live just as scared as you, have just as much to deal with.

"Why, just last night," he continued, "I read about a story of some rich guy in Europe. He had one son, and he made up his mind that *nothing* was going to hurt that kid. He raised the boy behind steel walls and shatterproof glass, gave him filtered air to breathe, and had him watched all the time by all kinds of doctors. Wouldn't let him have any kind of toy or tool that could hurt him. And you know what? One day the kid was sunning himself beside his private pool as a single engine plane lost power. Fell right on top of him from ten thousand feet."

"You're kidding," I said.

"That come as a shock to you? That there are no guarantees in this rat race? You want a guarantee, buy a toaster."

I had to laugh at that. "For that kind of advice you've become rich and famous?"

"How closely are you tied to Dawn?" he asked.

I had a pressure in my throat. "Pretty close."

"Be careful, Adam," he said at once. "*Very* careful."

"That's what Perry tells me *without* being a psychiatrist."

"He's got common sense, Adam. You could get hurt in this kind of situation, much worse than you did in the forest fire. By the way, have you had that dream again?"

"Yes, and it gets a little clearer."

"Tell me about it."

The dream had been pretty much the same

until three nights ago, and then it had been a little different. There was still the sound of men talking, and the fire swallowing me up, but something new had been added. It wasn't much, but I told him how I could hear some new sounds. Maybe they'd been there all the time, and I was too terrified to hear them.

"What kind of sounds?"

"Like . . . like thunder, Doc. Or maybe like big guns going off —"

I broke off so abruptly that he said sharply, "What's wrong?"

"I just remembered something else. In the last dream, I was carrying something."

"Carrying what? It could be important."

I racked my brain trying to bring back the flickering memory, but it was slippery. With a flash it came, and I said with some excitement, "It was a man, Doc! I was carrying a man on my back!"

He pumped me for a long time, but that was about it. Finally he said, "It's coming back a piece at a time, Adam. Every memory is important, like every piece of a jigsaw puzzle is important. Don't trust your memory. Every time something like this comes to you, write it down — and call me."

"Sure, Doc."

"Be careful."

I hung up, then called Cossey's office and was surprised when he answered at once. "Don't you ever go out looking for missing people?" I asked.

"Hello, Smith," he said lazily. "Naw, I just sit here waiting for idiots to call and ask dumb questions. What's up?"

"You think you could locate the pilot of that chase plane?"

"What, you think I'm some kind of dumb TV cop? I already *got* him. He's running a little crop dusting outfit in the valley. Why?"

"Maybe you ought to have a talk with him, Cossey."

"About what? We got his report."

"Maybe he could change his report. I don't like it."

He grunted and said, "I heard about a guy who had some X rays made. The doc said they showed he had a bad disease, that it would cost five thousand dollars for an operation. Guy said, 'How much will it cost to touch up the negatives?' "

"Funny. You think I want to change the truth?"

"I don't think you know what the truth is any more than *I* do."

"The New Testament says 'the truth shall make you free.' "

"Yeah, whatever," he said. There was a pause. "What's happening, Smith? You sound weird."

"Somebody came down on Perry. He's pretty well smashed up, in intensive care in Broken Bow. It was because of the Majors thing. I intend to get whoever did it, Cossey." He didn't answer, and I said, "Will you talk to that pilot?"

"Yeah. Who you like for hitting Perry?"

"Maybe Dane Taggert."

"Taggert's poison, so don't do anything stupid," Cossey spat out. "He's the best argument I got for having people put to sleep."

"I may try a little forceful persuasion."

Cossey groaned. "I'll get back to you if I find anything."

I briefly went back to the ranch to give Cora an update about Perry; then after a shower and a change, I returned to the hospital. There wasn't much sense in it — waiting hours to see him for five minutes, and he wasn't even awake. But there wasn't much sense in anything else right then.

He finally came to the next day. I saw him open his eyes and take me in, but he went right under again. The next visit, though, he was much better. I guess they were easing off on the drugs. He had a better color, and his eyes were clear. I asked, "How you doing?"

He licked his lips and said, "Better than I deserve, man." He tried to sit up, but when I held him down, he gave me a weak grin and whispered, "Life is full of goodies, ain't it? I feel older'n dirt!"

"You know who did it, Perry? We only have a few minutes."

"Oh yeah, I know that. They wasn't careful about wearing no masks."

"Who was it?" He took a couple of breaths carefully, and I could see his ribs were hurting.

"You 'member them two Nazis with Taggert at the restaurant? It wuz them."

"What I figured."

"You gonna go after them?"

"May have a few words."

"Yeah." He shook his head and added with a smile, "You is a stubborn cat." He blinked his eyes and reached out and took my arm, saying, "Hey, I got too much time invested in you to lose you. Don't get killed over this, hear me?"

"I promise."

He dropped off, and I put his hand down and left.

It was late when I got back to the ranch. I paced around my room, letting off some steam. I pulled out the Colt .38 I had found in the top drawer that first day. Checking it over, I made a decision and stuck it in my pants. Cora came in just as I was starting out the door.

"How's Perry?"

"Better. But I have to make a little trip, Cora. Should be back in a day — maybe two. Would you keep tabs on Perry for me? I hate to ask. . . ."

"Yes."

She stood there looking me over, and her single word spoke volumes. I knew if he got worse, she'd sit there twenty-four hours a day, nursing a man she barely knew and to whom she had no obligation. An endangered species, but there are still a few like her around.

She saw the butt of the gun sticking out of my

belt and lifted her eyes. I waited for her to ask about it.

"Who are you, Adam?" she asked without warning.

I guess I jumped at that. "What's that mean, Cora?"

"You're not what you say," she replied, catching me full in her clear-eyed gaze. "You're not just a stumblebum of a fighter. And I don't think you came to this ranch by accident. Why *did* you come here?"

I put my hand on her shoulder and said, "Cora, to tell you the absolute truth, I don't know who I am. It's a bit of a long story, but I guess you could say I'm trying to find myself. Like something from a silly soap opera. Why do you ask?"

"Oh, I don't know . . ." She hesitated, and for once she seemed flustered. She stared at me, then dropped her eyes and nervously picked at the front of her worn robe. "I think sometimes . . . when I look at you, Adam, . . . I think . . ." Then she sighed and turned, saying abruptly, "I'll look after Perry. You be careful."

When she got to the door she paused for a moment, then turned and looked at me, asking quietly, "Do you believe in God, Adam?"

I couldn't answer. It was as if I'd had the wind knocked out of me. Finally I just said, "I want to, but it's not easy." I pushed by her, piled into the Bronco, and tore out of the driveway. I waved at her as I left, but she just stood there watching me.

I made one stop before I went to Oklahoma City: Will Pentland's place. I'd managed to pump a few things out of him, but he knew more, and I intended to find out just what.

The lights were on when I got there. He must be a night owl. When I walked up on the porch, he seemed to be waiting for me . . . or someone.

"Who's there?" he asked nervously. "What do you want?"

"Adam Smith. I want to talk to you, Pentland."

"Smith? From the Majors' place?" He came outside, peering at me in the darkness. "How'd you find my place?"

"Not too hard. I have to talk to you for a few minutes. Won't take long."

"Well . . . come on in." He led me into a fine den with a bar and thick carpets, put the twelve gauge he'd been holding back in a rack, and asked, "What brings you up here?"

"I want to know about Dan Majors." I gave it to him blunt, hard and quick. He turned the color of old mortar and placed a big, shaking hand on his chest. "You may as well come clean, Pentland. The cops'll be all over this before too long."

That was a lie, but he believed it. "But . . . there's no reason . . ."

"Maybe we can keep it just between us," I said smoothly. "If you'll tell me what you know about the killing, I can try to keep it quiet."

"What *are* you?" he asked wildly. "You with the police?"

"Not exactly, but you'll be hearing from them if I don't get some good answers."

"But I don't *know* anything!" He began to weave back and forth, his mouth opening and closing like a dying fish. He reeled over to the drawer, pulled a small spray can from a drawer. Jerking off the cap he pumped some spray under his tongue, then stood there trembling until the stuff seemed to steady him. He muttered, "Bad . . . heart. I got a bad heart."

"Sorry to hear it," I said coldly. "About Dan Majors, Pentland, you might as well tell me the truth."

He sat down carefully and looked up with a feeble light in his eyes. "It's . . . it's hard for me to talk about it, Smith. That boy was like a son to me. They *both* were! Owen Majors was the best man who ever lived. He was . . . well, he was responsible for everything good that ever happened to me."

"And you still say that Dan killed Frank?"

He put a trembling hand before his face, and his voice was so weak that I had to lean forward to catch his words.

"It's horrible! I loved all of them, Smith! But the evidence . . ."

"You found Frank Majors, right?"

"Y-yes, I did and —"

"And then Renfro came in?"

"Yes . . . no, I mean. I called him and told

him. Then he came."

"And what then?"

"Well, we thought . . . that is, George thought that it must have been Dan who did it."

"Why'd he think that?"

"Well, Dan's gun was on the floor beside the body."

"Pretty careless, wasn't it? Leaving the murder weapon there?"

"Yes. I mean, I don't *know!*"

He was getting a bad color in his face again, but I kept right at him. "What did you and Renfro do next?"

"George said he must have taken the money and gone to get the plane — it was on the strip at the lake house. So George said we'd catch him there."

"Why didn't you call the police?"

"George said maybe we could get to Dan and, well, *fix* it somehow. . . ."

"How could you fix it, Pentland? Frank was shot to death."

"George said we could maybe make it look like a burglary or something."

"But you didn't?"

"We *couldn't!* We got to the house and Dan was leaving in the plane. Said he was going to Mexico to disappear. We tried to get him to give himself up, but he wouldn't listen."

"So what happened?"

"George was going to call the police, but Dan pulled out his gun and stopped him."

"I thought the gun was beside the body?"

Pentland hesitated, then looked away, saying feebly, "I . . . I guess he must have had two guns."

I stared at him, then said slowly, "You're *lying*, Pentland! You know it, I know it, and everyone is going to know it before too long." I wanted to let him stew in his own juices, so I turned to go, saying, "I'm leaving now, but I'll be back in a few days. And if you're still not ready to tell the truth, I can't promise you I'll be such a gentleman."

I went out the door without a backward look.

It caught me off guard to find that Dane Taggert was listed in the phone book. I thought I'd have to look under *Reptiles*, but there he was at the Admiral Hotel. I found it over on the east side of town, a good-looking place with the smell of prosperity oozing out through the desk clerk's face. Crime must pay. The clerk said Mr. Taggert was in room 203 and would I like to ring him?

"No, let me be a surprise," I said with my best smile, then went to the second floor, leaving him uncharmed.

It was about two A.M., and I could hear loud laughter and party noises through the door. I pulled the .38 out, checked the loads, then tapped at the door. Somebody hollered, "Come on in!" and I stepped inside.

Four guys were sitting around a table covered

with cards and chips. One was Taggert, two were the gestapo thugs, and the other one was a prosperous-looking fat guy with a bunch of diamonds on his thick fingers. I made a guess that he was a sucker, brought in to be fleeced. He did complicate my business, though.

"What you want? Who are you?" Taggert asked.

He was set up pretty well, with thick shoulders and a heavy neck. His face was flush with liquor. Throwing some cards down on the table, he angrily pushed back his chair and got up, knocking over a drink beside one of his goons.

"I don't recall inviting you. Get yourself out of here!"

The other two got up also, as if they operated by the same string, and one of them dropped a hand inside his coat.

I yanked the .38 free and trained it on his heart. "Go on, pull it. I guess you've had a pretty full life."

They all froze at the sight of the gun, and there was a breathy silence in the room. Finally Taggert cocked his head and asked, "You a cop?"

By this time the guy with the rings was losing it, sweating and breathing heavily. He wasn't in on it, so I waved the gun at the door, saying, "You can go now, Mr. Diamond Rings." He grabbed at his coat and disappeared.

"Okay, now, what do you want?" Taggert asked, not taking his eyes off me. "I don't know you, but you're in *big* trouble!"

He was a pretty hard article. I knew that without being told, and I also knew that the little glance he threw at the other two was fraught with meaning. They had a gun apiece. I had one. They were used to using them. I wasn't. The only thing I had going for me was that they didn't know what an amateur I was.

I knew I had to even it up quick, so I aimed right at one of the goons and said, "Give me your gun." He got a hard look from Taggert, but apparently not as hard as the barrel of my .38 special. He carefully placed the .357 on the table without a word.

"Push it onto the floor in front of me." It slid to my feet with a satisfying *thunk*.

"Now you," I said, shoving the barrel toward the second goon. He had a wicked-looking Python, which he menacingly surrendered. I waved my gun at Taggert. "Your turn."

He stared at me and cursed vividly. I said, "You watch your mouth, Taggert. I only have so much patience." He glanced at his buddies, then he pulled a nasty little .32 out of his shoulder holster.

"Now we can talk," I said pleasantly after making sure the guns were well out of the way.

Taggert stood and asked tensely, "Maurello send you? Whatever he gives you I give you triple."

"I don't know Maurello. I know Perry Jester."

I caught a slight flicker in his eye as he said

steadily, "Jester? I don't know no Jester. You guys know anybody named Jester?" They both shook their heads, and he said, "Look, why don't you just walk away from this? You have no idea what you're dealing with here."

"I know about you, Taggert."

"Yeah? Well, you won't always have that gun, slimebag."

I backed up, picked up the guns, and walked to the door of the suite's only bedroom. I tossed their guns in, then made a big show of throwing my own in after them. I shut the door and stood facing them, "I don't have a gun now."

It gave them a little shock, but Taggert gave the signal, and they moved in on me from two directions. One of them, the tallest, had been in the ring. He kept his chin tucked behind his left shoulder, his right cocked and ready to fire. The other one was just big — maybe a lifter. I knew I had to end it quickly or they'd wipe me out, so I let the tall one take his shot — a straight left with all his heft behind it. I caught it on my forearm, then stepped inside and blasted him in the middle with all I had, nearly fusing his belt buckle with his spine. He was out of shape, and said, "Whooosh!" before he collapsed, holding his stomach. I gave him a good one under the ear as he was falling, and he was retired.

A chop took me high on the head, and the room got a little dim, but I shook it off and turned around to see the heavy one coming at me with both arms open. He was slow, but dangerous as a bull, so I quickly gave him a forearm across the throat and watched him roll his eyeballs up, grabbing his Adam's apple urgently. From there I put him down with a straight left, and then two hard rights popped him into oblivion. He fell with a crash, and I turned to face Taggert.

He couldn't believe it. He stared at the two on the floor, then back at me. I moved over and lifted him by his lapels, and when he tried to give me one, I gave him one short, quick punch right on the sneeze nerve under the nose. It hurts about as bad as a punch can hurt, and his eyes watered up and pain filled his face. But he clamped his lips shut.

"Look, I can keep this up all night. I just want one thing from you — a little information. Then I walk out and you never see me again. Now, who sicked you onto Jester?"

He shook his head stubbornly, and I gave him one more treatment, harder than before, but he just shook his head. I tried it a couple more times. Still nothing.

He had me. I couldn't keep punching him, and he wasn't going to talk. I guess I felt a slight admiration for the ape. He wasn't worth dried spit, but he was *tough!* I knew that I could put the colt right to his ear and he'd *still* clam up.

I dropped him into a chair, walked into the bedroom and picked up my gun, then left, whipped. We didn't exchange any farewells, and I suspected he wasn't going to spend much for my Christmas present this year. All I'd done was belt a couple of guys, and I didn't have a thing. Except maybe a contract out on me. *What a waste.*

Revenge isn't all it's cracked up to be. Sure, I made them pay for busting up Perry, but I didn't enjoy it — if anything, it made me sick to my stomach — and I was certainly no further ahead.

A bumper sticker on a blue Mercury Cougar parked outside the hotel summed it up well: *ONWARD THROUGH THE FOG!*

Unveiled

THIRTEEN

I BARELY remember hitting the bed when I got back to the ranch just before dawn. I finally woke up and went to see Perry at the hospital late Tuesday morning.

Perry was in better shape than the doctors had dared to hope. He had nothing seriously wrong inside, so I brought him home. The doctor gave me some pills in case Perry needed help sleeping.

Perry walked like an old man, but the swelling in his face had gone down; and except for a lot of pain, he was in good shape. He did have nightmares, though, and the first night he scared me pretty bad when I woke up to find him thrashing and screaming. When I got him awake, he stared at me with fright on his face, dripping with sweat. "Man! I hope this ain't gonna be no permanent thing!"

"Take a couple of these pills," I said nervously. "They ought to put you out." He swallowed them as I went over to the drawer and got my gun. "Better keep this under your pillow.

274

Might have a visit from Taggert."

He put the gun under his pillow and asked, "What happened with that, anyway? You find out anything new?"

"No, but he might want to make another try."

"Maybe you better keep the gun."

"Nah. Don't like them, and it didn't do me any good last time anyway. Try to get some sleep, okay?"

"Yeah, but we can't keep going on like this forever, Champ. You got any long-range plans for us staying alive?"

"Sure, I plan to get into a telephone booth, whip off my clothes, and come out dressed in a blue body stocking with a big *S* on my chest and knock out all the evil people in the world."

"You ain't as good as you think you are — but then, neither is Superman," Perry said drowsily.

He finally got to sleep, but the next day he asked me to pick up some liquor, and I guess he kept himself pretty well out with pills and booze.

Dawn kept after me to meet her. "Look," I said once when she met me coming back from feeding the stock. "I've got to put everything on hold, Dawn."

"But I don't want to!" she cried and grabbed my arm with a fierce desperation. Dawn was a woman who needed a man. And I think I was in love with her. But Matt had seen me put my arm around her once, and the shocked look on his face was enough to keep me from betraying him. I already felt like a dog — not much different from the others Dawn had been running around with since Dan Majors had gone down.

Okay, so there it was. I loved Matt and I think I loved Dawn. The light at the end of the tunnel — the hope that I was Dan Majors — well, that light might turn out to be an oncoming train if I wasn't.

So my only hope was that I'd turn out to be Dawn's husband and Matt's father.

And if that rolled around, I'd probably wind up sitting in death row.

I tried to keep it all balanced. I talked to Cora about the ranch, spent some time with Matt, kept Dawn believing that we'd be together soon, made Perry as comfortable as possible, made calls to Doc Kimpel and Cossey, kept up communications with D.K. as I tried to ignore her barbed and accurate jabs about Dawn and me, and tried to think of some way to get the truth out of Pentland. All the time I kept an eye out in case Taggert paid a call.

Meanwhile periodic fragments of memory kept slipping into my mind. I was driving the tractor once, and without warning I suddenly had a vivid memory so real that I almost fell off the tractor. It only lasted a second, but I knew it was real. I was looking out at a large group of people — who were looking at me. I knew I was speaking, but that was all of it. I thought about it a lot. It was something that I had done once or maybe many times. Who were the people? I could have been a politician running for office, or a teacher. I didn't have a clue, but it was one more piece to the puzzle, so I wrote it down with other fragments that kept coming to me so I could give it all to Kimpel.

Once in the middle of all this, I thought of what Satchel Page once said: "If you hear footsteps, don't look back. They may be gaining on you!"

I guess it all had to stop sooner or later, and it did a few days after I got Perry home. I'd been taking some of the horses over to another pasture, and when I got back all hot and dirty and piled out of the vehicle, Cora was waiting for me. She had an odd look on her face, and I thought maybe Taggert had made a try, but she only said, "Come into the house."

I followed her inside, and Dawn was sitting on the couch with Matt. They both stared at me as if they'd never seen me before, and I asked quickly, "What's wrong? Perry worse?"

"No. He's asleep," Cora said. She came closer and searched my face carefully, not missing a thing. Then she touched my cheek as she had done once before. "I asked you once who you were, and you didn't answer me. I ask you the same now — who *are* you?"

I looked at Dawn and Matt, who were turned to stone, then back to Cora. "What's this all about, Cora?"

"Perry had a bad time, dreams and all. He drank all the whiskey you got him, and he went sort of wild. He was up wandering all over the yard, and I had to make him lie down. He was talking too, and it took a long time for me to figure out what he was talking about. But finally I did."

I waited for her to go on, but I saw pretty well what it was. "What did he tell you?"

Cora wet her lips, then said very slowly, "He said . . . he said that you are my son Dan!"

Dawn made a small cry of joy, then leaped up and threw her arms around me, and Matt stared at me, his eyes bugging out like Ping-Pong balls and his face white as paper.

"Why didn't you *tell* me!" Dawn cried. Tears were running down her face, and Matt was having a hard time as well. Cora was steady, but there was a tremor in her lips.

I pulled Dawn away. "I guess Perry was too drunk to tell it all," I said heavily. "What he didn't say was that I don't know *who* I am! I *may* be Dan Majors, but there's just as much of a chance I might be somebody else." They stared at me, and I made them all sit down. It took a long time, but I told them the whole thing — all of it except what I suspected about Will Pentland. When I was through, I felt weak as a rag. "I may be Dan Majors — I hope so — but all the evidence says he went down in that plane."

"If you are my son," Cora said slowly, her eyes fixed on me in wonder, "it's like someone come back from the dead."

"Not quite like that," I said. "The murder charge won't go away. They'd have me behind bars in a flat minute if they could prove I'm Dan."

"But you didn't do it, did you?" Matt spoke up suddenly. "You couldn't do a thing like that! I know you couldn't!"

He almost reached out to grab me, but not quite. He'd been hurt so bad, I guess he wasn't ready to take a chance on another ache. All he needed now was to go through it all again and see his father actually convicted — that would just about finish him off, I thought. "That's what I'm trying to find out, Matt. It's why I came here. I don't remember you and your mom. The doctors say my memory may come back like a flash, but maybe it never will."

"What if it does?" Dawn asked in a high nervous voice. "I mean, what if you do suddenly remember?"

I said, "Then I'll know either I'm Majors or I'm not. If I know I'm Dan Majors, I'll also know the truth about the murder of Frank."

"Dan would never kill anyone, much less Frank!" Cora said firmly. "But if he didn't, someone else *did*."

"That's right, Cora, and that's what I'm working on. But if anybody finds out that I'm Dan Majors — or even suspects it — that'd be the end of the ball game. You all understand that?"

"Sure we do!" Matt said swiftly. "I won't tell. None of us will!"

I took one look at his face and saw that in his mind it was all settled. I was his dad and I was innocent, and soon the whole family would be back together.

We stood there, and I guess I'll never forget that scene. All of them looked at me as if I were Lazarus back from the dead, and I was praying they were *right* about me. Who could have asked for more than a family like that? To a nobody man, it was the perfect answer.

Finally we broke up, but Dawn headed me off before I came in for supper. I was just putting on a clean shirt, and Perry was still asleep. She put her finger to her lips and pulled me to the far side of the room.

"Dan! I know that's who you are! I know it!" she whispered in my ear.

"You just *hope* so, Dawn." I smiled and shook my head. "So do I."

She shook her small head, sending the halo of golden brown hair flying. "No, I *know* it!"

I stared at her, and it occurred to me that she might have come up with something we might use. "You mean you got some evidence?"

"Well . . ." She dropped her face, then looked back and said, "Not evidence you could use in a *court*, but I just *know!*"

"How do you know?"

She said with an arch smile, "Do you think that a woman wouldn't know her own husband?"

I stared at her, saying, "Why didn't you say something before?"

"Why, I thought you were *dead*, of course! But

I knew all the time, from the very first! At least, I knew you were *like* Dan."

I knew what she meant, but it didn't mean much. I guess she was trying to help. It was pitiful in a way. I couldn't help thinking about all the guys she'd been seeing and wonder about them. Finally I said, "We'll just have to wait, Dawn."

Her eyes flew open and she asked, "Wait? Wait for *what?* You are my husband!"

"Not that simple," I said, shaking my head. I walked her firmly to the door, saying, "I'll talk to you later. After supper, maybe."

She gave me a long look, then left. As soon as she was out the door, Perry sat straight up with a grin on his drunken face.

"I feel like I been watching *Days of Our Lives* on the tube!"

"Why, you no-good Peeping Tom!" I half shouted at him. "Don't you have any decency?"

He thought about it for a long moment, then shook his head ponderously. "Nope," he said soberly.

I plopped down beside him and told him what was going on. He sat there, swaying back and forth, but his eyes were fairly alert. "Sorry I turned out to be such a blabbermouth, Champ. Didn't mean to let it out."

I shrugged. "May be just as well. When they get over the shock, they may come up with something that'll help."

"Something better happen quick. Taggert

ain't gonna wait forever!"

There was no action the next day. I wanted to go back to Pentland but couldn't think of any way to squeeze him. I couldn't think of anything to do but wait.

The day after that, I was sitting in the bunkhouse with Perry, and I heard a car pull up. I rolled off the bed in one motion, and Perry unlimbered the Colt .38. But when I took a careful glance out the window, I turned to him with a sign. "It's D.K."

She came right into the bunkhouse without knocking. "Don't bother to knock. We're just humble folk here," I said.

"Are you all right, Perry?" she asked and went over to put her hand on his shoulder, looking up at him anxiously. "I've been worried about you."

It suddenly bothered him. I guess Perry could take just about all the punishment you could dish out, but when this delicate, beautiful woman looked at him with concern, it caught him off guard.

"Well, I never saw you speechless, Jester," I grinned. Then I changed the subject. "So what's up, Darla Kaye?"

"Don't call me that!"

"*He* did!"

"He can do it — *you* can't!" she snapped.

"I *told* you I wuz special," Perry said smugly.

"I think I have something," she said in a businesslike way, and just then the door opened and Dawn walked in.

She looked hard at D.K., then walked straight over to me and put her arm around me. "Dan? Is everything all right?"

"Dan?" D.K. straightened up and stared at me. "You've got your memory back?"

"Ah, Darla Kaye." Perry rubbed his woolly head ruefully and said, "*You* think I'm perfect, but I do have just one small fault. I have been known to take one too many, and that's what I done. I spilled the beans about why we came here."

"So I know that Dan is my husband," Dawn said, taking a tighter hold on my arm. She ignored Perry and me, gazing directly at D.K. "A wife would know her own husband, wouldn't she?"

D.K. seemed to find something slightly amusing about that. "I have very little faith in marriage as an institution, Mrs. Majors. I think most husbands and wives never *really* know each other."

"*We* do!" Dawn gave her a brilliant smile. "I know this is Dan. No one could know that like *I* do!"

The statement sent the blood rushing into my stupid face, and D.K. was staring at Dawn as if she were an interesting specimen. Perry was suddenly very interested in staring out the window at a bird sitting on the telephone wire across the way.

Finally D.K. shrugged, saying, "Well, I'm a lawyer. The courts will have to have a *little* more than that, I'm afraid." Then she switched her gaze from Dawn to me. "You want to come to Tulsa? I think I've got a couple of things that will help us, but I need you there."

Dawn's grip on my arm tightened, and I knew she didn't want me to go. But we had to have more than her feelings. "What's up?"

D.K. hesitated, then said, "I'd rather tell you on the way." She gave Dawn a sweet smile and said, "It's what we lawyers call privileged communication, Mrs. Majors. Strictly an *intimate* relationship between lawyer and client."

Dawn turned pale, and her nails nearly met in my flesh. "You have a lot of clients, Ms. Wolfe?" she said, and the river never ran colder than her voice. She stalked out of the room without a backward glance, and I knew there'd be a price to pay for all this somewhere along the way.

"I'll go if you think it's important," I shrugged.

"I think it might be."

I got my stuff, and as we left the cabin, I took the gun from Perry and stuck it in my bag. "Ask Cora if she has a piece in the house that you can use. I might need this one while I'm away." I told him to stay off the whiskey and keep wary until I got back.

He made a fist. "No sweat, Champ. I'll take my best shot at anyone who noses around here."

I piled into the Volvo, and we drove out the gates in silence. After about half an hour of silence, she said, "Dawn's quite a fireball."

284

I just looked at her, not in the mood to talk about Dawn or any of that. But since she'd spoken, I decided to go ahead and talk myself. "What do you have?"

She paused, then said, "Maybe nothing, but I think if we keep on, something will come out of that small hunk of metal you gave me — the one the New Orleans cops gave you."

"What about it?"

"Well, the FBI examined it. I don't know what sort of new equipment they have, but they say they got something real this time."

"Like what?"

"They're in a blazing row about it, so they won't say. But I hear from my buddy there that they've got *something*. It should arrive tomorrow from Washington. That's why I wanted you here. Maybe it'll mean something to you."

"Sure, but . . ."

"Something else — I've had a whole gaggle of psychologists working on your case. They have a test for you."

"I've had a million of those stupid things already!"

"Not like this one." She dodged a dead possum with careless skill and shook her head. "This one is tailor-made for Majors. I fed all the stuff I could find out about him into a computer and gave the results to the doctors. They made up a test they *guarantee* will tell if you're Majors or not. If you can pass it, you'll know the same things that *he* knew, which is pretty close to saying you *are* him."

"Will a court accept it?"

"Not in a million years," she said cheerfully. "But *you* will. It'll just be one more thing to throw into the balance."

I slumped down in the seat. "I dunno, D.K. It all seems so involved."

She shrugged and we didn't talk for a long time. Finally she said in an offhanded way, "I talked to Cossey yesterday."

I sat up straighter. "You know Cossey?"

"Yes. I'm from New Orleans originally. I've been thinking of moving back."

"You mean . . . to be a lawyer?"

"Yes. I've got a love-hate relationship with the place. And I've never really liked it here in Tulsa." She hesitated, then said, "After this is all over, maybe we could see each other from time to time."

"I'd like that."

"Probably won't work out — nothing much does. Anyway, Cossey and I have talked several times. He likes you, Adam. You know that?"

I thought about it. "No, I didn't think he liked anybody."

"Well, he does. And I'd say that if a tough cop like that has a little faith in you, it gives me a little hope."

I thought about that and said, "You know, D.K., this is a pretty hard world, but I've found some good ones. Perry, Doc Kimpel, Cossey, the Majors . . . and you."

"I made the cut!" She turned to give me an odd kind of smile, her lips twisted slightly. "Want to hear what Cossey found out?"

"Shoot."

"He got to the pilot of that chase plane that saw Majors go down. Actually he was the copilot. I don't know how Cossey did it, but he got the guy to change his story."

I sat up and stared at her. "Change it how?"

"I think Cossey must have put needles under his fingernails or something. The transcript said they saw somebody at the controls when the plane went into the drink. Well, this guy now says that they got very close and that they never saw *anybody* at all in that plane."

"What?"

"That's what he claims now."

"But why did they say they saw somebody in it back then?"

"Aha!" she said and gave me a straight look. "That's the rub! According to this copilot — name is Roger Wood — they agreed on their story, that the plane was empty; but before they could file the report, the main pilot pulls him aside and says they've got to change their story. To say there *was* a man in the plane."

"But — why?"

"To earn the five thousand dollars they each got paid for telling that story and not the real one."

"Oh."

"Is that *all* you can say — 'oh'?" she asked scornfully.

"I could say 'Jeepers creepers.' " My mind was spinning with this new info. Suddenly we had more than just a wacky idea. We had *evidence*.

"It means there's no proof that Dan Majors was on that plane. It could have been anybody . . . or nobody," I said.

"Mind like a steel trap," she laughed. "Question is, who paid the money, and why?"

I thought about that, and we talked like purple-haired ladies at a bridge club all the way into Tulsa. D.K. parked in the lot of her apartment, and we got out. It was late, but I was excited and so was she. We went up, she made coffee, then we called Cossey. He was optimistic but refused to tell us how he'd gotten Wood to come clean with the story.

"It might be construed as unprofessional conduct," he said firmly. "I'm keeping him on ice, but I gotta see you, and soon. Can you come to New Orleans?"

"Sure, if you say so." We worked out the details, and I hung up the phone.

Then suddenly I got scared. Maybe I was so used to bad news that good news was too rich to handle. I stared at D.K. for a minute and said, "You know, D.K., this may sound silly, but I'm scared. Isn't that nutty?"

"Scared?" she said, and there was real surprise on her face. She moved closer on the couch and put her hand on mine. "I didn't think you'd be scared of *anything!* I mean, you never back up, Adam! You got out of that institution, fought in the ring to finance yourself . . ." She began to stroke my head, and it felt so good I relaxed. "You're not scared — you're tired."

She kept on rubbing the back of my neck, and I said, "But . . . what if I *am* Dan Majors?"

D.K. stopped her massage and was silent for what seemed like a long time; then she said gently, "Well, if you are, we'll have to face up to all it means for you to be him."

"I . . . I guess I've been so anxious to be *somebody,* it never really hit me that there's problems in *that* too."

"Don't you *want* to be Dan Majors?" D.K. asked. Her hands were firm, and I seemed to be floating as she continued the motion on my shoulder.

"Well, that Matt . . . he's a good kid. And he's going down the drain if something good doesn't happen soon. And there's Cora. She deserves something! I never knew anyone could be like that woman — tough, but gentle." I opened my mouth, then closed it again, because what I wanted to say was stuck in some kind of logjam. D.K. said it for me, though.

"You're not mentioning Dawn."

"Dawn?" I asked stupidly.

"You *do* remember her, don't you? Your wife, if you are Dan Majors," D.K. insisted gently. Then, "Do you love her?"

I suddenly was very uncomfortable. Standing

up, I walked over and stared down at the traffic. I turned and looked right into D.K.'s eyes. "I don't know. But it wouldn't make any difference . . . not if I'm really her husband."

She came up and put her hands on my arms. There was a gentleness about her face that was incredibly beautiful, and I wondered at it.

She said softly, "I know that. It's the way you are. You'd never leave her."

She didn't make a move, but suddenly I reached out and took her in my arms. She was so close, and it was so *easy*. I kissed her, and all kinds of things were mixed up in it. Not only was she so desirable it made me ache, but I was alone and pretty well scared and confused about everything. The strength of her arms was surprising, and I recognized the same loneliness in her as I felt in myself. We clung to each other, and what had been simply a need to feel the touch of another human was suddenly transforming, intensifying. The room was filled with the sound of thudding hearts — at least *I* thought so — and every nerve in me was suddenly alive. I gently drew her to the couch.

She whispered in my ear some term of sweetness, and there was nothing in her withheld. But then, somehow, something compelled me to pull back. It took every bit of strength I had, but I suddenly let her go, and she fell back with a gasp.

"No!" I cried harshly, though the harshness was intended more for me than her. But I saw her face turn pale, and her eyes suddenly glinted like steel.

"Why do you do this to me?" she whispered in a deadly tone. Slowly she got up and gave a shudder as she pulled herself into a rigid stance. "I thought women were the teasers. Get out of here!"

I didn't touch her but stood blocking her way. "Do you think I *like* this? Do you think for one moment this is easy for me? I would . . . but what *then?*" She crossed her arms as if waiting for more. "What if I am married to Dawn? What if tomorrow I remember everything. Where would we be then — you and me?"

"It happens all the time," she said slowly.

I almost shouted. "There's something in me that says no to this. I don't know what it is, or why, but we have to stay away from each other, D.K. You're . . . you're too strong in my blood! If I let myself go, I'd have to throw everything else away. That's what I'd like to do. Do you know that? Just let the world go down the drain. But I can't."

She was standing there, her face tense with hurt, but then she asked suddenly in a strange voice, "Do you know who Billy Sunday was?"

It caught me off guard, but I said, "Sure, he was an evangelist."

"What about Dwight L. Moody. Know anything about him?"

Again I paused. "Well, he was a preacher, about the turn of the century from Chicago."

She stared at me, and her face was softening into gentle planes. "How about John 3:16?"

"What about it?"

"Can you quote it?"

I shook my head, "D.K., I —"

"Can you?" she insisted as her eyebrows raised into a delicate arch.

I took in a deep breath and recited it without thought: "For God so loved the world He gave His only begotten Son, that whosoever believeth in Him should not perish, but have everlasting life."

She laughed at me. "You're a Puritan, Adam. That's what you are! That's why you won't make love to me. It's against your religion." And she added with a twist on her lovely lips, "And it's also why you're being 'faithful' to Dawn. You think she's your wife."

"That's crazy. I don't have any religion."

"Don't you?" she grinned crookedly. "You know all about obscure preachers from another century, and you can quote the Bible word for word. And you can't make love to a woman unless she's your wife because you think it's wrong. That's a pretty good definition of a Puritan." She shook her head gently. "You're like something out of the past."

She rose abruptly and said, "I'm going to bed. You can sleep on the couch or on the street or anywhere else you please."

She slammed the door to the bedroom, and I tiptoed out and got a cheap room for the rest of the night, back at the Elite Motel. I didn't sleep much, though.

The next day, well, we were about as relaxed as two mannequins in a store window. I wanted to say I was sorry, but for what? She took me to some clinic, and they gave me the test, which didn't seem much different from all the rest I'd taken. When I got through, she met me with a little smile.

"I think we'll make a trip. You won't be apprehensive that I have designs on your virtue, will you?" she asked tartly, but I could see she was relaxed.

"Where to?"

"The house of Mr. William Pentland, about forty minutes north of Broken Bow."

"Pentland? What for?"

"I have a few questions to ask him. Some of the books from SunCo are *very* interesting. In fact, if he can give me any sensible explanation about some of the items I've found, I'll be *very* surprised . . . and disappointed."

We left town and talked and talked as we drove. She tried to explain what the problem was, but I was just too dumb to understand it. "One thing is clear. I'm no bookkeeper," I finally said in despair.

She gave me a look and said, "That's pretty clear from the records. As I read it, Dan Majors was not able to get accounting. George Renfro made those decisions, and Pentland was there while he was making them."

I thought that over, and when we stopped for gas, I said, "I'm gonna go call Perry — see how he's doing."

"All right. But don't say anything to him."

I paused and asked, "Don't you trust Perry?"

"I don't trust anybody."

I shrugged and got the ranch. Cora answered so quickly I guessed she was waiting for me to call. "Cora —" I started in, but she cut me off.

"Don't talk, Adam!" she said instantly. "And don't come here."

"Taggert been there?" I asked at once.

"No, the FBI has. They took Perry with them. Don't come here."

"Right." I tried to think of a way to tell her where we'd be, and then I came up with one. "I have to get some accounting done, Cora. I think I know a good place to get it done." I hoped she'd think of Pentland, and she did.

"He is a good one. Get in touch with me."

I hung up and went back to the car. "The fat's in the fire. The FBI picked up Perry. They're looking for me."

She took that in at once and said, "You'll have to hide. I'll take you to my place."

"No, I can't hide forever. We have to find out the truth, D.K. I'm going to have it out with Pentland. But I don't want you to go."

"Why not?"

"I just don't. It's going to get messy — even dangerous. I don't want you mixed up in it.

You'd be some kind of accessory, wouldn't you?"

"Too late. I'm already in this up to my ears. You're stuck with me."

I stared at her, then had to grin in spite of everything. "One thing's sure. Whoever I am, I sure have winning ways!"

She didn't laugh, though. She looked at me and there was a vulnerability about her, a softness in her lips and something in her eyes.

"You have indeed, my boy! I'm in your power! Now, let's get to it, for better or for worse!"

It sounded like a marriage vow, and I thought as the Volvo plunged through the night that no matter how this turns out, I've met one fine lady!

Confrontation

FOURTEEN

D.K. kept the Volvo rolling through the night at a steady seventy-five, weaving to miss the armadillos and potholes with practiced ease. She'd found a Tulsa station that played only elevator music, and the bland sound was an improvement over the usual country sound that posed the eternal question, "Why did you mess around while I was gone?"

We hadn't said a lot, and finally she gave me a glance, asking, "What's the matter, Adam?"

I watched as we shot by one of those little outposts sprinkled across the flat plains of Oklahoma: a two-pump gas station, a small store with fiercely high prices, and a series of big billboards pushing cigarettes in that cryptic manner — lots of healthy green scenery with good-looking kids romping in the water and an epitaph in stark gothic pronouncing, *SURGEON GENERAL'S WARNING: CIGARETTE SMOKE CONTAINS CARBON MONOXIDE.*

As it flashed by I murmured, "I don't know, D.K. Nothing, I guess." Then I laughed shortly.

"After all, here I am, your typical amnesiac, with no more memory than a potato and a rap for murder one hanging over my head. Why shouldn't I be as happy as Rebecca of Sunnybrook Farm?"

"Know what's wrong with you? You don't have any parameters. No boundaries."

"What's *that* supposed to mean?"

"Only that almost all of us have our little book that we go by. Most of the time it's not actually printed, of course, but most of us know our parts. Take a football player, for example. I can't think of anything that's basically more meaningless than that — playing a game for a profession!" She shook her trim head vigorously, sending her coal-black hair wisping around in a short circle. "I mean, who *says* a football field has to be a hundred yards long? It wasn't handed down on Mount Sinai, was it? All the rules are just some things a bunch of grown-up kids agreed on, and if you change one of them, why, the world will still roll on. But the coaches talk about it as if it were a *religion!*"

"I guess coaches are saying pretty much the same thing about lawyers and the courts," I said.

"And they may have something, but I don't think so. Anyway, the point is that even athletes have their little goals, their rules. They have *boundaries* that make them feel safe, just like lawyers, plumbers, and even criminals in a twisted way. You don't have any boundaries, Adam, or at least you're not sure what they are."

I thought it over. "Guess you have something there." I watched the scenery for a moment. "I know a few rules, but I don't know what the game is."

"I don't think I do either," she said suddenly.

I glanced at her in surprise. She turned to meet my gaze, and I saw the darkness in her eyes, a bleakness I'd seen before but couldn't explain. When I met her eyes, it was like she'd opened a door that had been carefully barred for a long time, and it gave me a shock to see that under all the success and the trappings lurked a very unhappy woman.

"I guess your boundaries are a little shaky too. Maybe I've been feeling too sorry for myself to notice."

"No . . . I . . . I've learned to cover pretty well." There was a silence then, lying beneath the hum of bland music. I knew she'd go on if I kept still, and soon she said softly, "When I lost Jack, all I could think of was, 'It's not fair!' I mean, we'd been in love, but we kept all the rules. Saved it till marriage. You know, just like the preachers say we should. We helped each other through school, but all the time, it was like we were waiting in the wings. A dress rehearsal. And then finally we could at last get to the real thing. Only . . . we never got that far." Her hands were locked on the wheel, and she went on in a voice that was *too* steady, as if she had locked it up somehow. "He had to die and spoil it all. Selfish of him, wasn't it? Messing up my master plan!"

She clamped her teeth into her lower lip, and I asked finally, "It's still that bad?"

"Bad? Oh, I get by. Nice apartment, nice car, plenty of attention from men — whatever I want."

I couldn't think of anything to say. She was staring straight ahead, but I could see her face was set, and a silver tear was rolling slowly down her cheek. I wasn't sure how to handle things like that. Maybe there were people who knew the right words, but I doubted it. No matter what words are said, the funeral still goes on, doesn't it? On the newsstands I'd seen a pickup load of books all promising to get you through the bad times, but if the *right* book had ever been written, why all the others? Do you hand a tract to the guy who's just watched his life go up in smoke? Send him a Hallmark to show you cared enough to send the very best? Suddenly I thought of Cora. She'd taken the worst, and she could still smile. I wondered if she could say something to D.K. that might help. Maybe, but deep down I felt that every person has to scratch at his own peck of dirt — alone.

Finally I just said nothing but let my hand drop on her shoulder with just a little pressure. She turned to me at once and asked without preamble, "What about God, Adam?"

Her question stunned me more than anything she'd ever said. She had a hard surface, Darla Kaye did, but now as she took her eyes from the road and gave me a teary glance, I saw something else there I'd never seen in her. I guess it was vulnerability. She looked young and defenseless, and I saw that there was a hunger in her for more than she had. "I don't know much, D.K. I just know He's there. No other way to explain the way things are."

"I gave up on religion a long time ago. But lately I've been getting strange thoughts." She remained silent and then added almost inaudibly, "I think about Jesus Christ a lot, Adam, and for some reason that scares me."

I quickly responded. "I don't know what I am, but you can't read the New Testament without seeing one thing. Jesus loved people. And not just the good people. He loved even nuts like you and me."

She gave me a flash of a smile, and we just rode along without saying much for a long time. "I think both of us need to find our way," I said, and then we were at Pentland's house. It was nearly one in the morning when we pulled up, and I was pretty sure he'd hear us stop. By the time we'd made our way across the walk and up the front steps, a light popped on, and I wondered if he stayed up all night waiting for company. There were a couple of cars farther down the way, and one of them looked familiar, but it was too dark to see. I pulled the Colt .38 from my bag and stuck it in my belt, just in case. I zipped up my jacket to cover the gun so as not to give Pentland any cause for alarm.

The door opened just a crack, and Pentland

said, "Who's there?"

"Adam Smith. I want to talk to you."

I thought he'd try to keep me out, but he opened the door and stepped back. "Pretty late. Couldn't it wait until morning?"

"No. This is D. K. Wolfe. She's a lawyer from Tulsa. Got a few questions for you."

He didn't have the shotgun in his hand, but he looked just as scared as he had the last time I'd seen him, maybe even more. His hollow cheeks were furrowed even deeper, and his eyes were sunk back into the sockets so deep that they were almost hidden. He took another step back and raised a trembling hand to motion us toward the den. "Well, I guess you better come inside."

He threw a switch and the den lit up. It was all messed up, with papers and books everywhere, empty bottles all over the place, and the smell of cigarette smoke saturating the air. Pentland turned and said uncertainly, "I don't know what you want here, but I answered all the questions about Dan Majors at the hearing."

I nodded at D.K. and she moved in on him. He didn't look much better than the last time I saw him. I hated to probe at him, shockingly old and sick under the muted light, but there was no choice. She went at him in a steely, relentless voice.

"Mr. Pentland, I think you should know that the irregularities you were responsible for when you were head accountant for SunCo are not going to stay covered up. As a matter of fact, the firm of accountants I hired to look into the books already has enough evidence to satisfy the district attorney that the case has to be reopened."

Pentland folded up. He raised his thin hand again, putting it in front of his face as if to ward off a blow, and his voice was reedy and thin. "I . . . I don't know what you mean. I don't know anything about it." He shot a sudden frightened look at a door to his left, leading off to the rest of the house, I suppose, then suddenly sat down as if his legs wouldn't hold him anymore.

D.K. continued, "Your name is at the bottom of the audit." He flinched as if she'd put a knife in his ribs, and he'd have run for it if he'd been able. "The whole thing has been laid open by Bundy and Tibbs. If you know those names, you know that every figure has been analyzed and that the cover-up isn't covered up any longer. You're going to jail, Pentland. That's the bottom line!"

I didn't know a thing about all that. But it was obvious that Pentland was guilty. His eyes were dull, his mouth sunk into his cheeks like a dead man, and I thought he was going to pass out. He got up and made his way unsteadily to the bar, poured a drink, spilling most of it, then downed it. He choked and gagged for a long time, then came back with a little color in his waxy cheeks.

"You can't prove much," he said. He must have been a powerful man once, and a trace of the authority that had ebbed away with the years touched his face momentarily. "Oh, sure, there's been some juggling with accounts, maybe some question about this fund or that. But nothing you can put me in jail for."

I caught a glimpse of D.K.'s face and saw that he was probably telling the truth. "We don't want you in jail, Will. We just want to ask a few questions about the death of Frank Majors."

It was like touching a steer with a cattle prod, the way he jumped at this. His face twitched and he whispered, "You better leave, Smith! You don't know what . . ."

I sat down on one of the high stools in front of the bar, saying slowly, "This business isn't going to blow away, you know. I think you must have been waiting for it for a long time." He stared at me, and it wasn't a blind guess. Just the mention of it made his lips tremble and I hit hard at him. "You *must* have known that somebody would find out, didn't you?"

"No! I thought —" he started to say, then bit the words off quickly. He glanced at the door again and said, "I thought nobody —"

"You covered your trail pretty well," D.K. cut in. "Took the best accountants in the state to dig up the body. SunCo was in good shape, Pentland. Why did you alter all those accounts and shift all the funds around?"

"I don't know," he said, then sagged at every joint. He clung to the back of a leather chair, saying in a moan, "I told him it wouldn't —"

"You told *whom?*" D.K. was on him like a striking snake, and her question finished him off as he realized what he'd said. He stared at her, the nerves of his ravaged face working overtime.

"Why . . . he tol*d me!*"

I swung around, and the pieces all fell together.

George Renfro was standing in the open doorway holding a snub-nosed pistol in his hand. I knew with a sick feeling in the pit of my stomach that I'd made a terrible mistake by not being ready for this.

"You might put your gun on the desk," Renfro said.

"What gun?" I asked.

"The one you must have on you somewhere." He swung the muzzle of the pistol toward D.K., adding, "If you don't do as I say, Ms. Wolfe will bleed all over the floor."

He meant it. I carefully pulled the Colt out of my belt and placed it on the desk, then backed away.

"Just a couple more steps," Renfro grinned.

He must have read my mind. I'd hoped to stay close enough to the Colt to make a dive for it, but he was too sharp. He wasn't at all excited. I could see that mind of his ticking away and saying, *"Another problem to be solved. So many risks, so many gains. Add the credits and deduct the debits. "* The fact that he was dealing with human life wasn't a matter of consideration, and his face was a study in concentration as he stood there waiting for the answer to come around.

Finally he said with a shrug and a thin smile,

"I'm going to have to turn you in, Dan." He smiled at my expression, then added, "Oh yes, I know all about your little problem. Came as quite a shock, but now you'll have to answer for killing Frank."

He's going to kill us. That was the thought that washed through me. Somehow I'd decided from the look on his face that he was settling all the problems with a couple of bullets, and yet there was something digging at me — a thought that wouldn't stay quiet. It eluded me until suddenly I caught it. How did he know we were here? Cora was the only one who knew. I knew they'd pull her fingernails out, and she still wouldn't tell.

A movement behind Renfro caught my eye, and he moved slightly to one side, saying, "Come on in, sweetheart. Join the party."

Dawn came in, and somehow I wasn't terribly surprised. She must have overheard or been on the extension when I called and tipped Cora off about going to see Pentland. I knew the rest. Not too hard to figure. Her face was colorless, and she didn't look at me.

With her head down and in a beaten voice she said, "He made me tell, Dan. I couldn't help it." Then she began to cry, saying, "Cora wouldn't tell him . . . and he started to hurt her, and I . . ."

"Is Cora all right?" I asked quickly.

"Sure," Renfro answered easily. "You can't blame Dawn too much, Dan." He gave her a strange smile and said softly in a voice that caressed the words, "You never can help what you do, can you, Dawn?"

Dawn looked at me, and there was a touch of red in her cheeks, but she suddenly covered her face and turned away.

Renfro watched her, a peculiar light in his flat eyes; then he shrugged and walked over to the phone. "I got your story out of Dawn on the way here, Dan," he said and paused to stare at me. He shook his head, saying almost in a whisper, "Lost your memory. Well, I guess the courts will take that into consideration at your trial."

He dialed the first number, but Pentland suddenly said, "George, they know everything!"

Renfro paused, stared at Pentland, and his voice was smooth and reassuring as he answered the old man. "No, Will, they don't know anything."

"But — you heard what they said, George! They've had the books audited!"

"So what? Maybe they'll find a few shortcuts, but you know how that goes, Will. Happens all the time. We'll maybe have to pay a tax penalty and that's it."

"They'll find out, George!" Pentland moved toward Renfro, and his face was twisted with fear. "I always said we'd get caught! You know I did! They know about Frank too, and how —"

"Shut up, you old fool!" Renfro said, raising his voice for the first time. Then he gave a little shake of his head. "We have to keep our cool, Will, and it'll be fine." Then he cocked his head to one side and asked carefully, "You *can* do that, can't you, Will?"

But Pentland was too far gone to see that Renfro was making up his mind whether or not he could afford to let him live. He began to shake and wring his hands together, crying, "They'll find out, George! I always said they'd find out about Frank!"

He didn't realize he'd just signed his death warrant. Renfro slowly put the phone down, and there was a finality about it that sent a chill through me. He stood there with the gun in his hand, and I could see that he'd come up with the answer. I was pretty sure what it was.

I could hear the hum of the electric clock on the desk, and I heard Dawn's sniffling cry; but what I really heard was Renfro's whisper, barely audible, saying, "That's *it*."

I knew we were all dead. D.K., Pentland, me, and maybe Dawn. It was all my fault. I was sure it had to be Renfro. Every sign had pointed to him. But I did not expect him to know about me. I should have known that a man who could pull off a steal with the shrewdness he'd shown was no fool.

Renfro was staring at Pentland. He said quietly, "I guess you're right, Will. We can't let the police in on this — not right now."

Pentland thought he'd won a victory. He couldn't see that beneath the smooth exterior Renfro was a carnivore. The old man nodded, "Sure! That's right, George! Maybe they won't find out about it."

"Oh, they'll be coming around, all right. I'm sure Ms. Wolfe has left enough lying around to lead them here. But when they get here, I think they'll find something a little different from what she's told them."

"You don't have a chance, Renfro," D.K. said swiftly. "You can't cover up any longer."

"Oh, I think I can," he said with a cold smile. "I'm sure there'll be quite a story when it gets out that Dan here is alive. Somehow I don't think they'll buy the amnesia bit. But even if that were true, some bright cop can be led into the concept that he *recovered* his memory, came here to force me to give him money, and in the fracas I managed to get the gun and finish him off."

"What about D.K. and Dawn?" I asked. I'd been measuring the distance I had to cover to make a swipe at his gun, and it was too far. I had to get him talking, gain an inch or two even to have a chance. "You killed Frank, didn't you?"

"Why, yes, I did." He was talking to a dead man. I knew that, and I knew as well he definitely couldn't afford to leave any witnesses now. "As for Ms. Wolfe, it will appear that she was shot by her 'partner' in the scheme to embezzle me out of a fortune."

"You'll never make it stick," I said, inching forward as he put his gaze on D.K. for a second.

"Yes, I will. She'll be shot with your gun" — he motioned to the Colt lying on the desk — "and you'll be shot with mine. I tried to stop you, and she got the slug you meant for me. Then it'll all come out about how the two of you cooked up this scheme to get the company."

"What about Dawn?" I asked, and when he looked at her, I took another six inches. Not close enough. One more try should do it.

"Don't worry about Dawn, Dan. Worry about you," Renfro said.

I asked quickly, for I thought he might decide to do it right then, "How'd you do it, George. How'd you pull off this whole thing? Seems impossible to me."

He gave me a self-satisfied look, which I hoped meant he was ready to bask in the limelight for a bit. It must have been difficult for him to pull off such a stunt, then have to hide it from everyone. He relaxed, and I asked, "Why did you kill Frank?"

"He caught me stealing, of course. I had gotten in pretty deep with Taggert and his ring of gamblers, so I kept borrowing from the firm. I'd have gotten it all back if I'd had time. But Frank caught on, and when he told me he was going to turn me in, I had to do it." He turned to look at Dawn, and I took another three inches.

Almost enough, and I asked to keep him going, "But what about the rest of it? I can't remember it, you know."

"That's right, you can't." He smiled. "Well, you read the reports, and it's all there. Everything a sharp cop would need to get the answer. I took off for the coast and made one mistake. I pulled all the cash from the business and got ready to take off. Frank came to stop me and I had to kill him. Then you and Will caught me just as I was about to take off for Mexico with the loot."

"And then you shot me," I said.

"Actually it all worked out better that way," Renfro mused. "I think I could never have rested well just robbing you, Dan. You were so *nice* about it all. Even killing Frank . . ." Renfro's face twisted with hatred as he stared at me, and he said in a chilling voice, "I always hated you, Dan! You had it so easy! Everything I always wanted, you got." He glanced at Dawn, then smiled, "But not this time. You got the only woman I ever wanted, but it looks like it's my turn now."

"Dan . . ." Dawn pleaded, but Renfro cut her off.

"Shut up, sweetheart," he said, then looked at me with a puzzled expression on his sleek face. "One thing I can't understand, and that's how you lived through it all. I shot you right in the heart — or thought I did. Must have glanced off a rib."

"What about the plane?" D.K. asked. Renfro shifted his gaze toward her, and I knew she had spotted what I was trying to do. I took another three inches and knew that I couldn't get any closer. "Was Dan supposed to be on board?"

"That was the plan," Renfro agreed smoothly.

"I was going to put him inside, take off, and get it headed out to sea — and set the automatic pilot so that when the fuel ran out it would crash and sink."

"Why didn't you?" D.K. asked.

He kept his eyes locked on me this time, saying, "Because I was afraid that something might go wrong and the plane might not sink or something like that. If the body was found with a bullet in the heart, I'd have had a difficult time making my story hold water."

"So you did what?" I asked.

"Will and I drove to the Louisiana border and dumped your body into an old pit I'd found on a hiking trip a few years back. It was in some deep woods on government property, so I didn't think anyone would do any finding there." He stared at me and shook his head. "I can't see how you climbed out of that pit!" Then he laughed. "Must have been a pretty nasty shock — climbing out of there with a bullet wound just in time to get fried in that forest fire!"

"I couldn't help it, Dan! I thought you were dead — and Frank was dead — and George was going to kill me if I didn't help!" Pentland began to shake and sob, but Renfro's eyes were cold as he stared contemptuously at the old man.

"Good thing I had my hobby," Renfro mused. "Skydiving has its advantages in a matter like this. I just took the plane up with a quarter of a tank of gas, set the automatic pilot, then bailed out before I got to the Gulf."

"And you put all the blame on Dan?" D.K. asked.

"He was dead, so what difference did it make? I took the gun and put his fingerprints on it, then put it by Frank's body. Then Pentland fixed the books to make it look like Dan had been dipping into the till."

"You'll never get away with killing us all," D.K. argued. Her face was steady, and I was pretty proud of her right then. "There're too many in on it. You think you can trust Pentland? Or Dawn? Cora knows you're here. How many more?"

It rattled Renfro. The smooth mask slipped, and I glimpsed the wild desperation beneath. He raised his gun and said harshly, "Shut up! I don't care how many I have to kill! You hear me? I'm not going to be caught just because a nobody like you comes back from the dead!" Then he cast a cold glance at Pentland and said, "I'm sorry, Will, I can't let you go either."

"What? No! You *can't!* You can't shoot me, George!" Pentland made a quick rush toward Renfro, brushing against him, and I knew it was the best chance I was likely to get. Just as the old man came between us, I made a lunge, hoping to take them both to the floor and get the gun away from Renfro in the struggle.

But it didn't work. I got a piece of Pentland, and we both went down. Renfro must have been expecting me to make a try, because he pulled back from Pentland and the two of us sprawled on the floor right in front of him, Pentland underneath and me staring up at the .38 he was holding.

I stared into his eyes as he said, "So long, Dan. Just stay dead this time, will you? Just for me?"

"Don't . . . don't do it, George!" Pentland begged.

The muzzle of the silver revolver tracked back to me, and I knew that there was no hope. D.K. was crying something, but I could see Renfro's index finger whiten as he pulled down on the trigger. I waited for the world to explode. I wasn't really afraid — just sad that it was over with so much left undone.

The explosion rocked the room, making my ears ring. Out of the corner of my eye I saw Pentland shaking like a leaf, and I waited for another shot, thinking George must have missed, though I didn't see *how*, from three feet.

Then I looked up and saw Renfro. His face was frozen, his eyes rolling back. He was falling forward stiffly, and he kept his hand frozen on the gun as his face hit the floor with a crash.

He never moved except for a twitch in his left foot, and that stopped at once. A bullet in the head does slow one down. There was a lot of blood on the side of Renfro's head and face. I quickly dashed over and took the gun out of his hand. Then I noticed Renfro's chest heave suddenly. "He's still alive! D.K., call an ambulance!"

I looked toward the desk and saw Dawn

standing with my gun held in both hands, seemingly paralyzed. She looked like a cover on a pulp detective magazine with her wild eyes, her mouth open in a soundless scream. Then her hand opened and the gun bounced off the rug. She started to say over and over, "I didn't mean to do it. . . . I didn't mean to do it. . . . I thought if I shot over his head, he'd give up!"

Dawn made a step in my direction, took a look down at her handiwork, then turned pasty and started into a slide. I caught her before she hit the floor, and as I put her on the couch, she was muttering something I couldn't understand.

Pentland looked up, getting up on his feet. He moved over to stare at the body of Renfro and said slowly, "I'm glad! Even if I have to go to the chair. I hope he dies. It'll be better than what I've lived through since . . ." He dropped onto his knees and started sobbing like a lost child.

D.K. wasn't watching him.

She was watching me. I waited for her to say something, but she just looked at me with a strange look on her face.

"I guess that's the end of it," I finally said.

"You really think so?" she said, and I saw a sadness in her eyes that was so bad I wanted to take her in my arms. But then she gave a little shrug and said briskly, "You're not a nobody man anymore, are you?"

I stared at her, then shook my head. "I *feel* like one, D.K. I mean, what's so different?"

"You know you're Dan Majors. That's different." She glanced at Dawn and said tonelessly, "You have a family — a wife and son. There'll be plenty of money — everything a man could want."

"No, not everything." I felt like I was falling away into the darkness, and it took me back to when I'd first come out of it at the hospital. It was cold and lonely and I was afraid again. "I still feel like a nobody man, D.K. I'm still lost."

D.K. looked very tired, and she turned and went to the phone, her shoulders sagging.

I shook my head. The darkness was rolling up like huge thunderheads, and there was no joy, no life in me. "I don't think I'm going to live happily ever after, D.K. Why am I feeling like this?"

Family

FIFTEEN

"LOOK, grandma! look, we got six!" Matt ran ahead of me holding up the sack of dead rabbits for Cora to admire. It was almost dark, but I could see the flash of a smile that crossed her face as she looked down — not at the rabbits Matt was lining up on the ground but at his face, which was glowing with excitement.

"Dad got two and I got *four!*" he cried with a shy look at me to see how the word "Dad" took me. It had taken him a while to use it, but the thrill of that Sunday-afternoon rabbit hunt had allowed the tension to seep out, and he had finally lost the awkward manner he'd always had toward me.

Almost two weeks had passed since Renfro's body had been patched up and hauled off by the law, and things had moved so fast it had been like living on a souped-up merry-go-round. The press had swarmed the place so bad that I was afraid to even go to the bathroom without one of them snapping my picture. Finally Cora ran them off, saying with biblical tones, "Wherever

316

the carcass is, there the buzzards will assemble!"
I guess they were the buzzards and I was the carcass.

I spent about three-fourths of my waking
hours being interrogated by lawyers, judges,
policemen, and insurance investigators, which
was quite a trick, since I only had one answer to
any question they asked: "I don't remember."
That hacked them off pretty bad, and I think
most of them thought I was faking them out.

D.K. was working on the legal stuff and fighting with the FBI to get Perry released. Dawn was
still pretty shook up over the shooting and really
had to lean on Cora for support. But all the
excitement and confusion eventually died down,
and that afternoon I took Matt out to play a little
basketball. If I was going to be a father, it was
time to start learning how. Like I said, he'd been
awkward and unsure — but so was I. I could see
something was bothering him, so I said, "Let's
go make some lunch, son." He gave me a warm
smile when I called him "son," and we went back
to the house and started stripping the husks off
some corn. He was pretty quiet, but I knew he'd
come out with it if I just waited. And he did.

"Dad, there's something I gotta tell you . . .
but I don't want to." I waited a little bit, and he
gave me a troubled look, then said, "Maybe you
won't like me when I tell you what it is."

"I'll always like you."

"But — how can you say that until I tell you?"

I smiled gently at him. "I've got a crazy idea

that when you love somebody, it stays fixed. Matter of fact, once a fellow said, 'Love is not love when it bends . . . it is an ever fixed mark.' "

He thought that over and asked, "Who said that?"

"Shakespeare."

"I didn't know you knew stuff like that, Dad."

"Did you understand it?"

"Sure. It's like you said, when you love somebody you don't change — don't bend, as the poem says."

"Okay. Now that's settled. What's on your mind?"

He shuffled his feet and looked over my shoulder; then he set his jaw and met my eyes. "Well . . . when all the trouble happened, about the murder and all . . . and it looked to everybody like you'd done it . . . Well, I thought so too."

"Can't blame you for that. It looked pretty bad."

"Yeah . . ." his voice trailed off in worry. "But I hated you too."

I put my hand on his shoulder. "You were scared. Everything was ruined and I'd let you down. I wasn't the nice Dad you'd always thought, but a thief and a murderer. I betrayed you and your mother and the whole family. You wouldn't have been human if you hadn't hated me, Matt."

He stared at me for a long time, then began to smile just a little. He gave a deep sigh of relief and said, "I've been trying to think of a way to tell you that for a week."

Just then Dawn called us from the back door, and I gave his arm a punch. "We'll have lots of time to talk about it now, Matt."

We finished up and Matt went to his room, and I went to the bunkhouse. The bunkhouse, not my old bedroom in the house. It's a little sticky, but for some reason I was still living in the bunkhouse. The night we came home from the police station it was easy to say to Dawn, "Good night, Dawn, I'm bushed."

She looked surprised, then asked, "Aren't you coming with me?"

I stared at her. She was as enticing a woman as I could imagine, but all I did was shake my head and say, "I'll just bunk here tonight."

She stared at me, then whispered as she drew close, "But, Dan, I'm your *wife!*"

"We'll talk tomorrow," I said, and for a long time I lay awake wondering what in the world was wrong with me. The way was clear. What was holding me back?

But I was still in the bunkhouse after two weeks. Cora never mentioned it, and Matt didn't seem to think it was important. We were on the go all day, and usually we got home late so I could make my escape without attracting too much attention.

Anyway, I showered and went in for supper. The others were waiting, so I sat down. Cora said a medium-length grace, and Matt lit into the fried chicken.

"Boy, this is good!"

We looked like a typical American family, I guess. Suddenly I thought that Norman Rockwell could have used us on a calendar. Father and mother, young, handsome son eating fried chicken, and a wonderful white-haired grandmother with a sweet smile. Yeah, we looked good.

After supper, though, I noticed that Dawn was edgy. It was really the first time we'd had together, and I guess I was feeling a little foggy myself. Matt wanted to start right off to play Monopoly, and I said, "Sure, set the board up."

Dawn got up and paced around a little; then just as we were getting ready to begin, she said, "Dan, I don't want to sit around and play a game tonight. Let's go somewhere, get out of here for a while."

I looked up in surprise. "Go where?" I asked.

"I don't care — anywhere. Just drive around." She put her hands behind her and said, "I need to get *out* for a little while, Dan. Matt, you wouldn't mind, would you? We'll play the game tomorrow."

Matt ducked his head and said, "Sure, Mom."

I could see he was disappointed. I tapped his shoulder and said, "Maybe we'll go fishing tomorrow, real early before school. Just you and me." That lit his fire, of course, so he ran off to watch a rerun of *Home Improvement*.

We got our coats and piled into her car. As we

left the drive, I asked, "Anywhere special you want to go?"

"Sure!" She scooted over close beside me and said, "Let's live it up like old times, honey! Hit the high spots!"

"You name it." I was a little surprised when she mentioned a place over fifty miles away, but I didn't object. It was a nice enough place, and we danced, had a late snack, laughed a lot. The music was loud, and I found out I was a *very* poor dancer.

She only laughed and said, "You never were any good."

It was a strange evening. I felt as though I was some kind of impostor, out with some other guy's wife. Maybe the wife of a real good friend, but it still was strained. She kept throwing things at me that I would have known, I guess, if I had any memory. But I didn't, and I maybe never would — so this was a preview of coming attractions. It was miserable. Maybe Dawn felt how uptight I was, because she drank too much and tried too hard. Finally I managed to get her home. She was pretty unsteady as I took her to the door of the house. I opened the door and pretty well shoved her inside, hoping she'd find her way to the bed.

I hit the sack myself, depressed as an undertaker. On the other hand, maybe undertakers weren't depressed. How would *I* know? I must have thought about everything in the world, and then about thirty minutes later I heard a sound.

321

Before I could move she came in through the door. I immediately saw that under her robe she was wearing one of those French things they advertise in the junk mail catalogs — sheer black fancy lingerie that's effectively designed to get a guy's undivided attention. There was a set look on her face, and I felt like a mouse watching a cat getting ready to pounce.

She was out to get me, to establish her identity — the wife of Dan Majors.

I got up and said, "It's no good, Dawn."

She straightened up as though I'd belted her. Staring at me she asked, "But . . . what's *wrong* with you? What's *wrong* with me?"

"I can't answer that. All I know is that you have to give me more time."

"Time for *what?*" She was aggravated, and her voice started to rise, as did her favorite argument. "I'm your *wife*, Dan."

"You don't know what it's like! Not knowing a single thing about who I am. What you've done is . . ."

She stepped close to my face and said harshly, "What is it you think I've done?"

I was shocked to see how defensive she became. "I'm blank. You're a stranger to me, and so is everybody else."

"But you know who I am —"

I cut her off with, "I just know a name — that's all. And I know you're a beautiful woman, and I know you're funny and I'm attracted to you . . . but that's not love." I tried to soften my voice and loosen the tension. "You can remember me, Dawn, and all the things we did together. But I can't remember a thing. I've got to have more than that!"

She was a little unsteady. The drinks were getting to her. Suddenly she set her lips and said in a blurred tone, "I know what it is! I know all right!" Her full lips twisted with a painful thought, and then she raised her hands to my shoulders and whispered brokenly, "You do remember, don't you? I couldn't help it. You know I didn't mean it, don't you?"

I shouted at her. "Dawn! Don't say any more." She was about to make a confession that I didn't want to hear. "Look, you may have some bad memories about our past, and you may feel the need to confess them. Don't do it. If we have any chance at all, we have to start where we are right now! Understand?"

She nodded slowly, then whispered, "Do . . . do you think it will ever be all right, Dan? For us . . . like it used to be?"

She seemed like a little girl then, and I had the feeling that all her running around and wild living had been done out of fear more than anything else.

"We'll take it as it comes, Dawn," I said. For a moment we stood clinging to each other. Finally she turned and left and I hit the sack.

For a long time I wrestled with what was happening to me. I was not really happy, as I'd expected to be. Finally I drifted off into a fitful sleep, but out of the darkness came a dream, or something. The face I'd seen before when I was on the way to church with Cora and Matt came to me again. This time, it didn't swim slowly into my mind. It was just *there*. The same face, same features, and same half-smile. Something in the eyes revealed a deep wisdom touched by humor. He was wearing an old army jacket this time, and his face was younger, but I knew it was the same man.

For what seemed like a long time, I waited for him to speak, but he was silent. It was as though he knew what was going on with me, but still he said nothing. Finally his lips moved, and I was surprised to hear him singing. The tune was somehow familiar, but it was no pop tune. I knew that much. The words . . . were odd. He had a raspy voice and wasn't much of a singer. I tried to hear the words, but they weren't clear. Something about a river and a tragedy of some kind. Someone was dead, and as the song went on, I saw tears glisten in his eyes. He finished the song, then whispered, "Don't let the wind blow you wrong, Buddy . . . and don't let the river carry you into the wrong country. . . ."

And then I woke up, the tune drifting away like a faint wisp of fine smoke. I sat straight up, trying to remember the words of the song, but they were gone. But I whispered his words, memorizing them, "Don't let the wind blow you wrong, Buddy. And don't let the river carry you into the wrong country."

Whatever else, these were *my* memories, all mine. Somehow this man was my past, and what he was saying was for me — or had been once. I got up and stared out the window at the moon, a slice of silver, whispering the words over and over. *Buddy* he'd called me. Was that a real name — or just a friendly nickname?

I finally went back to bed, but a troublesome thought suddenly stabbed at my mind like an ice pick. Whoever that man is, he's not a Majors.

Matt and I got back from our fishing trip just before breakfast with a stringer of bluegills. D.K.'s Volvo was parked in the driveway, so we left the fish outside and went in.

D.K. wasn't there, but Perry was. I grabbed him and gave him a big bear hug. He staggered under my attention and said, "Hey Champ, careful wit' the merchandise."

He was still moving a little slow and had lost weight. I said, "Perry, your pants are so baggy you look like you're smuggling rice out of China!" He grinned with enthusiasm and gave me a shot to the arm. "You all right — all healed up?"

"Well I'm jus' about healed up. And you know, I didn't mind a night or two in da slammer. Keeps me in touch with my roots."

"They give you a hard time?"

"Well, the Feds was all right, but some of the local law is tough. I think a couple of them guards gotta be kept in some kinda cage when they off duty. But I guess we got all that behind us, Champ."

"Sure." I looked around and saw that Cora was putting plates on the table. "Let's eat."

"Mighty fine," he agreed. He sat down and Dawn came in, a little pale and sort of subdued. But she gave Perry a fair smile and touched my arm before she sat down.

Matt had always been a little tentative around Perry. But after about five minutes and a couple of funny stories, making himself the goat, Perry had Matt listening with both ears.

Then he turned to me and said, "Darla Kaye, she wants you to come to Tulsa, Champ."

"Oh? What for?"

He shrugged and said, "I reckon more of the same. You know how them judges and lawyers is — always wanting another meeting. Anyway, she say for you to come in."

"Dan, I wish you'd stay here today," Dawn said suddenly. She got up and came to stand beside me, a hand on my shoulder. "I thought we could all have a day together. We could go shopping, take in a movie — just like we used to."

I almost said yes, but Cora said, "We'll have plenty of time for that, Dawn. I think we ought to get the legal mess cleared up as soon as possible. Then we can get back to normal."

I hesitated, then shrugged. "I guess you're right, Cora." Then I turned to Dawn and said with my best smile, "How about tomorrow?"

"I . . . I guess so." Then she looked up at me and asked anxiously, "You'll come back tonight, won't you?"

"Sure." I got up and looked at Perry. "She say how long it would take?"

"No, sir, Boss. Just said for you to come."

I got cleaned up and went out to the car. Matt was there talking to Perry. Dawn and Cora were standing on the porch. I gave them a wave and said, "Tie a yellow ribbon 'round the old oak tree!" Then I said to Matt, "You're in charge. Keep these women in line, okay?"

He gave me a grin. "Sure. I'll wait up for you, Dad."

I got in the car and Perry pulled out. I twisted my head as we went through the gate. They were all watching me. Matt raised his hand to wave good-bye, but neither Cora nor Dawn moved.

I settled back and let Perry do the talking. He told me all about how the law had thought he was in some sort of deal with me, and how it seemed like they hadn't let him sleep for two days. Then he told how D.K. came busting the place apart when he had finally gotten word to her.

"Whoooooo! She is a *mean* lady when she get her back up!" he sighed in wonder. "I don't think the *police* gonna forget her right soon!"

We were halfway there when he said suddenly, "I reckon you and me are gonna split the blanket, Champ."

"What's that mean?" I asked in surprise.

He shrugged his bull shoulder and kept his eyes on the road. "Darla Kaye tells me that oil company is worth big bucks. She say you gonna own it when the smoke clears."

"I don't know, Perry. Maybe so."

He laughed and said, "With that kinda dough, you ain't gonna be doing no more fighting."

"I guess not, but that doesn't mean you have to leave."

"Whut I do, Champ? Lace your shoes? Open the door for you?"

"Oh brother, put a lid on it. You don't have to *do* anything. If I'm loaded, you and me can do what we please."

"Nope."

I stared at him. "What's the matter? You never turned money down that I ever heard of."

He didn't answer and I said, "Look, I'm a little shook up about all this stuff, Perry. You see, you're the only guy in the world I really *know!* I mean, you took care of me when I couldn't take care of myself. And if you hadn't brought me along, I'd still be in the hospital. Even if I was well, I wouldn't have found out I was Dan Majors if it hadn't been for you. Except for Kimpel you're all the *past* I got! Look, just hang in with me — just for a while, okay? I mean, well, to tell the truth . . . I need you, Perry."

He gave me a glance, then looked back at the road with a short nod. "All right. We see how it goes."

I leaned back, discovering I had broken into a

328

sweat. To cover up I said, "Look, when we get our hands on some of this money, let's *blow* it! I mean, just waste a big stack of bills!"

"Right! Les' get us a *Rolls!*"

"That's it — a Rolls-Royce! I wonder what one of those things costs?"

"One hundred and sixty-two big ones," Perry answered at once.

I swallowed, then laughed, "Well, I guess that's about right for us."

"You gets what you pays for, Champ," Perry nodded wisely. "That ol' assembly line don't move but a few inches a day. And over eighty thousand parts goes into a Rolls. Used to be they bragged that in a Rolls the loudest sound you could hear at sixty was the tickin' of the clock. Now with them digital things, they say all you can hear is your own heartbeat! Ain't that *elegant?*"

"I *like* it!"

"And you know that big silver grill? Well, it ain't silver — it's stainless steel. And there ain't but only thirteen dudes on this earth knows how to make 'em. And you know what else?"

"What?"

"All thirteen of them dudes is *black!*"

"Aw, Perry, I find that hard to believe!"

He leered at me and gave me the line. "Would you believe twelve blacks and one A-rab?"

"I would believe that!"

"And inside there's leather that comes only from foreign cows — Swedish cows. And they ain't never been behind no barbed wire, so's they won't scratch they pretty hides, you see?"

"Class — nothing but class! Maybe we ought to get two! A matched set!"

We went on with building our luxury holdings until we got to Tulsa; then Perry put me out in front of D.K.'s building. "I'll park the car. You go on up."

When I got to the office, Maury actually smiled at me. "Go right in, Mr. Majors. Ms. Wolfe is expecting you."

I stared at him in shock. He'd always looked at me before as though I were an unpaid bill. "Amazing how six million bucks can make a guy more charming, ain't it, Maury?"

I went inside, and D.K. looked up from her desk, which had papers all over it. "Here I am in my customary suit of solemn black," I said.

She smiled and got up. "Spouting Shakespeare again?"

"Just showing off."

She looked at me and said with a smile, "I've been doing my homework, Dan. How would seven and a half million dollars strike you?"

I guess she expected me to faint, but it was just a number to me. "Is that what SunCo's worth?"

"More or less." She looked at me and said solemnly, "It's not going well, is it?"

I slumped down in a chair and stared at her. "I don't know what's *wrong* with me, D.K. I just can't fall into it — being Dan Majors!" I stared out the window and she didn't say anything, so I went on. "All right, here it is. I can't just *say* I'm Dan Majors! I mean, it's just a *name* . . . nothing to do with me, D.K. I don't have any sense of it — nothing at all."

She didn't answer; then finally her face grew tense. She leaned forward over me, and her eyes were sad. Yet there was a softness about her mouth. "You'll have to settle for what you get. That's what most of us have to do." She started to say something else, but her buzzer sounded. She went to the desk and flipped the switch. "Yes?"

"Lieutenant Cossey is here."

"Send him in." She shot me a glance and said, "That's why I asked you to come in. Cossey called yesterday. I think he's got something."

The door opened and Cossey entered looking like an unmade bed. He gave me a strange look, then turned to D.K. "See you got him here."

"Hello, Cossey," I said. "That the same cigar you were burning last time?"

"Hello," he said and shook. "Gimme a drink, will you. I'm dry as dust." D.K. poured him a tall one as he turned back to me and asked, "How's it going?"

I tried to grin and didn't do too well. "Being a rich, healthy, and good-looking somebody?"

He chewed his cigar. "Opposed to being a poor, sick, and ugly nobody?" I nodded but didn't make eye contact. "Not too well, is it?"

"He'll be better when he gets used to it, Cossey," D.K. said. "A few million dollars does wonders for the disposition, I understand. And it won't be long. I've put a little pressure on a few people, and within about three months you'll have to tip your hat and say 'sir' to this loaded taxpayer."

Cossey regarded me carefully, taking a fresh cigar out of his pocket. I knew he had something in his head. He used those cigars for a prop, to take people off guard.

Finally he got through with the bit and said, "You're not Dan Majors."

It was as if the world stopped for a heartbeat. D.K. was taken off guard, and her lovely mouth dropped open. It didn't hit me that hard for some reason. I just met Cossey's steady gaze, and finally he grinned.

"You ain't *got* no nerves!" he said disgustedly. Then he pulled a brown manila envelope out of his inside pocket and handed it to me. I took it and he said, "We found Dan Majors."

"Let me guess," I said. "Pentland took you to the shaft."

"Got it in one," he grinned. "The old man won't last long. I don't think the law will get him bad, but he's a dead man anyway. Yeah, he took us to the general area, but he couldn't be sure of much. We got half of the state police force to look, with the National Guard and marines thrown in. Found it day before yesterday. It was almost filled in with brush and stuff, and it was *deep*. Had to send a guy down with rappelling gear. Almost forty feet down. Nobody would have climbed out of that, just like Renfro said, especially with a bullet in his heart."

"You have prints?" D.K. asked. "You could be wrong, Cossey."

"Nothing there but bones, of course. But we got this." He nodded at an envelope. I opened it and took out two X rays of a skull. Cossey tapped the one with a blue label. "That's Dan Majors' dental record. Right from the office of Dr. Jim Pellegrine in Broken Bow. Must be the only time he ever went to a dentist. He had great teeth. Pellegrine said he'd never seen such choppers! Had one little tooth about to give some trouble, so he took it out and stuck in a bridge. That dark one right there. See it?"

"What's this one?" I asked, holding up a print with a red label.

"That's *you!*" Cossey answered. "Got it from Kimpel. See anything funny about it?"

I stared at it. "I don't see anything wrong."

"That's *it!*" he said at once. "There ain't *nothing* wrong! No bridge. So even if we hadn't found Majors' body, you still ain't gonna be no millionaire."

I stared at the pictures and finally said, "Looks like I just lost a fortune." Then I saw they were looking at me with the same expression. Concern, you might call it. I gave them my best grin out of the side of my mouth, like Gable used to do it. "Win a few, lose a few."

Cossey studied me soberly, puffed on his cigar, then gave me a slap on the back that almost drove me to the floor. "Yeah, so what? It's only money, right?" He laughed again and added, "For some reason this reminds me of the guy who said, 'Every time we get a good war started, peace keeps breaking out.' "

"Yeah, well I guess peace just broke out for me," I said. "Back to the old drawing board."

He stopped, and a serious light came into his pale blue eyes. He sent a cloud of smoke toward the ceiling before finally saying, "Look, Adam, it ain't the end of the world. I want you to come back to New Orleans as soon as you can. I been doing a little probing around, and I think maybe we can come up with something. Now, don't get all excited, but I got a couple of things that maybe will help — like you wasn't *born* in that fire! You had to come from somewhere! I got a nice two-week vacation coming up next month. I think you and me can maybe use it together. We put our heads together, maybe we can plow up a snake?"

I knew he was a friend, and I had none to spare. "Sure, Cossey. I'll call you. Who knows? Maybe I'll turn out to be the long lost son of Howard Hughes, but probably not."

He laughed and waved his hand at D.K. just before he left. "Watch yourself with this one."

I smiled at her and asked, "Did he mean me or you?"

I was really feeling pretty bad. Maybe I wasn't sold on being Dan Majors, but being a nobody man again wasn't too great. She was looking at me with a strange heavy-lidded gaze. Then she came straight up to me and put her arms around my neck.

"Now . . . what about us?" she asked.

I stared at her. "Too bad about the way you beat around the bush, Darla Kaye."

She didn't smile. "I love you, Adam Smith. Whoever you are. I want you on any terms." Then she drew back and looked into my face. "But maybe you're in love with Dawn."

"No. That was just a try for the brass ring. I wanted a home, a family — and that was part of it. It wasn't *right*."

"*It wasn't right.*" She bit her lower lip and shook her head slowly. "Adam, you've got this notion about 'right' as if it were some sort of fixed line."

"Well, I think in some ways it is."

"Oh, come off it!" she said harshly. Then she put her hand on my cheek and almost whispered, "You're looking for a nice, clean world with everyone who's bad wearing black, and all the good guys wearing white. It just doesn't *work* that way." She closed her eyes and leaned against me. "I know it may not last forever, but it may be all we'll ever have. Why not take it? It's better than nothing!"

"*Carpe diem?* Seize the day? Gather ye rosebuds while ye may?" I held her tightly by her arms. "Do it if it feels good! Is that the rule you want to live by, D.K.?"

"Adam! You're hurting my arms!" she cried

out, and I looked down at her, then turned her loose. She rubbed her arms, then said in a brittle tone, "Got us all analyzed? Pinned down and dissected? But you won't be a part of all this nasty old mess! Not Adam Smith! Not the shining knight! Let everybody corrupt themselves, but there'll be one at least who kept himself pure!" Then her face began to break into planes of grief, and tears rolled down her cheeks. "Get out of here!"

I wheeled and rushed out of the office, hoping that Maury would take a swing at me so I could hit him, but he just stared at me. I floundered off down the elevator, then outside, but I was so shook up I couldn't remember much about the next hour. I must have walked twenty blocks before I finally came out of it. I wasn't mad — just confused.

I walked around for a long time; then finally I turned and went back to D.K.'s building. I went to her floor, but I guess Maury was gone for the day. The office was empty, and I stood there feeling like a fool, trying to get up the nerve to face her again. Finally I pushed the button on the intercom. It rang and I had about decided she had left, when a light went on and she said in a tight, muffled voice, "What is it?"

I said, "There's an ugly frog lurking in your outer office. It will take the kiss of a beautiful and wonderful woman to turn him into a handsome prince. Would you be interested . . . ?"

She came sailing out before I could finish, and

we managed to turn me into a prince — of sorts.

We walked around for the remainder of the afternoon, sitting on park benches, feeding the pigeons, and talking.

Finally we got to her place. We always did. Most of the night we talked — or *I* did. The words practically spilled out of me. I talked about how I couldn't just wipe the Majors family out of my mind, especially Matthew. Then I talked about my relationship with Dawn and the intensity of that struggle. It had all caught up to me, and my throat was thicker than I'd ever felt it — at least that I remember. I told her about my memories of the man in the army jacket and all about the dream of the fire.

Finally I ran down and put my hands over my face. "I get so *lonesome* sometimes, D.K."

"Me too. So does everybody," D.K. said quietly. She was sitting beside me, and I felt her hand touch my arm. "Look, Adam, a street-wise cop like Cossey, a genius like Doc Kimpel, a smart lawyer like me, and an operator like Perry can find out *anything*. We could probably find out the enigma of the sphinx! I think all of us ought to be able to find *you*."

"I . . . I don't like to think about tomorrow, D.K. I've got to make a living."

She said confidently, "Well, I've decided to move my practice to New Orleans, and I've got an idea of expanding. A rotten place like that needs lots of lawyers, and I've been thinking for a long time about starting a new security agency.

I'll need a couple of tough guys with muscles and enough brains to find their way home. You and Perry might have a shot."

I looked at her, and suddenly I knew she was doing it for me. She said nothing, and I cleared my throat. "It . . . might be all right. Better than getting punched in the ring."

I would have gone on, but she suddenly kissed me. Then she put her arms around my neck. I buried my face against her, and she stroked my hair gently. All of my problems grew soft and out of focus. I closed my head and muttered, "I am in your power. Be *nice,* Darla Kaye!"

Escape

SIXTEEN

SOMEWHERE I'd read or heard that in a war, some men get terribly wounded but don't seem to know it. Shot to pieces, they keep on fighting, totally oblivious to the fact that their life is dribbling away. Something like that happened to me after I learned that I was just a nobody man again. In a way it was almost worse. I had so put my hopes on being somebody and having a place and having people that it was somehow more terrible than when I first came out of the black tunnel. Then at least I didn't have any expectations — just a faint hope of finding out who I was. This time it was different, and it hurt worse than anything I'd experienced so far.

I moved back into my home away from home, the Elite Motel in Tulsa. I finally called the ranch and left a message on Cora's answering machine, briefly explaining things. It was Sunday morning, so I knew she'd be at church, and Dawn asleep. I didn't even leave my phone number.

The next day I called Kimpel and we talked for

a long time. I guess I must have seemed listless because several times he asked me what was the matter. He explored my dreams until there was nothing left to say about them. Finally he took a deep breath, then asked abruptly, "What are you going to do about the Majors family, Adam?"

It took some effort for me to concentrate on what he was saying, but a thread of surprise ran through me. "What do you mean by that, Doc?"

"I mean exactly what I ask. You act like you're half asleep or back in a coma. You've already been there and done that. Wake up! What are you going to do about Cora, Dawn, and Matt?"

Anger ran along my nerves. "There's nothing to do. I'm not Cora's son, and I'm not Dawn's husband, and I'm not Matt's dad."

"So you're just going to kiss them off, is that right?"

"They'll be all right. D.K. said that they're going to get a big settlement from all the SunCo properties."

"And money settles everything, doesn't it?"

"What do you want out of me, Doc?"

"I want you to wake up."

I could tell he was upset, and I imagined him bouncing up and down on his chair, the fat quivering all over his body. But I still didn't understand what he was getting at.

I said, "Look, I'll send them a Christmas card. Is that all right?"

"You can't kid around about this. You'll hurt

340

them if you don't go back, but you'll hurt your-self worse."

"I don't see how I could hurt myself any worse than I've already been hurt."

"Having a nice little pity party, aren't you? Well, let me tell you how you can hurt yourself. Things need to be closed. Doors need to be shut. Good-byes need to be said. That's why we have funerals — to say good-bye. I've seen it too many times — people dying and the bodies never recovered. The survivors go on for years denying it, half hoping that somehow their loved ones will walk through the door. You must have read about the MIAs in Vietnam. Men just disap-peared. Most, if not all, of them are dead, but there are a lot of people waiting for their hus-bands or their sons or their brothers to reappear. It's not going to happen. Once you have the funeral, as tough as it is, you close the door and move on to something else."

I knew he was right, and wearily I drew a hand across my brow and said, "Okay, Doc. Okay. I'll say my good-byes to them."

"And bury Dan Majors."

D.K. had been out of town on business for the whole week, but she had loaned me the Bronco, so I was able to drive out to Broken Bow.

When I pulled up in front of the ranch house, I saw Cora sitting out on the front porch. She stood up when I got close to her, and she put out both hands. I took them. It was a strange gesture

for Cora Majors. She was not given to demon-
strations. There was a concern in her fine eyes
that I didn't miss. "Hello, Cora," I said.

"Hello, Adam. I'm glad to see you."

"I almost didn't come back, but a friend of
mine told me I needed to."

"I'm glad you did."

"Are Dawn and Matt here?"

"They've gone to town. They'll be back in a
few minutes. Just went to get a few things. Here.
Sit down. I'll bring you some tea."

She brought the iced tea and I took it. "That's
the first thing you did when I first came here —
gave me a glass of tea. Seems like a million years
ago."

"It's been a difficult time for you."

We sat there, neither of us knowing much
about what to say, until finally Cora said firmly,
"I'm sorry it turned out this way, Adam. I
haven't had much hope lately, but when you
came into our lives — and then when I thought
you were my son — it was a new day for me."

"For me too."

"You're like my sons and like my husband."
She hesitated a moment, then said, "Dawn's in
love with you."

There it was. All set out on the front porch.
Cora was a straight-speaking woman, and I
knew she had spoken honestly. I knew also that I
had to speak just as honestly to her. "I'm not
sure that she is."

"Well . . . as much as Dawn can be in love with

any man. She's got problems, Adam. You know that as well as I do."

"Well, it's a big club. We've got our problems too, haven't we, Cora?"

"Not like hers. She doesn't know the Lord."

"I'm not sure that I do either."

Cora stared at me suddenly. "What does *that* mean?"

"I mean I don't know if I'm a Christian or not. Maybe I was saved before I was in that fire, but maybe not."

Cora rocked slowly back and forth in a motion as old as time itself. She folded her hands and did not speak for a long time — for so long, in fact, that I thought she wasn't going to answer.

Finally she turned her head to me and said quietly, "You're a Christian, Adam."

Her certainty jarred me for a moment. "How can you know that?"

"Because of the way you acted with Dawn."

I felt my face redden. "I didn't think you knew about that," I mumbled.

"I hate to say it about my daughter-in-law, and I wouldn't say it to anyone but you, but Dawn's one of those women who can't leave men alone. Matt never saw it, but I did. I saw her go out to your place many nights and come out almost at once, and I also saw you leave and go off wandering after she'd made her little visits. And besides, just the way she looked at you, I knew she was after you. . . ."

"But at the end she thought I was her husband."

Cora accepted this, although we both knew it had nothing to do with the case at hand. Cora merely said, "You're a strong, healthy man, Adam, and any time a man like you turns away from a woman who offers herself so freely, it's because of something in his heart. The natural thing would be for you to take what she offered, but you didn't. I watched for it. I think I would have known instantly, and I dreaded it. So when I saw you turn from her, I had hope that maybe it would all work out. But I know you've got the Lord in your heart, for no man could have withstood that kind of temptation unless he had help from Him."

Suddenly I felt an unexpected release. "Do you really think that, Cora?"

"Of course I do. You're a clear thinker, Adam. Why did you think you were saying no to her? Why did you say no to her?"

"There was something in me that I couldn't turn away from. When everything in me was crying to reach out for her, still something said don't do it."

"That was the Holy Spirit. He teaches us things. He warns us against sin, and He's kept you from a terrible wrong. It would have destroyed you, I think."

A combined feeling of relief and release came sweeping through me then. I took a deep breath, held it, and then expelled it. "Maybe you're right, Cora. I hope so." I would have said more, but suddenly I looked up and saw a car coming down the highway. It turned off on the road leading to the house.

"There they are," Cora said. "Dawn bought a new car."

The shiny new Corvette pulled up in front of the house. It didn't take Dawn long to use that money, but I said nothing. The doors opened, and at once Matt came toward me slowly. I stepped forward and said, "Hello, Matt."

"Hi. I'm glad to see you."

Dawn was only a step or two behind him. She was pale, I thought, and was wearing expensive-looking new clothes. Her voice was somewhat breathless as she said, "Hello, Adam. Have you been here long?"

"Not long."

Dawn's face suddenly reddened, and she looked at Cora, then dropped her head. "I'll get the things out of the car, Matt. You entertain Adam."

"All right, Mom." Matthew gave me an odd look and then said, "I've got a new colt. Would you like to see him?"

"Sure would."

The two of us left the house, and soon I was looking at the fine yearling, a sturdy quarter horse glistening and glowing in the sun. We talked about the horse for a while, and finally Matt said, "Going to be all right, Adam." He somehow had matured, and there was a certainty about him. He looked older than his years, although it was nothing in his appearance. Something in his eyes was different, a peace that hadn't been there before.

"I'm glad to hear it, Matt. I've been worried about you."

He said instantly, "Ever since I found out that Dad wasn't a murderer, it's been different. I'll never get down on myself like I did before."

"He was a fine man. Any son of Cora's would have to be." I grinned and said, "How's it going to be?"

"How's what going to be?"

"Being rich. Think you'll like it?"

He grinned at me then, and there was an ease in his manner. "Better than being poor. What about you?"

"Oh, I'll muddle along."

"If you need money, we can get it for you. Some of it's left in trust to me. You can always have anything you want if I've got it."

A warmth came to me then. I stepped forward and put my arm around his shoulder. "That sounds like you, Matt. I may take you up on it if I need it."

He looked up at me and said abruptly, "Mom's got problems, but she's going to be all right. I'm going to look out for her. And she really wants to change."

The two of us talked a little more; then when we went back to the house, Matt instinctively knew that I had to see Dawn alone. He sat down on the porch beside his grandmother, and I stepped inside and moved through the parlor. I met Dawn coming in from the hall, and she seemed flustered. There was no point in dragging it out, so I said, "Dawn, I'll be leaving now, but I want to wish you well."

Her face looked strangely tense; then suddenly her lips quivered and tears sprang to her eyes. "I'm going to try, Adam. I'm going to try hard."

"You'll make it. Stick with Cora. Matt's going to be a fine man, and somewhere in this world there's a guy just made for you. You need a good one, and I'm going to pray that you find him."

"What will you do? Will you be around?" She suddenly flushed and shook her head. "I'm not making a play for you or anything like that."

"I know that, Dawn. I'm just not sure where I'll be, but we'll keep in touch." I put my hand out and she took it. "Take care."

I stepped out on the porch. I knew it was time to leave. "I've got to go. A few errands, but I'll be in touch. Matt here has offered to finance me. So I may let him finance us a trip to the Rocky Mountains to go deer hunting."

Matt's eyes glowed. I came over but didn't put my arms around him — because Cora was there — and I shook his hand as if he were a full-grown man. I did put my arm around Cora, whispering, "I'll be in touch."

As I drove away, I knew that I would see them again. But somehow the incident was over. As Kimpel had said, the door was closed, and I knew that it was for the best.

It had been good to see the Majors, and I felt that they were going to make it now, but for the next two days I went into a spin. I missed the Majors. I missed D.K. but felt afraid to get any closer. I was like an animal that had been wounded, I guess, and just wanted to crawl off somewhere and not be bothered.

As a matter of fact, that's exactly what I did. I caught a bus to New Orleans, rented a hotel room, and again got in touch with Kimpel. Told him I'd be in to see him sometime, but I put it off. Kimpel had said that Perry was also back in town, but I couldn't bring myself to contact even him. I didn't go out except to eat, and even then I wasn't really hungry. I lay on my bed most of the time and stared at the ceiling.

My third night there, the fire dream came back full force. But this time there was something new. I knew it was some kind of a military scene. There were machine guns, missile batteries, and screaming jets overhead. It could have been from an old war movie I'd seen, but I felt it was too real for that. I woke up screaming, "Tim, you got to get out of here! Come on, Tim!" I lay there wrapped in my sheets, focusing all my attention on the memory of the dream and trying to see a face. It almost came once, and I knew that Tim was somebody very important in my life. Could he be the man I had seen so clearly at the church?

Early the next morning, still in bed, I was lying there thinking about the dream when a hard rap at the door came. I got off the bed instantly, startled, for it sounded as though someone had used a hammer. When I went to the door and opened it, there stood D.K. She came breezing right by me and stopped in the middle of the floor to look around. She took a big sniff and wrinkled her nose. I could see she was not happy, and I said, "You want to sit down, D.K.?"

"No. Get your clothes together."

"What?"

"I said get your clothes together."

"How'd you find me?" I demanded.

"Kimpel called me. He said it's time for you to break out of your prison here, so I've come to get you. Now get your clothes together."

"Where are we going?"

She was wearing a light green linen suit consisting of a short, form-fitting jacket with long, narrow sleeves and a V neckline through which showed a crisp white wrap-around blouse. The narrow skirt ended just above the knees, and she wore matching shoes and carried a leather purse.

"You ask too many questions." She stood in the center of the room and made me feel like a ten-year-old as I gathered my few clothes together and threw them into my bag. When I was ready, she said, "Come on," and walked out the door without another word.

She had parked in a No Parking zone, and I threw my stuff in the backseat of her Volvo and then climbed in. She started the engine and pulled out of New Orleans. We crossed the Mississippi River, hit Highway 10 going east. She drove like a race car driver. The speed limit was seventy, but she didn't pay a great deal of attention to that. We stopped once at Gulfport, Mississippi, to get coffee and gas, and she told me about a case she was working on. I answered as best I could with a series of grunts, and when we got back in the car the silence continued.

We passed through the rest of the state and before long we got to Mobile, went over the causeway, and D.K. said, "Does this look familiar?"

"No. Doesn't ring any bells."

We passed by a huge battleship in the bay, and she informed me, "That's the battleship *Alabama*. Someday we'll come and look it over."

"All right."

If she was troubled by my lack of words, she didn't show it. Just outside of Mobile we took Highway 59 and started going down through little towns — Loxley, Robertsdale, Summerdale, and Foley. "Gulf Shores is up ahead," she said.

I didn't comment, but the road played out in a dead end where you had to go east or west. She turned left and said, "It's not far now."

We passed through the little town, which was mostly composed of restaurants and souvenir stores. I got a glimpse of the blue waters of the Gulf and the white sand.

"Where are all the people? I thought it'd be crowded at a place like this."

"Not the season," D.K. shrugged. "Come here July the fourth and you couldn't find a parking place for love or money."

We passed by condo after condo and finally went across a huge, curving bridge spanning an expanse of blue water. "This is Perdido Pass. That's Perdido Bay. You know what Perdido means?"

"Lost, in Spanish, isn't it?"

"That's right. Lost Bay."

Ten minutes later we pulled off to the right on a dirt road. A hundred yards away a house sat on pilings. Her eyes twinkled as she said, "Well, what do you think of it?"

It was painted pastel pink, which somehow amused me. "Did you pick the color out? It's sweet."

"No," she said coolly. "It belongs to my aunt."

I followed her up the stairs, then waited while she rang the doorbell. Squeals of delight came from behind the screen door as D.K. was recognized.

I quietly ascended the stairs.

"Who is this handsome young man?" asked the pleasant-looking white-haired lady in the doorway.

"Aunt Hazel, this is Adam Smith, a friend of mine. Adam, this is Aunt Hazel."

Aunt Hazel searched my face for a moment. I must have passed her test when she said, "Wel-

351

come to my humble home, Adam. Come on in! I'll just skedaddle out of you kids' way and let you get settled."

When I walked in I saw that the whole other end of the house was glass. The effect was striking in its beauty. I walked over and looked out. The sun was shining, and the sand was as white as could possibly be. The sea was as green as a sea ought to be, and overhead the sky was blue and hard enough to scratch a match on. White clouds drifted over, and a big sailboat went by about a mile out, gliding over the waters almost magically.

"Why haven't you mentioned this place before?" I asked.

"I use it for a hideaway," she said. She walked to the glass sliding doors and opened them. The sound of the sea came whispering and roaring as the white waves broke. "A lot of surf today. We'll go down to the beach after a while.

"Adam, before you ask the inevitable question, Uncle Walt died a couple years ago and Aunt Hazel doesn't mind us being here." She turned and walked down a short hallway. "That's your room," she said, then turned her head to one side and motioned to the other door. "That's mine. But you don't have to worry. I won't come scratching at your door in the night. After all, Aunt Hazel has omnipresent ears, and she doesn't like anything untoward happening in her house." She smiled then, with a little mischief in her eyes. "Okay, Adam?"

I could never ignore her smiles. "Okay," I said with obvious surprise in my voice. I opened the door and went in. The furniture was all white wicker and the walls were white. Overhead a white ceiling fan began to spin as I turned to see that D.K. had turned it on. The bed was queen size, and I had a good view of the Gulf through the large sliding glass doors that opened onto a balcony. "This is beautiful," I said, and I meant it. There was something restful about it.

Aunt Hazel insisted we visit around the breakfast nook next to the kitchen. She was a wonderfully warm hostess who immediately made me feel like one of her family.

Later we went down so D.K. could show me what there was of Gulf Shores. "Pretty typical Gulf town," she said as we walked along beside the highway. "Life abounds on the highway, of course. Everything draws its life from this one street." She motioned toward the Gulf on the south side of the street. "That's what draws the people — white sands, blue-green water. On the north side you have the bars, fish houses, liquor stores. The town is all shaped around the highway. Apart from the beach, it wouldn't be any different from an Oklahoma town."

It was growing dark and we went back to the house. Once we were inside, she said, "I'm tired. Good night."

"Wait a minute." I went over to her, and apprehension came to her eyes. She acted as if she were about to be propositioned, but I said,

"Thanks, D.K. I think I can get myself back together here. The beach and the waves will be like a salve for my mental wounds. Good night."

I turned and went into my room and sat for a long time out on the balcony, looking at the moon as it washed over the waters. I breathed slowly and was aware of a deep stillness within me, a profound and familiar peace that I suddenly realized was fundamental to my identity. It was the presence of God. I had sensed it vaguely during my dark times in the hospital; I had felt it in my hunger for the Bible; I had seen it reflected in the life of Cora; in the repentant woman at the Broken Bow church. It was the reason for my sense of right and wrong — my "Puritanism," as D.K. would say, and it was wonderfully clear in the beauty of creation, the infinitely soothing sounds of the lapping waves. I thought about how they'd been making those sounds for thousands and thousands of years, and finally I fell into a deep, dreamless sleep, sitting in the deck chair.

We settled in, and for the next four or five days I knew a quietness that I hadn't ever experienced in my new life. We roamed the beach a lot together. Sometimes I went by myself to take in the peaceful rhythms of the surf and the blue herons that swooped down to collect the leavings on the sand.

After another leisurely stroll together Saturday night, we went inside. I said suddenly,

"I'm going to church tomorrow. I wish you'd come with me."

"All right. I will." She laughed suddenly at the expression on my face. "You expected me to stay behind, didn't you?"

The next morning we got up, and D.K. said, "You don't have to dress up for anything down here. Not even for church."

"I don't even know where one is."

"I do. I'll show you. I don't know what kind it is, though."

"Doesn't matter."

We found a little church off Highway 59 that looked as though it had been there a long time. There were less than fifty people there in the white frame building, and the preacher, one Brother Buck, was an older man. He preached on the woman at the well. I'd read it many times, but it always did something to me. The woman was a sinner. She had done nothing good in her whole life and everything bad, but after she met Jesus at the well everything changed. At the end of the sermon, the preacher's eyes lit up and he said, "She went back to her friends and said, 'Come and see a man who told me everything I did.' That's what Jesus is. He knew everything this woman had done, every wrong thing that she ever committed in her whole life. Every sin, but somehow she was excited, for He had told her that He was the Messiah. I think she got saved right at that well. I don't think she ever had another illicit affair. She went back telling her friends, her family, her neighbors, 'Come and see this man.' " He hesitated; then his eyes fell on us. We were the only visitors there. "I guess I would say to anyone who doesn't know Jesus, 'Come and see this man.' He will do you good."

The invitation didn't last long, and afterward as we filed out, we were greeted warmly by many of the members. The preacher's hand was hard and strong, and he said, "I'm glad to see you. Come back if you can."

Afterward D.K. said almost nothing for the rest of the day. As soon as we got home, she said, "You'll have to get your own lunch. I'm going for a walk."

That was usually my line, so I looked at her with surprise. "Do you feel all right?"

"I feel fine." She changed clothes, and I sat on the deck and watched her as she disappeared down the beach.

She didn't come back for a long time. It was nearly four-thirty, and I was getting a little bit worried about her. When she came back she merely grunted and went right to her room.

I'd learned to cook a little bit, so I put together something and knocked on her door. "Supper's ready, D.K."

A long silence and nothing, so I turned and walked away. However, just as I sat down she appeared. Her face was swollen but I didn't comment on this. Something was bothering her. She sat down and I said, "I don't know if you can eat this or not. I'm not much of a cook."

"It looks all right."

I bowed my head and asked the blessing, something that I had determined to do. It was short enough, and when I looked up, I saw that she was watching me strangely. She let her eyes drop and we ate in silence.

Afterward we went outside on the deck. She did not sit down but stood at the rail looking over at the water. It glistened and sparkled under the red rays of the setting sun. I went to stand beside her and she did not move. Finally I said, "Is there anything I can do, D.K.?"

It was as if I had touched a switch. She turned to me and reached out blindly and I put my arms around her. She began to sob, great, trying sobs that seemed to almost tear her in two. I held her, not knowing what to say, but she didn't need any words. She just needed someone to be there. Even I had sense enough to know that and wisdom enough to keep my mouth shut. It lasted for some time, and finally she pulled away from me and fished a handkerchief out of her pocket.

"I'm sorry," she whispered. "I haven't done that in a long time. It was the sermon," she said. "If I'd gone in there and he had preached hellfire and damnation, I probably would have walked out. But when he talked about how Jesus loved that sinful woman, it got to me. That's what I am. A sinful woman. It's that simple."

I didn't say a word for quite some time. Then, tentatively, I asked, "What happened on the beach?"

She turned to me and the wind blew her hair about her shoulders. "I prayed," she said simply. "The first time I've prayed since Jack died, or even before that. Maybe since I was a little girl. But this was different. Jesus loved that woman," she said, and her voice was quiet and almost reticent. "The disciples didn't care much about her, but He did."

"Yes, He did."

"And so I walked and walked until finally I prayed. I wanted to be that woman at the well. I've done so many bad things I've stopped keeping count. That well woman got another chance, despite who she was. And you know what? As soon as I told God I was lonely and empty and asked Him to forgive me, He did it."

A joy came to me then, and I knew somehow that this was not the first time I had seen a human being find freedom from sin. "Tell me some more about it."

And then D.K. began to talk. It was another woman that stood there before me. Gone were the hardness, the selfishness, the meanness, all the things that I had disliked. Now there was a gentleness and a softness and a tenderness, and after a long time I reached out and took her hand. "I'm glad, D.K.," I said simply. "I can't think of anything that could please me more."

We talked long into the night. She was apprehensive, thinking maybe it might pass away, that it was just an emotional experience. Somehow words came up in me, words that I didn't even know were there. But I realized that I had said words like this before to others. I assured her that she might have some grief along the way, but when Jesus came in He came to stay.

When I said this, something like a mischievous smile touched her lips. "Going to change my law practice a little, I think. Well, it needed changing. Come on. Let's go walk along the beach."

New Life

SEVENTEEN

WELL, I guess D.K.'s breakthrough was one of the more dramatic I'd ever heard of in my limited memory. For the next three days after she came back and told me she had found peace with God, we lived in a world of our own. It was as if a huge glass dome had been slipped over us, and the world outside had nothing to do with us at all. We got up, ate, then read the Bible together and talked and even prayed together.

It was on the third day when I had my own private breakthrough. Not as dramatic as D.K.'s, but to me it was something. I was sitting on the sand just looking out over the water that stretched along the white beach. It was colored differently. The water up close was a greenish strip about ten yards wide, while out farther it was a gray blue, almost the same color as the sky only darker, as far as the eye could see. There was no surf, and the water wrinkled slightly like a huge sheet of cellophane. No, not quite like that. It was like nothing else I can think of. It was almost as smooth as a lake.

Gulls, the world's greatest moochers, gathered around me as I fed them bread. I gave one a piece of bread, and two minutes later the whole flock descended on me. I got up and let them hover in the air almost motionless; then one of them swooped by and picked off the bread. I even tried putting it on my head, and they didn't even hesitate. They made harsh, rasping cries as they gracefully danced about in the air.

I'd just given them my last piece of bread when suddenly without warning, as if I was watching a video, a memory came back. I was standing in a gymnasium decorated for a dance. I knew it at once. It was my senior prom, and I was dancing with Joanne Melton.

That memory was crystal clear. I could see Joanne's dark brown eyes and the yellow dress she wore and even the little mole on her right cheek.

I yelled, got up, and ran down the beach where D.K. was walking along picking up shells. She turned to me and for a moment she seemed afraid. "What is it?" she cried.

"Joanne Melton," I said. "I went to my senior prom with Joanne Melton. She had a mole right here. I touched her face, and she wore a yellow dress."

"Adam, you remembered!"

"It all came back. I wasn't even trying." I stopped then and said, "I can remember everything about that night. I borrowed Dad's car, a Chevrolet."

D.K. smiled, then put her arms around me and pulled my head down and kissed me. "It's coming back, isn't it?"

"Yes." I stood there holding her, pressing her against my chest, and said, "I think if I hold you like this long enough, I can remember more. And the kiss seemed to be helpful too." I kissed her again, and she laughed and pushed me away.

Taking my hand, she said, "Tell me some more about that night."

We walked along the shore, and the sand-pipers ran before us. I exhausted the details of the memory rather quickly. And try as I might, I couldn't dredge up anything else.

Finally we turned and moved back. D.K. said, "I wish we never had to leave here. It's safe."

"As long as your money holds out, I guess we can. Otherwise I'll have to get back in the ring again to make a buck."

"No, Adam, you must never do that again! Promise me."

It wasn't hard. I shook my head. "I promise. Scout's honor."

"Were you a scout?"

Suddenly I stopped dead still. "Yes, I was. I remember the night I got my Eagle Scout award. I remember going to scout camp in Texas in a place called Runaway Bay. I remember everything about it." I was off again in a race against a fleeting memory. Squeezing every drop of the story, I reveled in its telling.

It was a miracle of grace to me, and for the first

time I really believed that it was going to be all right.

Suddenly I was too full of joy to speak, my throat was full, and I said, "D.K., I don't know where we're going or what's going to happen. But I think I'm going to get my memory back."

D.K. looked down and was silent for a moment. When she looked up her eyes were filled with something like fear. "You may be married," she said quietly.

"It's possible." I knew I was in love with her and couldn't imagine loving any other woman ever, and I think she felt the same about me. But now there was the prospect of a woman in my life, a wife somewhere. Maybe children.

We said nothing more but went back to the house. We fixed lunch and D.K. made a good bisque, Cajun in origin I guess, and we ate crab salad. It was delicious. We were almost through with the meal when the phone rang.

D.K. went over, picked it up, and said, "Yes?" She was still for a long time, and then said, "Of course, Doc. We'll be expecting you." Putting the phone down, she turned to me and stood very still for a moment. "Doc's coming out."

Something in her voice caught at me. "Is it some kind of bad news?"

"I think it's some kind of news. I don't know whether it's good or bad. Cossey's coming with him."

The time passed slowly, for it took at least three hours to get from New Orleans to Gulf

Shores. Several times I went out and walked up and down, watching a charter boat as it moved slowly by, trolling for the big ones. The solitude had been the best thing I'd ever known, but now it seemed shattered. Whatever it was Kimpel was bringing, I couldn't imagine it being any better than what I had.

I began to pray hard. I couldn't pray that God would not give me my memory back, and I couldn't pray that I wouldn't have a wife. The memory would come, I knew that now, and as for the wife, if I was married, that was the end of it. The Scripture was too clear about the nature of marriage. It was forever — at least forever on this earth.

Finally at three-thirty we heard a car pull up and a horn sound once. "They're here," D.K. said. She got up and her face was tense and drawn and somewhat pale. She waited for the knock, then walked over, and when she opened the door, Kimpel stepped in and right behind him the massive bulk of Cossey.

Kimpel embraced D.K., exchanged pleasantries with Aunt Hazel, and then came over to me. "How are you, Adam?"

"Fine." I shook his hand, then walked over and studied Cossey's face. He was excited, although he tried to hide it by rolling his cigar and looking around the house. "Nice little place," he said. "How have you been?"

"All right."

An awkward silence reigned over the room

then, and it was D.K. who broke out nervously, "What is it, fellas? Don't keep us in suspense."

Cossey was wearing a pair of baggy tan pants and a white T-shirt, the biggest in stock, no doubt. He shifted on his feet and looked at me. "Doc and I have come up with something. He wants you to meet someone. Well, two some-ones as a matter of fact."

I have never seen Doc Kimpel so jumpy. Even Cossey's hands weren't steady when he reached up to take the cigar out of his mouth. I didn't think anything could shake him up, but he was nervous. Well, now I was infected. Somehow I felt that the next few moments would settle my destiny. That sounded like a literary way to put it, but that's what came to me. I said quietly, "Sure, Doc. Are they outside?"

"I'll get 'em," Cossey said. He ducked out the door and shut it behind him. Doc Kimpel started to say something, then cleared his throat and shook his head and remained silent. I looked over toward D.K. She had backed up against the wall, her hands behind her, and her body was as tense as possible. I knew she was sending me some kind of a message, and there were fear and uncertainty in her eyes.

We heard footsteps on the wooden steps, and as the door opened I turned to face it. Cossey came in first, blocking out the two who were with him, and then he stepped aside, and a man right behind him stepped forward and stopped dead still.

I wish I could properly explain what happened at that moment. It was like nothing else that ever happened to me, before or after the fire. I'd been wandering around a nobody man for a long time, but as soon as I saw the man's face, every bit of my past just seemed to jump into focus. Like a door crashing open and a fresh breeze whooshing in to sweep away the fog.

"Hello, Dad," I said, and my voice cracked as I pronounced the words.

It was the man I had seen in my dream, and instantly tears came to his eyes. He was a big man, as tall as I was, but his face was weather beaten. He wore an old army fatigue jacket, like the one I had seen. He came forward at once and put his arms out.

"Davis," he whispered. "It's really you."

His arms were around me. We were two big men, but we hugged each other without thought. Tears ran down my cheeks. He smelled like the out-of-doors and leather and faintly of some kind of shaving lotion that I recognized. Finally we stepped back and I looked over his shoulder and gasped, "Tim!"

"Hello, Davis." The man who came forward was wearing the uniform of a colonel in the United States Army. He did not embrace me at first but put his hand on my shoulder and stared at my face. "Is it you?"

"Yes."

"I'd never have known you in a thousand years." His face broke and I saw that his eyes softened; then he reached forward and we embraced.

We held each other for a moment, then stepped back, and I said, "D.K., I'd like for you to meet Colonel Tim McKeown. He was my commanding officer in the army."

Colonel McKeown nodded and then said, "More than that. I'm the fellow who won him the Silver Star. If I hadn't gotten myself in a fire, he wouldn't have been able to jump in and haul me out of there."

I turned to D.K. and said, "And this is my dad. Dad, this is D. K. Wolfe."

My dad moved over to stand next to her. "I've heard a lot about you, Ms. Wolfe. I'm Nolan Trask."

D.K. seemed to be in a daze. She took his hand and studied his face. "You have the same eyes as Adam."

"No, it's not Adam. It's Davis."

I looked at her, at my father, then over at Cossey, and Tim, and Kimpel. They were all looking at me strangely, and I nodded and said, "Yes. That's who I am, D.K. I'm Davis Trask."

The moon was high in the sky, covered by skeins of tattered clouds. The waves had died down somewhat, but the glow of the moon made an inverted V shape on the waters as D.K. and I walked along.

Suddenly I said, "I'm so tired I can hardly walk."

She turned and nodded. "I think it's the emotional strain. I'm pretty weak myself. Let's sit down for a while."

We sat down on the remains of an old trunk half covered with sand, and for a while neither of us spoke. "I like your father."

Quickly I turned to D.K. "He likes you," I said. "I can tell."

It was almost midnight. The visitors had all taken a motel room, and we were due to meet for breakfast to hear the rest of the story. We had gotten bits and pieces of it, but there had been so many people talking, and I had been distracted by all of it. The moment I had seen my father's face all of my family flashed in. My mother was gone, but I remembered my two sisters and my brother, all the aunts and uncles.

Doc had taken a long time to explain it, saying, "In cases like this when you struggle a long time, sometimes just one familiar face opens the door for all the memory to come back."

Around the breakfast table the next morning, we all talked. Cossey explained how he had gone to the FBI and gotten the results of that melted piece of metal that had been found on me. After much analysis, they determined that it was a medal of some sort. They finally came up with the possibility that it was military. So Cossey had gone from there. It had been a hard chase, but he had somehow found a high-ranking military official in the Pentagon who was willing to listen. Cossey chewed his cigar and said, "It was real lucky. That man had served with your father, and they still kept in touch. He heard about a missing son who had come from Oklahoma. So I went down to see him.”

Dad said, “I didn’t believe it at first, but the longer the lieutenant here talked, the more I thought I’d have to come and see.”

“Tell your story, Davis. How did it all happen?” D.K. said, “Listen to me. I called you Davis. It’s the first time I’ve been able to do it. It’ll take a while, but tell me again.”

“Well, I’ve told you about the fiery dream. That was all related to the Gulf War when I was recalled to the army.”

I sat there and told her about my past, amazed at how easily it came. “I was pretty rough and wild for a while when I was younger, before I went in the service. Spent some time on the amateur boxing circuit. Dad was in the army, so we moved around a lot but ultimately settled in Oklahoma. We ended up in Oklahoma City after trying for a time in a little town called Harris. Believe it or not, Harris is only ten miles south of Broken Bow!”

“What happened in the army?”

“I planned on a military career, but there was a chaplain who led me to Christ. I remember it now. God put His hand on me and called me into the ministry. So I got out and went to Bible college, got my degree, and then Desert Storm came along and I got recalled. I was in the reserves as a chaplain.”

"Tell me about saving Colonel McKeown's life."

"February 25, 1991. We were stationed in the rear in Al Khobar, Saudia Arabia, near Dhran. Far enough from the action to feel safe." I paused, eyes watering from the memory. "Out of the blue came one of those Iraqi Scud Missiles. The warning sirens. The anti-missile batteries going off in rapid-fire mode. *Boom! Boom! Boom!* But one of the Scuds got through and exploded in the base. Twenty-eight dead and ninety-eight wounded that day.

"I was running for shelter with Tim when the missile hit. A fuel tank nearby was pierced by slugs of molten shrapnel. The explosion caught us in the open."

I shuddered suddenly and looked across the table at Tim. He nodded, so I continued, "He was burning, D.K. His clothes were on fire and he was just lying there. The gas and oil were burning everything around us. I pulled him out."

Tim leaned forward. "I don't remember any of it, but witnesses say Davis was on fire too. He jumped on me and rolled to put the fire out. Then lifted me on his back and ran me to safety."

D.K. reached out and touched my hand and asked, "And you got the Silver Star for that?"

I shifted uneasily.

Tim replied proudly, "I quote, 'For gallantry and heroism in action against an enemy of the

United States while engaged in military operations.' "

Continuing, I said, "My arms and the back of
one leg were burned pretty bad. It sure made me
afraid of fire. But something else happened to
me, D.K. I'm not exactly sure, but I think they
call it post traumatic stress syndrome. I was restless and couldn't settle down. So finally I went
out to Belize."

"Belize!"

I grinned at her, and she tightened her grip.
She was firm and warm and smelled good, as
usual. "You go to Mexico and turn left," I said.

"What did you do there?"

"I had a friend there, a missionary and his
wife, James and Murlene Golden. I just wanted
to get away, so I stayed with them for a long
time. They both saw something was wrong with
me. I got to where I'd wander off into the jungles
to spend some time ministering to the Mahia
Indians. Couldn't even speak their language," I
chuckled. "But I was able to help them build and
plant."

"What happened then?"

"Well, it was strange. Suddenly I had the
notion that I had to get home. So I went. I didn't
even tell the Goldens. Just got on the airplane. It
never occurred to me how that would seem to
them. I'd been out in the jungle, and I flew back
to Oklahoma City. I wanted to see Dad, but
when I got there I decided to take a week and
visit our place in Harris. It seems like a coinci-

dence now, but I stopped off in Broken Bow on the way. While picking up some supplies I must have seen Dawn and Matt Majors, which explains why they looked familiar to me later.

"After Harris, I decided to drive through Texas to the edge of Louisiana and hike in the hills. I was a bit out of sorts and was determined to get things straightened out.

"To my shame, I didn't know that the Goldens were worried sick about me. Dad now tells me that they thought a jaguar or something had gotten me. You know, I just went out one day and never came back."

"How awful!"

"It was awful. I've got to get back to them. Dad's already sent them a telegram, but I'll have to make my peace with them."

"And that's it. You were caught in a forest fire and burned."

"That's it. Roamed the hills and got trapped in that forest fire and that wiped me out."

Doc Kimpel pitched in, "Amnesia is such a bewildering thing. Many times it's from a blow to the head. Who knows? Maybe Davis got hit by a falling tree. My theory is that after being burned in the war and continually suffering from post traumatic stress syndrome, the forest fire was too much. Not only was he physically hurt, psychologically he just shut down. Too much terror for his mind to handle. A kind of defense mechanism."

"So no one even knew you were in the hills

near Louisiana?" asked D.K.

"No. Dad went to Belize and searched the jungles for me — had the local forces out and everything else. They thought maybe I'd gone for a swim and drowned. They were looking for me down there. That's why no missing report ever turned up in the States."

We all sat there for a while enjoying one another's company. Cossey said, "I have to take these guys back to catch their plane. You want to come with me?"

I looked over at D.K. and said, "No, I think I'll say my good-byes and catch up with you later."

Dad and I bear-hugged. After shaking Tim's hand, I turned to Cossey.

He growled, "Don't you get all sentimental with me, buddy."

"Just wanted to say thanks. If it weren't for you . . ."

He just waggled that cigar around and with a glint in his eye, grunted.

"Doc, what can I say? Until Dad showed up, you were like a father to me."

He smiled broadly and said, "Just make sure you come see me. After all, Perry's back working at the hospital, moping around with a long face. I suspect he'll be anxious to spar with you again."

"It's a deal."

They drove off as I stood in the driveway watching. I stayed there for a time thinking of all this, and suddenly D.K.'s voice turned me around.

"Davis? You still haven't told me, and nobody said anything. Are you married?"

I pulled her into my arms. "Nope," I said. "Never been married or even engaged." It did something to her when I said that. She was tall and shapely, and her eyes mirrored some kind of wisdom. She looked at me silently, but I was pretty sure that a woman's silence could mean many things. It pulled me after my own solitary life. And then I saw she drew away the curtain of reserve and had a provocative challenge in her eyes. D. K. Wolfe was a complex and striking woman.

Her lips were near, and I saw them move and become heavy. Then her eyes darkened. She turned her face up to me. As I squeezed her in my arms, my mouth came down on hers. I held her like that over the lengthening moments and felt the surrender soften her. Then she pulled her lips away and she was silently crying.

"What's to cry for?" I asked.

"Nothing. It's just a woman thing. You wouldn't understand it."

We stood there holding each other, and finally she asked, "What are you going to do now, Davis?"

"That depends on you."

"On me?"

"Yes. If you marry me, we'll live happily ever after, just like in the storybooks. If you don't, I'll become a miserable man and die unhappy and lonely."

D.K.'s lips turned upward in a smile. "I couldn't let that happen," she said. "I'll marry you out of pity."

She pulled my head down, kissed me again, and then we turned and walked down to the beach. The water whispered on the sands, and there was something whispering inside me. The whispering said, "For now we see through a glass, darkly; but then face to face: now I know in part; but then shall I know even as also I am known."